HANG FIRE

A STEVE MARTINEZ MYSTERY

HANG FIRE

HENRY KISOR

FIVE STAR

A part of Gale, Cengage Learning

GALE
CENGAGE Learning®

Detroit • New York • San Francisco • New Haven, Conn • Waterville, Maine • London

GALE
CENGAGE Learning®

LIBRARY OF CONGRESS CATALOGING-IN-PUBLICATION DATA

Kisor, Henry.
    Hang fire : A Steve Martinez mystery / Henry Kisor. — First edition.
        pages cm
    ISBN-13: 978-1-4328-2685-7 (hardcover)
    ISBN-10: 1-4328-2685-9 (hardcover)
    1. Sheriffs—Fiction. 2. Teachers—Crimes against—Fiction. 3. Teton Indians—Fiction. 4. Upper Peninsula (Mich.)—Fiction. I. Title.
PS3611.I87H36 2013
813'.6—dc23   2012047123

First Edition. First Printing: April 2013
Find us on Facebook– https://www.facebook.com/FiveStarCengage
Visit our website– http://www.gale.cengage.com/fivestar/
Contact Five Star™ Publishing at FiveStar@cengage.com

Printed in Mexico
1 2 3 4 5 6 7 17 16 15 14 13

For Emmet, Ellie and Alice

CHAPTER ONE

Angel closed the shutters against the night air, snapped on the banker's lamp above the ancient oak rolltop desk that served as an armorer's bench, and reverently lifted the Hammer of God from its pegs on the barn wall.

The heavy flintlock musket had been in the family for many generations, and a long-ago forebear had carved the name in the polished maple stock. The Hammer killed Redcoats at Cowpens, Monmouth, and Yorktown after service in the French and Indian War, Daddy had said before his lingering death from cancer. A Texan ancestor had used it in the conflict with Mexico.

After that the musket was retired from war, but from time to time a grandfather took it out of a closet or down from the wall above the mantel and caressed it while telling its family stories to the grandchildren. Sometimes it was taken outdoors for a little target shooting. Afterward the musket would be thoroughly cleaned, then oiled and replaced in the closet or atop the mantel.

In this fashion the well-worn weapon had been lovingly maintained down through the more than two hundred fifty years of its existence, and was as ready for action as it had been the day it emerged from the armory in the Tower of London. The Hammer would now return to slaying the Nation's enemies.

Before setting to work Angel cued the iPod to an old favorite.

*Mine eyes have seen the glory of the coming of the
Lord:*

He is trampling out the vintage where the grapes of
    wrath are stored;
He hath loosed the fateful lightning of His terrible
    swift sword:
His truth is marching on.

With a slight tilt Angel rolled a heavy cast lead ball across the surface of a hand mirror, watching its path for telltale jitters and hesitations from flaws on the metal. When the ball bounced ever so slightly, Angel picked it up and peered at it through a loupe, searching for a dimple or ridge in the metal that might alter its trajectory. An emery board took care of the worst and a thorough polishing with jeweler's rouge the rest. The ball gleamed in the soft light from the banker's lamp.

Angel was pleased. Each ball had been hand cast from the finest lead alloy and finished painstakingly. The expensive black powder that propelled it came from a small factory in Switzerland famous for the precision ammunition it produced for the best marksmen in the world, both competition target shooters and military snipers. Angel measured out the powder not in a rough flask the musket's previous owners had employed but with a small precision chemist's scale, and carefully poured it into the muzzle of the Hammer so that not a single grain would be lost.

Glory, glory, hallelujah!
Glory, glory, hallelujah!
Glory, glory, hallelujah!
His truth is marching on.

From a small pile of round patches made of striped pillow ticking Angel selected what seemed to be the most perfect circle of cotton. The patches were not custom-made, but came from a big mail-order company in Kentucky. Though they had been carefully punched out from the cloth with steel dies, some patches bore imperfections almost imperceptible to the naked eye, and Angel quickly plucked and threw out the rejects.

Nestling the leaden ball dead center within the patch, Angel brought it to the muzzle of the musket and fitted it inside with a single sharp roll of a polished maple sphere a little larger than a golf ball, then shoved the patch-shrouded projectile an inch deeper into the barrel with a metal-tipped wooden nub attached to the sphere. Finally, with a single smooth stroke of the musket's wooden ramrod Angel drove the ball deep into its breech. Two brief taps with the ramrod seated the patched ball firmly against the charge.

> *I have seen Him in the watch fires of a hundred*
> *circling camps,*
> *They have builded Him an altar in the evening dews*
> *and damps;*
> *I can read His righteous sentence by the dim and*
> *flaring lamps:*
> *His day is marching on.*

Angel reversed the musket to bring its trigger, hammer and primer pan within easy reach, then filled the pan with another carefully weighed dose of powder ground finer than that of the main charge. Then Angel lowered the lid of the frizzen onto the pan.

With the loupe Angel examined the surface of a thumb-sized stone that had been selected from a pile of rough flints and carefully knapped with a staghorn, making sure it carried a sharp edge that would strike a strong spark against the steel of the frizzen and ignite the powder in the pan. That in turn would fire the main charge in the breech and send the ball to do the work of God.

I have read a fiery gospel writ in burnished rows of
steel;
As ye deal with my condemners, so with you my
grace shall deal.
Let the hero born of woman crush the serpent with
his heel,
Since God is marching on!

Making sure the forked hammer bearing the flint was safely caught at half cock, Angel hefted the heavy musket and sighted down its barrel at the Devil in an old framed print of the Lord smiting His enemy.

Two more stanzas of the *Battle Hymn*, and with practiced care and profound reverence Angel returned the Hammer to its place on the wall. Around it nestled, like apostles at the Last Supper, a dozen other muzzle-loading weapons, all of them loaded, oiled and shining, ready for action in the looming battle.

He is coming like the glory of the morning on the
wave;
He is wisdom to the mighty, He is honor to the brave;
So the world shall be His footstool, and the soul of
wrong His slave.
Our God is marching on.

Angel was a soldier of the Lord.

CHAPTER TWO

Cops live by hunches. Call them premonitions, intuitions, suspicions, inklings, divinations, educated guesses or just strange feelings in one's bones, these not-quite-rational insights help police officers bridge the chasm between a meager collection of clues and the revelation of a sequence of events that had ended in crime. Sometimes hunches are born of long experience in sifting seemingly conflicting facts. Sometimes they just appear mysteriously on one's mental doorstep.

The trouble with hunches is that most of them just don't pan out. For every criminal caught within that critical first forty-eight hours by means of a brilliant insight seemingly plucked from the sky, dozens go free because the detectives looking for them waste valuable time chasing down dead ends. Hunches are also expensive things to follow, often requiring heavy manpower and lots of money. In the North Woods of Upper Michigan, we cops have lots of hunches but precious little resources to follow through. Sometimes we just get stuck in a deep hole of uncertainty, unable to claw our way out, like a frustrated otter scrabbling in a trap.

The humid air hung hot, still, and gray, as if nature was holding its breath on a suddenly hazy day in late July in the deep woods of the southern shore of Lake Superior. I took in a deep lungful of pine-scented forest air as I contemplated the victim lying in the still water before me. Tiny green frogs chortled *eep, eep, eep* in chorus on lily pads as scattered dragonflies soared and dipped, their iridescence sparkling in the faded sun. A cloud of mosquitoes probed my collar and cuffs. I slapped my neck and sighed.

She had collapsed on her left side on pebbled shale that stood an inch above the water in an eddy of the Mullet, a shallow backwater in a bend in the Porcupine River, deep in low second-growth forest a mile south of Porcupine City. Her arms, clad in the billowing sleeves of her white cotton blouse, had been flung above her head. Her ankle-length gingham dress and petticoats lay rucked above a leather jerkin. Except for one finely tooled moccasin bedecked with Indian beadwork and a soft leather fringe, she was naked below the waist. Her other moccasin had fallen into a shallow puddle a foot from the body.

Blood clotted around an entry hole three-quarters of an inch in diameter in the right side of her jerkin, just below her rib cage.

"She was probably squatting to wash when the bullet hit, Steve," said Alex Kolehmainen, the long, lanky Michigan State Police detective sergeant we in the Porcupine County Sheriff's Department always called in for homicides. The troopers are better equipped than we are in the forensics department, and even though their bosses in the capital at Lansing ride hard on their meager budget they're still a lot flusher than their country cousins.

"But where's her underwear?" I said as Alex trained his big digital camera on her.

"Don't know. They haven't found any," he said, glancing at the dozen deputies and troopers who had been searching the banks on both sides of the Mullet, a good hundred feet wide. "Maybe she didn't wear any."

"Why do you suppose?"

"Don't know." Gently he turned the corpse onto her back, her legs falling open slightly. Rigor had not yet set in.

The victim had been attractive. She was not an utter

knockout, but she would have been more than passable as a Rockette, worth turning one's head for a long second look. The beginnings of crow's feet suggested she was perhaps thirty-five years old. Her long blonde hair drifted in a bright fan in the still water.

"Look at this."

Alex's tone was flat and neutral, that of a veteran cop no longer surprised by anything, but with a slight rising inflection at the end of the sentence. Some Canadians talked this way, and so did many denizens of the Upper Peninsula of Michigan, but with Alex I knew it meant he was slightly irritated by what he saw, as if it were just one more link in a long chain of unchallengeable evidence that civilization was going to hell in a handbasket.

Golden light winked from the junction of the woman's legs, and my eyebrows rose, as much from the pain she must have suffered to be pierced for her vanity as from the profound cultural gap the jewelry bespoke between her generation and mine. I was not really surprised, having been a cop for two decades and having seen just about everything.

"God in heaven, Sheriff Martinez," said a strained voice behind me. "Can't you cover her?"

The Reverend George Hartfelder had found the body and called in the alarm. Short and broad-shouldered, balding, bearded and pushing fifty, George was an experienced woodsman, a veteran deer and bird hunter and a hard-shell Baptist, an eager infantryman in the culture wars he believed had infused Christendom with the stink of the Devil. He could be a nuisance to more liberal Porcupine County denizens with his sulfuric fulminations from the pulpit and in letters to the editor of the *Porcupine County Herald* against homosexuality, evolution, abortion and Harry Potter, but he was also a Christian who believed in being one.

He was quick to befriend gay men and lesbians—"everyone sins," he said—and was always first in line to help every time anyone, a member of his flock or not, needed aid and succor, whether in the form of a large bag of groceries or a month's supply of firewood. He and his wife Edna had taken in a troubled teenage girl who had been thrown out of the house by her parents after going to Detroit for an abortion. He often dropped by the county lockup to see if an inmate needed spiritual counsel, often offering a Bible to those he felt troubled in heart as well as mind.

Once he had taken a covered dish to an old enemy when she was laid up with a broken ankle. She was a well-to-do former student radical and retired political-science professor from Chicago whose ideology matched the color of her fiery red hair. An encounter with the leather-lunged professor was about as relaxing as a conversation with a clenched fist, but on that occasion, witnesses said, she was utterly nonplused.

I couldn't help liking and respecting the Reverend Hartfelder. He was "George" to me, as he was to everybody else in the county, but on official occasions I always used titles.

"What are you still doing here, Pastor?" I had already spoken with him and learned little. But he had had the sense not to touch the body while waiting for the authorities to arrive.

"Well, you know it's my land on this side of the river," he had said. "Or almost." His property line ended at the edge of the trees on the east bank of the Mullet. A local contractor owned the land on the west bank.

"What were you doing when you found her?" I had asked.

"I was walking the dogs, looking for partridge cover for when the season starts, and looked through the trees and there she was. I scrambled down the bank and went over to her. It was obvious she was dead, so I went back to my house and called the sheriff's department."

"Did you touch anything?" I said.

"No. But those are my tracks across the sand."

I shrugged. Though his footprints technically had contaminated the scene, they'd be easy to identify and dismiss.

I returned to the present. "Pastor, we can't cover the body until the troopers have done their job. No need for you to see everything close up—could you please go stand behind the yellow tape?"

He complied, shaking his head in dismay as much over what he had seen as well as the presence of unfortunate death. We belonged to the same generation and shared some of the same values.

I turned back to Alex.

"Whatcha make of that?" I asked, nodding toward the corpse in general and its decoration in particular.

"Maybe kinky."

"You think that just because she didn't wear pants?"

"That, cousin, and the rings."

Alex and I may have been country cops, but we were hardly unfamiliar with the fashions of the pierced generation.

"Maybe pioneer women didn't wear anything under their dresses?" I said, just to suggest another possibility. "Easier to pee."

"What about all those petticoats?"

"Don't know," I said, irritated with myself that I was beginning to sound as monosyllabic as Alex. "The Mountain Men do, probably."

The entire Midwest Chapter of the Society of Mountain Men of the United States of America was encamped in a meadow on the other side of the Mullet not a hundred yards away. They had chosen Porcupine County this year for their rendezvous, as they called their annual gathering in period costume. They reenacted the life of American hunters and trappers of the age of Lewis and Clark, an era that spanned the years 1800 to 1840.

"Do we know who she is?"

"Gloria Lake. Two-twenty-five Ash Street, Madison, Wisconsin. Thirty-seven years old by her driver's license," Alex said as he thumbed through the cards in her buckskin-trimmed leather purse. "A teacher," he said, holding up an elementary-school staff ID card.

"Never had a teacher like that," I said.

"Times have changed," Alex said.

"Credit cards? Money?"

"Visa, MasterCard, Discover . . . all here. Hey, there's quite a wad of cash. More than five hundred bucks in small bills, mostly fives and tens."

"Wasn't a robbery."

"No. Probably an accident. The shooting range is just over there, y'know."

The range lay just two hundred yards away over a ten-foot-high earthen berm, covered by low brush, hiding the meadow opposite. Before the rendezvous opened, a couple of my deputies had helped the Mountain Men stake signs both upriver and downriver warning hikers not to proceed past safety points during shooting contests. The berm was high, but not enough to stop stray bullets from ricochets and the like. Somebody was supposed to be manning each of those points to prevent campers, fishers and townsfolk from blundering into the line of fire.

"If that's a ball from a muzzle loader in her side," Alex said, again voicing what we both knew, "we're never going to match it to the rifle that shot it."

I stood, turned and gazed at the berm. A crowd of several dozen Mountain Men of both sexes, dressed mostly in buckskin, calico and muslin, stared back. Scenes of violent death, especially urban ones, tend to draw lively, almost jaunty crowds that often remind me of old stories about onlookers at beheadings, burnings and hangings, chatting gaily among themselves as if the spectacle of execution was nothing more than a town festival. If the victim of homicide, however, is a colleague or neighbor the audience had known, the crowd often is subdued, even fearful in a but-for-the-grace-of-God-there-go-I sort of way. This bunch was quiet and sober, even morose. The victim not only had been one of them, but, I suspected, also well known and well liked.

CHAPTER THREE

Two afternoons before, I had paid a visit, along with half of Porcupine City, to the opening day of the encampment on the Mullet where upwards of five hundred Mountain Men had pitched bleached white canvas tents and tepees along an eight-block grid of streets mown out of a hayfield. Because the encampment was bound to be a boon to the flagging economy of Porcupine County, the county board had asked that I do what I could to make things go well.

As I emerged from the sheriff's Blazer at the encampment, the place rang with booms of muzzle-loading rifles from the range, clangs of steel on iron at the smithy, thumps of axes on wood, metallic scrapes of kettles and cook pots, shouts and cries of small children, and snapping and crackling of flags and banners in the wind. The stiff breeze couldn't carry away a delicious aroma of frying bacon mixed with the scent of burning stove wood and black powder.

On the encampment's main street clumps of men and women in period costume chatted quietly. From time to time a burst of eager bartering between customers and shopkeepers issued from tents ringed with displays of canvas cloth, cast-iron utensils, wooden furniture, beads, bows and arrows, handcrafted muzzle-loading rifles and other trade goods.

The Mountain Men, I had learned, were an offshoot of the National Muzzle-Loading Society of the United States. They were gun enthusiasts of a particular kind: collectors and aficionados of replica muskets, rifles and pistols of a technology more than two hundred years old. The weapons used black powder and flints or percussion caps to shoot lead balls tamped down through their muzzles. I suspected that the Mountain Men originally had been founded to give the shooters' spouses and children something to do while the big boys made noise with their toys.

At least some of the members had other interests, I discovered when I met the "booshway"—a word corrupted by the original mountain men from the French "bourgeois"—or the "boss" of the encampment, in front of his spacious tent. Richard Crockett, a rotund septuagenarian in a powdered periwig, looked like Ben Franklin in Paris in blue brocade knee breeches, waistcoat, long jacket and a tricorne hat as well as old-fashioned octagonal pince-nez spectacles that gave him the wise-old-owl look Ben had in all those paintings. Only the button of a hearing aid belied his modern origins.

"We don't just shoot up the place," Crockett protested, when I, in my sheriff's way, shook his hand in friendly fashion but also inquired about his motives as a Mountain Man with a muzzle-loading rifle.

"Are you supposed to be Davy Crockett?" I asked.

"Does this look like a buckskin outfit?" he replied. "My persona is a frontier banker."

"Persona?"

"Yes. Each of us chooses a persona, or a role, to play in our gatherings. Some are trappers, some are traders, some are missionaries—we are anyone who ever traveled to the West during the early frontier age. We try to dress in the most authentic clothes and live the most authentic ways we can during rendezvous. We trade with each other and with the public that comes to visit us.

"We also have classes in Indian pottery making, weaving, dry-ing beef jerky, clothes making, leather tooling, flint knapping, all sorts of things the mountain men of the early eighteen-hundreds did. Some of our members sell these items. Others teach informal classes in the history of the times. You're a Native American, aren't you? We have a former Episcopal priest, a historian from Ann Arbor, who serves as the unofficial chaplain of our outfit. He specializes in Midwestern Native American history."

I nodded. The question follows me around all the time, like a small dog. I look uncannily like Iron Tail, the Minniconjou Sioux chief who was a model for the old Indian head nickel. Mahogany skin, black hair, hooked nose, hooded eyes. Unmistakable. A poster child for all the tribes. Everybody noticed, especially since I stand six feet three inches, tall for an Indian. I couldn't do anything about it except answer the curious questions as politely as I could.

Sometimes folks ask if I participate in local powwows, if I was a traditional Ojibwa. I'm not. I was born Oglala Lakota on the reservation at Pine Ridge, South Dakota. Not long after my birth parents died in a drunken automobile accident, I was adopted by white missionaries who took me back to their home in upper New York State and raised me as Steve Martinez, a black-haired Methodist with a deep tan. I may look like an Indian, but emotionally and culturally I'm a white guy. My surname tricks some people into thinking I must be Mexican, but my adoptive father was descended from Spaniards who settled in Florida centuries ago and quickly assimilated with the Anglos.

"What do you do in real life?" I asked Crockett.

"Real life?"

"You don't consider this real life?" I said, sweeping my hand all around.

"Well, it used to be real life, didn't it?" Crockett said with more than a hint of asperity.

"You have a point there," I said with a grave nod.

He chuckled and changed his tone. "I own an electrical-supplies company in Chicago, actually. This is my hobby. Come, I'll buy you lunch."

He led me through a mass of Mountain Men to a large tent bearing a rickety wooden sign emblazoned "FRY BREAD." The tent shaded half a dozen long, hand-hewn wooden tables and benches as well as a huge wheeled cast-iron stove fueled by wood. The scent of fry bread, shaped like elephant ears and bubbling in hot grease, made me hungry.

Suddenly a large woman—more than six feet tall, built like a squat concrete silo, frizzy salt-and-red-pepper hair caught up in a huge bun behind a remarkably sunburned face—pressed past me and leaned her muzzle loader against the stove. I caught a whiff of freshly burned black powder, and recognized the weapon as a delicate Pennsylvania rifle, maybe of a small squirrel caliber such as .36. In her massive hands it must have been as light as a matchstick.

" 'Scuse," she said expansively, like a merry earth mother. "Lunch hour is coming up and I gotta feed multitudes."

"Freddie Barnes," said Crockett, "this is Sheriff Steve Martinez. Steve, Freddie owns and runs the restaurant. We call her Big Freddie. She operates a high-school cafeteria in Waunakee in southern Wisconsin and spends her summers feeding Mountain Men at rendezvous all over the country."

"Pleased," I said, proffering my hand. It disappeared into her calloused and commodious fist, but she had the manners not to squeeze any harder than necessary to let me know she could probably take me in a cage-fighting match.

"Freddie is a fine markswoman, too," Crockett said.

"Woman?" Freddie said archly.

"Marksperson?" Crockett offered a little nervously.

"You could just have said a hell of a shot," she said, and broke into a broad smile as she tied on a greasy apron.

"Well, that too," Crockett said. "She usually wins the women's matches."

"You separate the sexes in the competitions?" I said. "In this day and age?"

"It's not exactly this day and age that we commemorate," Crockett said. "Two centuries ago there was no feminism, you know."

We seated ourselves on benches and dug into the tucker that Freddie had brought in a huge pewter platter and placed on the table with remarkable delicacy for such a large person. She and my equally elephantine deputy Chad Garrow, I thought, would have made splendid bookends.

I bit into a slab of fry bread filled with blueberry preserves, an earthen mug of lemonade on the side. The thick and chewy bread was both remarkably tasty and remarkably caloric—the kind of thing to be eaten sparingly if one was not to become an instant obesity statistic. I could see that a steady diet of it probably shortened the lives of the original mountain men by a decade or two. This was not a dish I would eat more than once in a lifetime, but I'd certainly remember it.

After a few mouthfuls I looked up. Freddie was gazing at me from behind the stove. She seemed upset, I thought, or maybe she was just being pensive or suffering from dyspepsia. It was hard to read her mood.

Suddenly she noticed my glance, and her expression instantly changed from whatever it had been to one that I interpreted as a frank and concupiscent leer. That alarmed me, so much so that I dropped my eyes and tried to hide behind a tent pole. Romance with Big Freddie was too frightening to contemplate.

At that moment a long-legged blonde visitor in tight white shorty-shorts sashayed by the cook tent, followed by the yearning eyes of a dozen men—and of Freddie, whose gaze lingered on the young woman in unmistakable fashion. This earth mother, I thought, swung both ways.

"Of course you have security?" I asked Crockett.

"Yes, we have a dozen Dog Soldiers."

"Dog Soldiers?" I was starting to irritate myself with my own terse questions.

"From the Cheyenne term for camp policemen," he said. "They wear coonskin caps, red sashes, and, like you do, six-pointed stars. But we're a peaceable bunch and they don't really need to keep us in line, so they're more like firemen and paramedics than cops. They can do both jobs, though." He whistled. "Jack!"

A large, shaven-headed man with a handlebar mustache and the beginnings of a muffin belly detached himself from a small gang of buckskinners grunting to erect a tent and sauntered over.

"Jack Seymour," Crockett said. "Sheriff Steve Martinez. Jack is the chief Dog Soldier and will get hold of you if anything happens."

Jack's equally large paw enveloped mine. "Steve," he said cheerfully. "I'm Des Moines PD."

"I'll leave you two to the shop talk," Crockett said, fishing a point-and-shoot digital camera from inside his silken waistcoat. "Got to get some pictures for the Web site."

"Web site?" I said, incredulity in my voice.

"Yes," Crockett said. "The Mountain Men of old weren't Luddites. Like everybody else, they used the newest tools they could find, and so do we, when we're not being Mountain Men. See you later, Sheriff."

I turned to Seymour, who was grinning at the humor of the situation. "We can always use another detective around here," I said. "We're always shorthanded."

"Uh . . . I'm a traffic officer."

I laughed. "That's what we mostly do in Porcupine County. Traffic stops. You'd fit right in." Then I said more seriously, "What are the usual problems you have during an event like this? Booze?"

"Once in a while," said Jack. "Some of the guys like to take nips now and then and get noisy, but we squelch 'em. This is a family-oriented outfit and we aim to keep it that way. Once in a long while there might be a little theft, but that's rare, very rare. We mostly know each other, although new people come to every rendezvous from all over."

"Yeah. A little bird told me some of you like to pass the jug late at night," I said. It stood to reason that some of the Mountain Men made moonshine and brought it to the encampment, but if the revenuers weren't following them across state lines, I wasn't going to, either. Too much on my plate.

"Well, yeah," said Jack. "Gotta keep an eye on them, too."

"I've heard that at your rendezvous some of the local women have been seen sneaking out of the tents at dawn and going back to town," I said.

"No law against that, is there?"

"Nope," I said, chuckling, then changed the subject. "You carrying?"

Jack nodded and patted the flintlock Kentucky pistol at his belt.

"Loaded?"

"God no! It's just for show. We Dog Soldiers do compete in pistol events and that's the only time we load with powder and ball."

"Your service piece?"

"In my truck, locked in the glove box."

"Shield and ID?" Seymour's police shield and identification would establish not only his bona fides but also the federal right of a police officer to carry a concealed weapon from state to state.

"Yep."

"May I see?"

"Yep. Come with me."

We walked through a copse of trees to a hidden parking lot and Jack's big Chevy pickup. Jack's ID was good. I wouldn't have to worry about him.

"What about the other Dog Soldiers?" I asked on the way back.

"None are cops. Doubt they brought anything that isn't loaded from the front end."

" 'Kay. Thanks. Come see me if you get tired of this stuff and we'll bust a speeder or two together."

Jack chuckled, and I left him as he picked up a small girl, dressed in a simple white shift, and swung her around as she chortled in glee.

"Sheriff?" whispered a feminine voice at the same time fingers tugged at my sleeve. I turned. It was Audrey Moilanen, a tiny, blue-haired octogenarian from Porcupine City. Sharing her severe expression were two other women whose faces I knew but whose names I didn't.

"Yes?"

"Look at that Indian!"

I followed her eyes to a tall, pale fellow selling handmade arrows. He wore his long blond hair in two lank braids on his chest, Sioux fashion. A hawk feather completed the 'do. Around his chest he wore wampum and around his bare loins a loose breechclout and leggings. Way too loose, I saw as he took a step to the side.

"That's disgraceful," Audrey said. Her companions nodded. "There are children around. Can't you do something?"

I sighed. "All right."

I strode over to the make-believe brave, carefully keeping my gaze on the arrows, not wanting the approach to seem official and threatening. I picked one up.

"Nice fletching," I said. "Do yourself?"

"You bet," said the pretend Indian. "Knapped the arrowheads, too."

"Uhh," I said, still examining the arrow, "some of the town ladies are a little upset over your, uh, air-conditioned attire. Think you might be able to tighten it up a bit?"

He drew himself up in a huff and looked down his nose directly into my eyes. "Sheriff," he said, "I am dressed in absolutely authentic fashion. The Native Americans of two hundred years ago wore these for protection, not for modesty. Loose clothing did not mean loose morals. It enabled them to move quickly, unencumbered by what they wore. And who are the complainants?"

His spiel was a little too glib for me, but I turned and glanced at Audrey and her retinue. They watched us, heads together, giggling.

"Never mind," I said. "Carry on. Sorry to bother."

"Um, Sheriff," said the fellow. "You're Native American?"

"In a manner of speaking," I replied softly, changing the subject as unobtrusively as I could. "And I can't imagine wearing what you're wearing in this blackfly country," I added. "How do you stand it?"

"Oh, lots of bug dope, hundred-percent DEET."

"*That's* authentic?"

"You got me there." He laughed. "But we really, really try to live the way people did almost two hundred years ago," he said, sounding like an uncanny echo of Crockett. These folks, I thought, must have memorized stuff to tell the tourists. "We're not crazy, though. We use modern sanitation"—he pointed at a palisade of eight-foot-tall stakes behind which, I knew, lay a dozen fiberglass porta-potties—"and we bring in bottled water. For two weeks every summer we do try to live the lives of the mountain men and their Native American allies, but we can't forget that we're modern people also."

"Modern enough to use the term 'Native American,' " I said. "I just call myself an Indian. Most of us do."

"Ojibwa?"

"No, Lakota," I said. Might as well go along with the thought. People are going to think what they want, and there's no percentage in arguing.

"Long way from home."

"You said it."

"Enemy territory, in fact."

"You do know your Indian history," I said. Until the middle of the eighteenth century the Lakota tribes, or the Sioux as the French called them, lived and hunted in Upper Michigan until they were driven out by the more warlike Ojibwa, themselves hounded out of the East by even fiercer Iroquois tribes. The Sioux fled to Minnesota and the Dakotas, where they became horse Indians and hunted buffalo on the Great Plains.

"Sure do," the pretend Indian said with a smile, holding out his hand. I took it and smiled back.

"Now I gotta sell some arrows," he said, swiftly turning as a fresh knot of Porcupine Countians strode up. His breechclout lagged in the turn, I saw, and I glanced back, looking for Audrey and her friends. They had wandered away, no doubt looking for something more interesting to occupy my professional time.

A chuckle resounded over my shoulder and I turned to confront a tall and gaunt-cheeked man in his early forties. He wore the long black cassock of an eighteenth-century Anglican missionary. He carried a long, slim flintlock rifle in the crook of his arm.

"I couldn't help overhearing your exchange with that guy," he said. "We're used to his dress, but tourists and townspeople always do a double take. Don't worry about the youngsters. They might snicker at him but they'll quickly put it out of mind. After all, our generation enjoyed looking at naked native women in old *National Geographics*, and I daresay that didn't corrupt anyone."

I chuckled back. "I'm not planning to bust him," I said, holding out my hand.

The man in missionary dress took it with a firm and dry palm that held mine a moment too long. "Bill Du Bois," he said. "They call me Father Bill here, but I'm no longer a priest. I teach American history at the University of Michigan."

He smiled with oily sincerity, in the fashion of inspirational speakers who peddle banalities to the credulous. A bit of a put-on, I thought. Maybe a ham actor.

"Yes, the booshway mentioned you," I said. "Former Episcopal priest, he said."

"Indeed. The church hierarchy and I had a parting of the ways long ago, but I'm still an Episcopalian."

"Did missionaries shoot guns?" I said, glancing at his rifle. "I thought they fought hostiles with the crucifix."

"They did and many perished for their cause," Du Bois said, drawing out the phrase dramatically, "but a few of them decided Indian raids weren't a good time for martyrdom and defended themselves as best they could. That's the kind of priest I'm portraying in this rendezvous. Besides, it gives me the chance to make smoke on the range with this little beauty. I've always enjoyed target shooting."

"Are you good at it?"

He smiled. "Won a few turkeys."

"Turkeys?"

"Frozen ones. Usually first prize in a shoot."

"May I see your rifle?"

"Sure." He handed me the weapon. Its freshly oiled barrel and action gleamed. So did the long stock of highly polished bird's-eye maple, a wood prized by custom gunsmiths.

"What kind is it?"

His stagey manner suddenly yielded to a childlike enthusiasm.

"Fifty-caliber Tennessee. Handcrafted. Cost a fortune to have it made but worth every penny."

"Why do they call it that?"

"The gunsmiths who came to eastern Tennessee in the seventeen-nineties to eighteen-tens had no brass to make the fittings and mountings, so they used the local iron instead," Du Bois said. "You can tell a Tennessee rifle by that. On most of them there isn't any shiny metal like brass or silver to reflect sunlight and spook the game."

"Or the enemy," I said.

Du Bois looked into my eye and winked. "Or the enemy."

"Thanks for showing me," I said after a moment. "Gotta go do sheriff stuff."

"Go with God, my son," said Du Bois, hamming it up, suddenly Father Bill again, making an elaborate sign of the cross. He strode away, rifle cradled in the crook of his arm, black robe billowing.

CHAPTER FOUR

The body of Gloria Lake having been dispatched in a hearse to the state police forensics lab at Marquette, the Mullet seemed once again suffused with color, the now-bright sun heightening the greens of the forest, the yellows of the meadow and the blue of the sky, as if the removal of the corpse had lifted a curtain and brought the stage back to normal. The presence of death always subtly alters the atmosphere of a scene, fading it into a dry grayness.

I had first encountered the phenomenon in Kuwait during Desert Storm, when battlefield smoke parted over a row of rocky entrenchments destroyed by carpet bombing, and my column of military police rolled in dusty Hummers past blasted bodies of clueless Iraqi conscripts caught by B-52 bombs before they could surrender to us. Since then, each time I had encountered the victims of violent death, the same subtle and colorless pall had enveloped the surroundings. Maybe it was just a psychological quirk but it felt so real to me that I shuddered involuntarily.

Alex and I strode into the encampment. At our orders, all movement in and out of the Mullet had been closed by my deputies after the body had been discovered on the riverbank. They'd started preliminary interviews with the Mountain Men who had been using the rifle range that day.

"Talk to me," I told Chad Garrow, the deputy I'd put in charge of the detail. Jack Seymour stood next to him, resplen-

dent in Dog Soldier garb, but Chad commanded all the attention. Chad is six feet six and shaped like a stout water heater.
He is heavy, but his is a hard, muscular fat, like that of a pro
football tackle.

Jack had offered to help in the interviews, and we had accepted. That had made Chad's job easier, having Jack to smooth
things with the Mountain Men. Many stood or sat on boxes
nearby, watching us, their expressions somber and concerned. A
few seemed vaguely hostile, as if they had something to hide.

"Nothing unusual, they said. Nobody missing from the range
this morning. Everybody was where they were supposed to be."

I thought a moment. "Any hang fires?"

A hang fire occurs when a flint or percussion cap fails to fire
the main charge of black powder in a muzzle-loading weapon.
Sometimes, with flintlocks, the primer in the pan goes off but
does not ignite the powder in the breech of the gun, hence the
term "flash in the pan." A careful muzzle-loading rifleman
experiencing a hang fire must point the weapon at a safe place
in the ground for a full minute to make sure a smoldering grain
of powder does not set things off and propel a leaden ball into
the crowd.

"Quite a few," Chad said, "and some went off, but everyone
said they fired into the ground, and witnesses backed them up."

"Ricochets?" Occasionally a ball could bounce off a nail in a
stake and howl away into the distance.

"None that anybody says they remember."

"Any interesting fellows?" I meant persons of interest, possible suspects, but didn't want anyone overhearing to draw that
conclusion. The field on the Mullet was not a crime scene. Not
yet, and maybe never.

"Just one," Chad said.

"Who's that?"

"Guy named Ray Mitchell," Chad said, checking his notepad

and handing it to me. "From Grosse Pointe Fields down by Detroit. Claims to be a national champion in muzzle loading. Said it was impossible his hang fires could get loose 'cuz ain't nobody else in the country got his skill and experience."

"Big head?" I said.

"Well, I don't know, maybe, but . . ." That was unusual. Large and clumsy as he may be—strangers often mistook him for an overgrown Barney Fife—Chad is not easily baffled. Natives of rural Upper Michigan are often sharp and smart, though without much book learning beyond high school.

"Point him out?" I asked.

"Over there. Tall fellow in leather hat and skins. The one in the canvas chair."

I looked, and the man in fringed buckskins so crisp and well-fitting they looked as if they'd just come from a bespoke tailor returned my glance from the handmade camp chair with a direct but relaxed gaze. I strode over.

He stood up, or, rather, unfolded himself like a reverse human origami, and offered his hand for a shake. Tall, tanned and with deep vertical furrows in his long cheeks, he could have been mistaken for the actor Gary Cooper in some long-ago Western.

"Ray Mitchell," he said pleasantly. "Do you for?"

"My deputy says you were on the firing line when the incident happened," I said, returning his grasp. His hand was cool, dry and firm.

"That's right, Sheriff."

"No hang fires? Ricochets?"

"Not from me, Sheriff, as I told your deputy." He stood casual and relaxed.

"How can you be so sure?"

"Sheriff, not to boast, but I am one of the best fellows in the world with a muzzle loader. I have more awards than I can count. I haven't been defeated in a match for, oh, four or five years now."

The words were those of an egotist, but he delivered them in a surprisingly quiet, even humble voice.

"Hmm," I said. "What does that have to do with what happened today?"

"Just this," Mitchell said. "You don't get as far as I have without being very, very careful and very, very painstaking. Accidents just don't happen to shooters like me. I know that sounds conceited, Sheriff, but it's the truth."

"What about the others?"

"The others?"

"The other shooters in the competition this afternoon. They didn't have your skills, did they?"

"Some come pretty close but a lot are almost beginners."

"So one of them could have made a mistake?"

"I'm afraid so."

"Any idea which one?"

"Not really. When I'm shooting I don't see anything but my sights and the target. I'm too focused." He nodded slowly in grave emphasis.

I didn't have anything to say to counter that, so I busied myself studying Chad's notes. "Grosse Pointe Fields. You're from there?"

"I live there now, but I'm originally from Maine."

"Ayuh," I said, mimicking the stereotyped Maine dialect for "yes."

Mitchell smiled at the joke, although he must have heard it thousands of times.

"What do you do?"

"I own a series of large automobile-repair centers," he said.

"Garages?" I said with a belittling tone, just to be provocative. A small needle sometimes brings a revealing reaction.

"They used to be called that," he said without rancor. "But mine are far more full-service. They all have attached car washes and some of them also have short-term day care for mothers who want to run errands. I employ about four hundred people."

"Okay," I said, closing Chad's notebook. "We've got your phone number and your license plate, and if we need to ask you more questions we'll be in touch. Have a nice day."

Mitchell nodded deferentially. "I hope," he said, "that we all can put this tragedy behind us." He thrust out his hand again and I took it.

I looked around at the small canvas settlement. "Where's the booshway?"

"In his tent breaking the news to Gloria Lake's people down in Madison," Chad said. "He maybe shoulda left that to us, but I didn't think it'd hurt."

Crockett, sitting on a trunk in the back of his tent, turned, snapped his cell phone closed and stood as I entered.

"Do those things work this far upriver?" I asked.

"Yeah. We're on a bit of a rise."

Cell-phone coverage in Porcupine County is spotty at best, even though the phone company had erected a new tower recently. Phone companies understandably dragged their heels putting up new facilities in a place where the population fell by ten percent every decade.

"Did you get through to the relatives?" I asked.

"Yes. There's only her mother in a nursing home. I'm not sure she understood what I told her. She barely seemed to remember her daughter. What a horrible, horrible business."

"Mr. Crockett, what do you plan to do?"

"We'll take a vote tonight on whether to break camp or stay. I think I can safely say we'll stay. We've experienced tragedies before. Two years ago a child drowned in the Indiana lake where we camped and his parents wanted us to carry on. This is what typically happened on the frontier and we have to be strong and go on, like the mountain men of old."

That sentence sounded as if it had been plucked from a high-school history textbook, but all I said was, "You really believe in being authentic."

"It's a moral authenticity, too."

I didn't quite see his point, but we had more important things to talk about. "Tell me about Gloria Lake."

"She was well liked," Crockett said. "She'd been a member of the Mountain Men for a while and this was her second rendezvous. She's from Madison and is—was—a first-grade teacher there."

"Husband? Boyfriend? Did she come with anyone?"

"No, she always came alone in a minivan and had her own tent. Her persona was as a seamstress. She sewed very well-made women's and children's clothes of authentic designs, and sold a great many of them to other members as well as the public."

"Anything unusual about her?"

Crockett paused for a moment. "Not really," he said. "Apart from being an unattached woman—usually the women here are the wives of shooters, but some of them are shooters them-selves."

"Was she a shooter?"

"She brought no weapons, but she occasionally borrowed a rifle and participated in the women's matches. She wasn't a bad shot, either."

"Boyfriend?" I repeated.

"Never mentioned one to me."

"Family?"

"Only her widowed mother I just spoke to."

"Can I have her name and number? We may have to follow up."

Chad already had that information, but it never hurts to stay a boat-length ahead of the fellow you're talking to. Crockett did not strike me as being slippery and evasive, but I am often driven by old habit.

With a crude lead pencil made from a twig, Crockett quickly scribbled the name and number on a fragment of foolscap and handed it to me.

"I don't know if this is significant," I said, "but Miss Lake wasn't wearing any pants, or bloomers or whatever underthings women wore at that time. What could that have meant?"

He hesitated before answering. It was a small hesitation that could have meant something, or nothing. Slowness to answer sometimes suggests a conscious cover-up of the facts, but it can also mean the subject wants to clarify them in his mind before speaking. Quick glibness can mean the subject has already thought of the question and prepared an answer designed to divert attention. I filed the hesitation away in my mind.

"Nothing, really. Frontier women of those times usually wore nothing under their long skirts and petticoats except for a chemise, a slip, for ease of hygiene. Miss Lake probably was just being—"

"Authentic?" I said.

"Yes. She was a real stickler for doing things the old way. Left her cell phone at home."

"May I look inside her tent?" I didn't have to ask—standard police procedure would be to just go in, look around and photograph the contents—but a little politeness goes a long way for cops as well as for civilians.

In the middle of a row of tents on the edge of the encampment, Crockett led me to Miss Lake's tent, a small white canvas structure bearing a crudely lettered wooden sign: GLORIA

LAKE SEAMSTRESS. We strode inside.

In the front sat tables piled high with homespun and calico, with two women's blouses displayed atop dome-topped maple chests. In the back, a sheet hanging from a horizontal wooden pole screened a thin mattress on a canvas cot that was covered by a soft brown cotton quilt. Another dome-top trunk stood by the cot.

With a pencil I tipped open the lid to the chest. Inside it lay needles, thread, a wooden-handled toothbrush, a tin container of tooth powder, no cosmetics except for a modern deodorant stick, a glass jar full of washed agate pebbles, and a box of a hundred condoms of a brand popular for its dry lubricant. I pulled a small point-and-shoot camera from my shirt pocket and took several photographs of everything in the chest as well as the background. Finally and without comment, I closed the chest and paused for a moment.

"However you vote tonight, Mr. Crockett, it would be helpful to us if everybody could stay here for at least the next couple of days," I said. "This of course looks like a tragic accident, a stray ball from a rifle on the range, perhaps, but until that's officially been declared, it's an open case. So we'll have to follow up."

"There will be no problem with that," Crockett said with deep sincerity in his voice. I could tell that he was a shaken man and wanted to cooperate as fully as he could. Or at least leave me with that impression.

"Okay, then," I said, and stood up to leave the tent. I stopped. "By the way," I said, "did anybody here know the vict—er, Miss Lake—well?"

Crockett paused. "Yes, I think so. That would be Sheila Bodey. She's a quilter, has a tent right next to Miss Lake's. They've been—were—friends for many years. Miss Lake said the other day that they were teachers together in Madison. Sheila lives outside Masonville near Ironwood now."

Masonville is about an hour from Porcupine City to the southwest, near the extreme western edge of Upper Michigan.

"Thanks, Mr. Crockett," I said. "I'll speak with her."

Sheila Bodey sat silently in a camp chair just inside the flap of her tent, sewing a fringe onto a brightly colored quilt utterly unlike the plain muslin ones on display in front. Her eyes were rimmed with red, and her face had paled behind the slight pink that fair-haired people often display even after just a few minutes in the sun. A large straw hat billowed over a pile of folded quilts atop a crate next to the chair. A brass-bedecked flintlock I recognized as a Hawken, a lightweight Plains rifle, leaned against the crate.

Underneath her blue-and-white gingham blouse and billowing canvas skirt Miss Bodey appeared short, stocky and buxom, and in her early forties, with red hair, a kewpie mouth and a strong jaw that gave her a certain maternal appeal, like an older aunt who had retained some of her youthful beauty. She did not look up as I entered, but held herself rigidly, eyes fixed on her work, the picture of a stunned woman trying to control her emotions.

"A word, Miss Bodey?" I said, showing my star. "I'm Sheriff Martinez."

"Yes, I know who you are," she said, a slight quaver in her voice.

"I understand you were a good friend of Miss Lake," I said, keeping my tone soft.

"Yes."

"I'm very sorry for your loss."

"Thank you."

"It appears to be a terrible accident," I said, "but I need to ask you some questions."

"Okay," she said, relaxing slightly. "What do you need to know?"

"What sort of person was Miss Lake?"

"What's that got to do with what happened?" She looked up at me and fixed her hazel eyes on mine. She was quite right. She knew I was just fishing, floating a bobber down a lazy stream to see if an unseen trout might dart out from under a sunken log and change the dynamic of the day. Sometimes the people I talk to can see right through me. But Sheila Bodey's gaze was not hostile, just concerned.

"I don't really know," I said with a wry smile. "But it might help explain why she was where she was when the accident happened." That was the truth.

"She loved rivers and the shores of ponds. She liked to wade in the water and look for pretty stones. Over the last couple of days she found a few nice agates in the same place where she— where the accident happened. She said she planned to walk along the beaches on Lake Superior and find some more."

"People liked her?" I prompted, returning to the original question.

"Yes. She was a lovely, lovely person. Always friendly, always giving of herself. People liked her a lot."

"Anybody *didn't* like her?"

"You don't think—"

"No, no," I said. "I'm just fishing. Never know what might turn up." Sometimes it's best to own up to your intentions, just to get the witnesses on your side. Keeps them relaxed and their memories flowing.

"She didn't have an enemy in the world. Not one."

"I heard you were teachers together in Madison."

"Yes. She taught second grade and I taught kindergarten."

"Good teacher?"

"The best. Conscientious and creative. She loved the kids

and they loved her, even in her Sunday school."

"What church?"

"A little Pentecostal one called the New Rising Church."

Suddenly she brightened for the first time in our conversation. "Do you know Jesus?"

That's not an uncommon question in wilderness country, where religion helps people cope, and I'd long ago developed a vague answer, one that usually didn't offend the fervent but deflected their curiosity. "God and I have an understanding," I said.

It worked with Pastor Hartfelder, who often asked me if I had yet been saved. I always gave him the same answer. He just patted me on the shoulder and said, "Someday, Steve."

It worked with Sheila Bodey, too, even though she wasn't fooled. She grinned.

"In other words, He minds His business and you mind yours."

"I wouldn't quite put it that way, but it's something like that," I said.

"That's okay," she said, dimples wreathing her cheeks. She looked like a cute chipmunk. "You're a private man. Never mind. I'm sorry. I get carried away. It's an evangelical thing."

"That's okay, too," I said, and returned to the task at hand. "Boyfriend?"

"Me?" she said with genuine astonishment. "A boyfriend?"

I could see no visible reason why she might not have one. "No, no, I meant Miss Lake," I said.

"She had one for a while, sort of, not terribly serious. She broke up with Teddy a few years ago. He's a fellow teacher at her school in Madison. They're still good friends."

"Teddy?"

"Teddy Gillson." I did not write down the name but committed it to memory, as I often did while questioning witnesses, later inscribing such facts in my notebook. Keeping the tone informal and conversational often helped witnesses to relax and open up.

I drew up an empty camp chair and plunked myself in it. Making oneself comfortable in the living room is another cop trick. It tells the witness that you find her story interesting and that you have all the time in the world to listen to it. That can turn a tense interrogation into a relaxed chat.

"I'm told you live in Masonville now," I said.

"Yes. I found a very good job in the schools there and moved up four years ago."

"You kept in touch with Miss Lake?"

"Oh yes. We saw each other a couple of times a year, usually at Mountain Men encampments."

"How'd you get involved in the Mountain Men?"

"Three years ago Gloria saw a rendezvous near Black River Falls—that's in Wisconsin, too—and just fell in love with the idea of historical reenactment. She'd been a history minor in college. She told me about the Mountain Men a little while later and the idea just drew me in. That's when I started quilting. She was a seamstress, so she did a lot of sewing for me."

"Did she shoot?"

"Yup. Gloria and I often shared that Hawken there."

"Good shot?"

"She was coming along. She was a quick student. I didn't have anything more to teach her."

"Did you shoot this afternoon?"

"No. I've got to finish this quilt by tonight. I'm making it for a woman in Porcupine City who runs a bed-and-breakfast."

"Your quilts *are* lovely," I said truthfully as I looked around the tent, admiring the precise needlework in decorative floral comforters that were an unseen riot of color in an encampment dominated by blacks, whites, browns and grays. "But why do you keep the pretty ones inside and the plain ones outside?"

"Tell you the truth, Sheriff," she said with a wink. "The frontier of the first half of the nineteenth century was no place to find pretty quilts. The materials are heavy and bulky, and there was only so much room in the pioneer wagons for nonessential things like chintz from India. The early settlers used hastily made quilts of homespun muslin when they weren't sleeping under woolen blankets or bearskins. Only later, just before the Civil War, did bright colors and patterns finally arrive from the East."

"Ah, so the quilts out front are historically correct?" I said.

"Yes. But *this* is what the tourists want to buy today," she said, smoothing the chintz in her lap. She smiled and shrugged. "What can I say?"

"I'd like to get one of those for my lady. I'll bring her in in the next day or two."

"That will be nice," Miss Bodey said, her eyes shining. "I'm sure I'll have just the thing for her."

"Thank you," I said, standing at last. "Miss Bodey, I'm sorry for your loss. Miss Lake must have been a great friend."

"Oh, she was. I am going to miss her."

Her eyes welled and a tear trickled down her cheek. Sheila Bodey returned to her quilting and I departed.

CHAPTER FIVE

The next morning I pulled up in my ancient Jeep at the sheriff's department, a long, low and lumpy single-story concrete-block fortress that looked as if it had been quickly and cheaply constructed, as public buildings often are in impoverished rural counties. For months I had been bugging the county board to approve the purchase of a few buckets of gray paint for the jail trusties to slap on the peeling concrete exterior. "Yeah, yeah, Steve," the commissioners said every time. "Pretty soon."

The phone rang as I reached my desk, where I had been picking over the proposed next year's budget, trying to find a few more pennies to squeeze before submitting it to the county board. For more than two years we had been two sworn deputies short, unable to pay their salaries and benefits, and the ones we did have were racking up so much overtime to fill the gaps that we were getting close to the point where new hires would be cheaper. I'd been working long days myself, filling in on patrol on my own time to relieve my overworked underlings. More than once I yearned to move down to the mitten of Michigan and become a state police detective, fighting crime rather than spreadsheets.

Such is life for a sheriff in a far northern rural county whose population has been shrinking for more than half a century. Most county departments simply downsized as people left, but our workload had for a long while remained much the same: traffic stops, legal servings, domestic violence, substance abuse, theft, outdoors accidents, barroom assaults, an occasional homicide. There were fewer felony crimes but far more social problems involving the elderly, unsurprising since our population was aging rapidly. We had to be social workers as well as crime fighters.

The caller was Alex.

"Check your e-mail," he said without preamble, as he always does on the phone, never bothering to identify himself. "Sent you a copy of the pathologist's report."

He didn't have to say about what. We have so few homicides in the North Woods that we can truncate our references, the way native-born Yoopers like Alex shorten sentences by leaving out their subjects.

"Okay," I said, punching a few keys and calling up Alex's message.

For the most part the report revealed nothing I didn't already know. The shapeless leaden slug the pathologist had removed from the victim weighed 625 grains, consistent with a .75-caliber muzzle-loading ball. That was no surprise. At the time of the contest at the Mullet, at least twenty of the riflemen had been shooting modern replicas of the Brown Bess, a heavy .75-caliber flintlock smoothbore musket that was the standard shoulder arm of the British in the Revolutionary War and was common among Continental soldiers as well.

No rifling marks were visible on the slug, only a few faint microscopic crosshatches from the cloth patch used to snug the ball in the bore of the musket. Chad and his deputies had gathered and bagged a few tattered and charred remnants of the patches from the firing range, but I knew that most muzzle-loading riflemen bought their patches from a handful of mail-order companies, and that most such outfits obtained their patches from one manufacturer. They weren't going to help us identify anything.

Nor, said the pathologist, was there a short-starter mark anywhere on the slug. Most muzzle-loader shooters start the ball down the barrel by first placing it on the muzzle, then rolling it inside the bore with a small wooden ball. Into the ball is stuck a wooden peg with a brass ferrule at the end. The peg is used to seat the ball deeper down the bore. Finally, a ramrod drives the ball home to the bottom of the breech.

The end of the ferrule often leaves a distinctive mark in the soft lead of the ball. Sometimes in flight a ball from a smooth-bore weapon like the Brown Bess will turn slowly back to front so that the part of the ball marked with the short starter survives more or less intact. That hadn't happened yesterday with the projectile that killed Gloria Lake.

It was the section of the report about the vaginal examination that caught my eye. The pathologist had carefully but nonjudgmentally described the jewelry he found there, as well as noting the lack of semen. Rather, he said, there were unusually large deposits of a dry silicone lubricant common to certain brands of condom, including the one I had found in Gloria Lake's tent. This was, the pathologist wrote dryly, "consistent with numerous sexual encounters in the forty-eight hours preceding death."

"Steve?" Alex said. He had remained on the line while I read the report.

"Yeah?"

"What do you know about the Brown Bess?"

"Big old smokepole," I said. "So big it makes a pretty good war club when you run out of ammunition."

"It's even got a literary history," Alex said. "Do you know Kipling's poem 'Brown Bess'?"

I steeled myself for one of Alex's lugubrious mini-lectures. "No, but you're going to tell me, aren't you?"

His voice deepened dramatically—Alex is a very good amateur thespian—and he declaimed:

"In the days of lace-ruffles, perukes and brocade
Brown Bess was a partner whom none could
despise—
An out-spoken, flinty-lipped, brazen-faced jade,
With a habit of looking men straight in the eyes—
At Blenheim and Ramillies fops would confess
They were pierced to the heart by the charms of
Brown Bess.

"Though her sight was not long and her weight was
not small,
Yet her actions were winning, her language was clear;
And everyone bowed as she opened the ball
On the arm of some high-gaitered, grim grenadier.
Half Europe admitted the striking success
Of the dances and routs that were given by Brown
Bess."

"Um," I said, "that's pretty good, Alex, but . . ."
"Oh, there's more. Listen."

"When ruffles were turned into stiff leather stocks,
And people wore pigtails instead of perukes,
Brown Bess never altered her iron-grey locks.
She knew she was valued for more than her looks.
'Oh, powder and patches was always my dress,
And I think I am killing enough,' said Brown Bess."

"Shall I go on?" Alex said. "There's several more stanzas."
"If I need to, I can go look them up on Wikipedia and print them out too," I replied. "Let's get to the stuff in the vagina."
"Was waiting for you to remark on that," Alex said.
"Thank you for giving me the chance," I said with heavy irony. "I think there's more to this than meets the eye."

"Is there?"

"Gloria Lake was more than a seamstress."

"Yeah?" The same flat tone.

"I think she may have been a prostitute."

"What tells you that?" Alex said with feigned astonishment.

"That 'numerous sexual encounters' in the pathologist's report. Could have been one guy, but is that really likely? Think of all the small bills she carried and the brand of condom. It's very popular among sex workers." I deliberately used the neutral sociological term for "prostitute."

"How do you know?" Alex said, mock skepticism in his voice. I knew he knew the answer. He is a veteran detective familiar with the workings of the sex industry. But he likes to put me on the spot, just for the hell of it. I played along. Our didactic little dramas sometimes helped us solve crimes.

"Dry lubricant just feels better to the guy wearing the rubber," I said. "The feeling's more intense. He gets off faster. That's why hookers like these brands—they save time and maximize income."

"Very good," Alex said, chuckling. "Your expensive education wasn't wasted on you."

I'd graduated from Cornell, then studied criminal justice at City University of New York before serving my ROTC obligation as a military police lieutenant in the Army, rounding up those Iraqi POWs under that gray sunlight in the Kuwait desert. Then I'd come to Porcupine County as a deputy. I'd sunk roots in the place and had been the sheriff for little more than a year.

"I'm going to go further my expensive education some more out at the Mullet this morning."

"Why?" Alex knew the answer to his own question, but Alex is Alex.

"Those guys were telling the truth," I said. "But not the whole truth."

★ ★ ★ ★ ★

When you've been a cop long enough, you know instinctively when you're being lied to. A clue might be that almost imperceptible hesitation, shiftiness, too much care in choosing words, maybe just a sideways glance. It might be a slow awareness that something was being left out, that you haven't been told everything, that not everything has been explained. Or maybe it has been explained way too easily. You may never know exactly why, but you know when a lie is hanging in the still air. It's a kind of hunch, but one that's easy to follow up.

CHAPTER SIX

Twenty minutes later, without knocking—there's nowhere on a tent to knock—I swept back the front flap of Richard Crockett's canvas domicile and strode in as the booshway looked up in surprise.

"Sheriff? Have a seat."

I already had. I gazed at him silently. Ginny, my girlfriend, calls me "Old Stone Face" when I do that. We Indians are very good at it. We lower our lids, tilt our heads back slightly and fix an expressionless gaze upon our targets without blinking or uttering a sound, like Dirty Harry in maximum dyspepsia. Sooner or later they wiggle and squirm and perspire. What do I know that they don't want me to know? Sometimes everything, sometimes nothing. Cops of every kind thrive on scenes like this. It's human nature to want to break a silence, to fill the threatening emptiness with words.

"Is something wrong?" Crockett said as a bead of sweat broke out on his forehead.

I remained silent and held my gaze.

"Uhm . . ."

"You lied to me."

"I did not!" Crockett said, but his indignation carried no force. "Everything I told you was true!"

"It may have been—I don't know that for sure—but you did not tell me everything," I said. "That is lying by omission."

A defense lawyer might challenge that statement, but there

was no lawyer around. That occurred to Crockett, too.

"Do I need an attorney?" he said, wringing his hands. He was scared. Good. A little fright often lubricates a rusty conscience.

"If you think you need one," I said slowly. "That is your right."

He fell silent and studied me.

"What's going on?" he said. He wasn't going to lawyer up until he found out why I was there.

"You are not a suspect in the death of Gloria Lake," I said. "But you may be involved in obstruction of justice. That's what I mean about not telling me everything about Miss Lake that you knew."

"What—?" Crockett stammered.

"Her sexual activity," I said. "You knew all about that."

Crockett finally broke, shoulders slumping. "Yes. It was part of her persona."

"As a seamstress?" I said incredulously.

"As a camp follower. Many of the women who traveled with the hunters and trappers in the old days also did a little monkey business on the side. Some, of course, were full-time whores."

"We have evidence that Miss Lake did a lot of that."

"What is it?"

"That's confidential for the moment."

"Oh, God. I hope this doesn't get out. It could ruin the Mountain Men."

"If this is an accident," I said, "it likely won't get out. We can't suppress the evidence but we don't have to volunteer it to the press. You can help here by telling us everything."

"Okay."

"Did everyone in the encampment know about Miss Lake's, ah, supplementary persona?"

"No. Only a few of the guys. She was very discreet, and so were her, um, customers. After all, there are families and children out there."

"Who were those customers?"

"Do I have to say?"

"It would help you if you did."

Twelve names tumbled out one by one as Crockett searched his memory. I jotted them down, then opened my briefcase and checked the names against Chad's interview list of the day before. They were all on it, including Ray Mitchell. Ten had participated in the musketry contest during which Gloria Lake had been killed. If this were murder, I knew, none of them could have fired the fatal shot—there was no way a shooter on the range could have seen what was over that berm. Only if it were a genuine accident could one of them have done it. That left two names.

"What about these two guys?" I said. "Dale Suppelsa and Dick Trenary?"

"They're both shooters," Crockett said, "but they volunteered to man the sentinel posts that guarded the rear of the shooting range."

I checked Chad's list. No surprises there.

"Is that everyone?"

"Everyone?"

"Everyone you know who had sexual relations with Miss Lake."

"Yes."

"Think there were any more you don't know about?"

"Possibly. Probably. But I wouldn't want to guess."

"All right," I said. "But one more question."

"What?"

"Did you pay for sex with Gloria Lake?"

"I want a—" Crockett began, then fell silent. After a moment he nodded.

"Is that a yes?"

"Yes," he said, his expression abashed.

Deep down I felt a touch of amusement and even admiration. The man may have been in his seventies, but he was still frisky.

"All right. I think you're telling the truth now."

"My wife doesn't need to know, does she?"

They all say that, the johns, when they are caught. It's pathetic.

"Don't think so."

"Please."

I ignored Crockett's plaint and gazed at him without a word. Sometimes a little silence is punishment enough. He squirmed. I shook my head, stood up and swept back the tent flap, then stopped and turned.

"Ah, Mr. Crockett?"

"Yeah?"

"What did she charge?"

"Ten dollars."

"Only that?" Every self-respecting hooker I had ever heard of demanded at least twenty times that sum, sometimes a thousand dollars or more if she catered to a wealthy clientele.

"Yes. The camp followers of the old days charged about that in the equivalent of the times."

"So she was being authentic?" I couldn't keep the sarcasm out of my voice.

"Yes." He closed his eyes in embarrassment.

"God." I also thought, but didn't say, that she must have enjoyed the work, too. To put that into so many words would have been tacky, even sexist. But maybe it was true.

"That's all," I said. "For now."

Dale Suppelsa was an easy interview.

"I talked to Deputy Garrow yesterday," he said. "Something wrong?"

He was, according to Chad's report, a twenty-seven-year-old

from Mount Pleasant, Iowa, who worked in his dad's feed store and, by his own admission, had no desire to rise higher in life. With shoulders like an ox yoke he was almost as big as Chad, handsomer, although my deputy was hardly an eyesore, and as unassumingly pleasant but far more eager to be liked, a clumsy puppy hoping for attention. He had the grace to blush when I asked if he had had sex with Gloria Lake. He did not deny it, either. He wasn't married. He wouldn't be in trouble if anything got out. Except maybe with his mother or girlfriend, if he had one.

"How did it happen?" I asked.

"The accident?"

"No, the sex."

"The usual way, I guess," the lad said cheerfully.

I stifled a grin. This young fellow was not the sharpest knife in Iowa's drawer.

"I meant how did your relationship with Miss Lake come about? Did you go to her?"

"No, actually she came to me."

The afternoon of the first day of the encampment, Suppelsa said, he had stopped by the seamstress's canvas emporium and introduced himself, as he had done with everyone else. This was his first Mountain Man rendezvous and he wanted to get off to a good start with his fellow participants. He and Miss Lake had talked for a while and then, he said, she had asked if he had a girlfriend.

"Never really had one," he had told her, and she had put her hand on his leg and giggled. "Maybe that'll change," she said.

Asleep in his tent that midnight, he said, he had awakened to the soft sound of a canvas flap being opened. He looked up and against the starlight watched as Gloria Lake slipped off her clothes and slid silently under the covers beside him.

"I don't know how much I should say," Suppelsa said.

"Whatever you're comfortable telling," I said.

"Well, she kind of grabbed hold of me, not hard, but the way girls do, you know."

"And?"

"She said I had to give her ten dollars before the fun could commence. That's how she said it."

"Were you surprised?"

"Was I ever." A slow grin crept over his face.

"She tell you why?"

"Yes. She said she wanted to pretend that she was a, you know"—he groped for an appropriate term—"*party girl* from the old days."

"Kind of a part-time whore?" I said bluntly.

Suppelsa nodded. "I know people here want to do things the way they were done on the frontier, but that seemed a bit much."

"But not too much, eh?"

"No. Sheriff, I had a good time. I think she did, too." His tone was not boastful, just matter-of-fact, as if he were a younger version of Ray Mitchell.

"Did it happen more than once?"

"No. I suggested it, but she said she had other 'friends to take care of,' as she put it. Maybe later in the week."

"Did you use protection?"

"Yes. She brought some."

"What kind?"

Suppelsa named the brand. I nodded to myself. This young man was being forthright and truthful.

"Did you hear anybody say anything bad, negative, about her?" I asked.

"No. Everybody liked her. She was a nice lady, even though—"

"Even though?" I repeated encouragingly.

"Even though she sold herself," the young man said, a cloud

suddenly forming over his face, as if he realized for the first time the moral implications of what had taken place in his tent. Young men faced with the prospect of getting lucky never think about the circumstances, let alone the consequences. "That was a sin. A terrible sin."

He looked up. "Will the Lord ever forgive me?"

He was not being ironic. He meant it. Immediately I decided he was an open and decent young man with normal urges and a normal conscience.

I shrugged and patted him on the shoulder. I'm a sheriff, not a padre, although we're both confessors. The one deals with facts and the other in spirituality.

Time for more facts.

"What kind of a gun do you shoot?" I asked.

"A thirty-six Kentucky squirrel rifle," he said, "and a fifty Hawken."

"May I see?"

Suppelsa dragged a long pine crate out of a corner and opened the top. Two well-kept replica rifles lay within, snuggled in brown velvet. There was, I saw, room for only two weapons. No Brown Bess.

"You were doing picket duty on the Mullet during the shoot, I understand."

"Yes, Sheriff. I do all right at that, but compared to the better shots I'm not all that good and I don't really compete very much. So I volunteered to be a sentry, it being my first rendezvous and all."

"Didn't see Miss Lake by the river?"

"Nope. Just a couple of Mountain Men and ladies who were a little late to get out of the way before the shooting contest started. No problem with them."

"All right, Dale. That's all I need to know, and thanks for your help."

The boy—overgrown as he was, he was still a boy—stood and held out his hand. I shook it. Why not? In his own naive and uncomplicated way he had been a gentleman.

Dick Trenary was no gentleman. When Chad and I confronted him in his smoky, cluttered and tattered tent, he did not rise from his chair to greet us but glowered up from it, like a wolf bearded in his lair.

"I already talked to that deputy," said the dark, wiry little man, who not only looked like an unshaven eighteenth-century *voyageur* but dressed like one, in rough woolens and a stocking cap with a pompom. "What more can there be?"

His tone was defiant. I decided on a frontal assault.

"Did you have sex with Gloria Lake?"

Trenary hesitated a moment, then plowed on without blinking. "Who didn't?" he said, spitting on the grass. "She peddled her bony ass to everybody."

"*De mortuis nil nisi bonum,*" I said quietly, biting back disgust.

"What's that mean?" Trenary, I knew from Chad's notes, worked as an aviation mechanic in La Porte, Indiana, and hardly could be expected to have had a classical education.

"That's Latin for 'Speak no ill of the dead,' " I said.

"Ha. An Injun who knows Latin!" Trenary said. "Who'd ever think of that?"

"Did you solicit the sex?" I pressed, stifling a violent urge to splay Trenary's nose all across his churlish face. I hate cheap comments about my ethnicity. I feel them, but can't let them affect an investigation.

"No, she gave it to me for free," he said. "She said I'm better in the sack than any of the others."

"Where did it happen?"

"Her tent."

"So you went to her?"

"Yeah, she came up to me on the firing line and whispered that she was putting out."

"What did she charge?"

"Fifty—hey, I said I didn't pay, didn't I?"

"All right." He was lying, and he knew I knew. But he stared me in the eye, challenging me. I had no evidence that he had committed an infraction of the law, except one so piddling and technical that it wasn't worth pursuing. Being a jerk isn't a crime. Good thing, too, because if it were, Trenary would be a capital offense all by himself.

"I'm told she charged the others only ten," I said with a mocking smile, trying to provoke Trenary into further indiscretion. "I guess she had to make you worth the trouble."

He shot me a look of naked hate.

"She sure wasn't worth *my* trouble. She was a lousy fuck."

I did not respond, although Chad stiffened in disgust. I checked my deputy's notes from the day before. "You were doing sentry duty on the southwest side of the Mullet during yesterday's shooting contest?"

"Yeah. And like I said, I didn't see her at all. She either came from the east side, or maybe had already been out there in the woods before we set up our posts."

That corresponded with what witnesses had told Chad. Gloria Lake had last been seen in the encampment fully two hours before the shooting contest. No one had seen her walk off into the forest, but that was unsurprising, given all the coming and going in the camp.

"One more question. How come you weren't in the shooting contest yesterday?"

"Don't need to win another trophy," Trenary said. "I got me lots of those. On a good day I can beat them all."

"You own a Brown Bess?"

"No. Just that Kentucky and the Tennessee in that there rack. Besses are too big and heavy for me."

The long, slim and elegant Kentucky and Tennessee designs of muzzle-loading rifles shoot smaller-caliber balls, typically .36, .45, .50 or .54, not huge .75s. I plucked each rifle out of the rack and sniffed the primer pans. There was only a smell of gun oil. If they had been fired recently, they had been cleaned immediately afterward. This fellow took care of his tools.

"All right. Never mind." Without a further word I turned on my heel and turned my back on Trenary, stepping outside the tent.

Chad followed, but stopped at the tent flap and turned to Trenary.

"Does it just come natural," the big deputy said with a growl, "or did you have to go to asshole school?"

I turned, grasped Chad by his elbow, and gently shoved him in the direction of his cruiser, parked at the entrance to the rendezvous.

"I'm sorry, Steve," Chad said. "I don't know what came over me."

Shortly after I had taken office, I had issued an order reminding all deputies to treat everyone with careful respect, even suspects, despite provocation. That was not so much an act of kindness as it was common sense. Polite cops gather fewer brutality complaints and help the prosecutors win more cases.

At the cruiser I turned, faced Chad, and said quietly, "Don't do it again."

The deputy stood crestfallen. "Yes, sir."

I patted Chad on the shoulder and said, "Never mind. He *is* an asshole."

I was about to follow Chad into town when I remembered Sheila Bodey. She wasn't on Crockett's john list but she did know Gloria Lake. I decided to shake her tree a little and strode to her tent.

She was pinning an Amish-style hex quilt to the inside of her tent when I walked inside.

"A word, Miss Bodey?" I said quietly. There was no need to sound confrontational.

She nodded quietly and sat, taking the same chair she had occupied the day before. I took the other and gazed at her with a thoughtful expression and without speaking. For two beats she returned my gaze, then sighed in resignation.

"You found out, didn't you?"

"Found out what?" Never tip your hand too soon.

"Gloria's pro-cliv-it-ies," she said, enunciating every syllable of the word, as if she had practiced but not quite mastered it.

"Those being?"

"Sheriff, let us not be coy. You know I am talking about her sexual habits."

"Why didn't you tell me about it yesterday?" I said, carefully keeping accusation out of my voice. "You must have known for a long time."

"It was an accident," Miss Bodey said. "I didn't want her to be remembered for her . . . her . . . sin. Only God can judge."

"Selling one's body is illegal," I said. "Maybe in this case it's only a technical crime, and I'm sure some of you would say she was just being historically accurate, but the fact remains that in her historical persona, or whatever it's called, Miss Lake practiced prostitution. I'm not going to arrest anybody here, but I do want to have a more accurate picture of what happened."

"I *told* her not to," Miss Bodey said with a groan. "Lust is an awful sin. And what she was doing could be dangerous. She might get hurt. But she wouldn't listen. She said she loved . . . loved indiscriminate coupling with men."

"Did she put it that way? 'Indiscriminate coupling'?"

"No. She said 'fun.' "

"How far back did this activity go?"

"As far as I know, she didn't sell herself until she joined the Mountain Men. But when we were teachers in Madison and went out on Saturday nights, she never came home with me—for a while we shared an apartment—but spent the night with a man. A different one every time."

"So the, ah, 'fun' was her personal inclination," I said.

"Some people would say she was sick," Miss Bodey said. "I think the Devil had taken her."

It occurred to me that in these enlightened days getting lucky every Saturday night was now as much a female prerogative as it was a male one, but this was neither the time nor place to say so.

"Well, that does it for me," I said. "Thank you for being forthcoming."

"Anytime, Sheriff." Relief flooded Miss Bodey's face.

I picked up my hat, shook her hand, and departed.

Across the meadow I spotted Father Bill Du Bois sitting alone in his black robe at the fry-bread tent, sipping a mug of coffee. I walked over and sat down on the rough bench next to him.

"How well did you know Gloria Lake?" I whispered, confident that no one else could hear.

He shot a sideways glance at me and whispered back. "Depends on what you mean by 'know.' "

"In the Biblical fashion," I said.

He straightened, gazed without expression in the direction of the Mullet, and said, "You found out."

"Please answer my question," I said.

"Yes. The flesh is weak." It was a simple statement without self-justification or pleading, as if he was a forthright man who had no need to cover his tracks, but with a certain studied manner that impelled me to keep on fishing.

"You weren't at the rifle range yesterday, were you?" I said.

"No. I was in town at the historical society talking to kids." That would be easy enough to check, and if necessary I would do so.

"You have a Brown Bess?"

"Only the Tennessee you saw," he said. Suddenly his manner changed. "Sheriff, you don't think foul play was involved?"

"Not really," I admitted. "Everything points to an accident."

"It's a tragedy," Du Bois said. "She was such a beautiful girl."

"I'd have said 'woman.' But yes, she was very pretty."

"A waste . . . of life," he said, hesitating perceptibly.

I stood and nodded. "Thanks for your time," I said, and left.

On my way back to the cruiser I saw a knot of Dog Soldiers, Jack Seymour among them. "A word?" I asked him. We stepped out of the street onto the trampled grass as a knot of chattering women passed without pausing, each one of them sneaking a sidelong look at us.

"Why didn't you tell me Gloria Lake was a hooker?" I demanded.

"Dog Soldiers don't police private morals," he said. "We police antisocial behavior. What she did was not against the law on the frontier."

I rolled my eyes. Authenticity was starting to wear on me.

"Even so," I said, "as an actual cop you know that what she did could conceivably have had something to do with her death. It's material information."

"It could have," he said with a slow nod. "But did it?" He spoke quietly, without hostility.

"I don't know the answer to that."

Even though Jack's name was not on Crockett's list I decided to ask anyway, to see if there was a personal reason for not volunteering information.

"Did you have sex with her?"

A wry smile spread across the big man's face. He leaned close and whispered.

"Steve, I'm *gay.*"

Spotting Big Freddie Barnes at the cookshack across the meadow, I wondered about her. We had not interviewed her immediately after the incident on the Mullet, because we knew she competed in the contests with a Kentucky rifle, not a Brown Bess musket. But maybe she kept a Bess in her gun box and pulled it out to shoot from time to time. That was a loose end left undone. And maybe Gloria Lake plied her trade with both sexes, as was common in real life.

I was not eager to talk with Freddie but decided to beard the lioness in her den. Composing my face into as stern an expression as I could manage, I strode over.

"Good morning, Miss Barnes," I said.

She looked up and beamed. "Sheriff! What brings you here?"

"I think you know," I said. "Word travels fast."

Her smile faded. "What can I do for you?"

"Did you know Gloria Lake?"

"Oh, yes," Freddie said. "Everybody did. Nice gal. Fun-loving, too." The bright leer briefly returned to her face, then slid into the shade.

"Fun-loving?"

"Sheriff. You know what I mean."

"Why don't you tell me?"

"Sex isn't a crime, is it?" Freddie said.

"Well, the way Miss Lake apparently performed it, it technically was," I said.

Freddie threw back her head and laughed. "Man, that's a

stretch. For ten bucks? Gloria was just role-playing."

I pounced. "Is that what she charged you?"

"Yup," Freddie said utterly without guile. "It was funny. All I had was a hundred and Gloria had to go back to her tent to make change."

"Anything else?"

Her tone changed and a cloud darkened her face. "Not unless you really, really, really have to know, Sheriff. Do you have to have details? I liked Gloria, and would rather leave it at that. She was a very nice person."

I could think of no response to that and said, "Tell me, do you own a Brown Bess?"

Her expression did not change, nor did her voice. "Nope, only a thirty-six Pennsylvania. Don't like them smoothbores."

"Okay. Thanks for your time." I stood.

"Come by tonight?" she said with a grin so wicked I nearly had to laugh. "I like guys, too."

"Sorry. Got a date with my girlfriend," I said, thanking my stars that I actually did and didn't have to lie. But I did return to my vehicle wondering what Gloria Lake's experience in the sack with Freddie Barnes must have been like.

Later in the afternoon, back at the sheriff's department, I reviewed everything I knew and finally and somewhat regretfully concluded that the unfortunate demise of Gloria Lake indeed had been an accident. She had either missed or ignored warnings of danger and had been wading in a stream out of sight, but still in the middle, of the line of fire during a riflery competition. She had been killed by the kind of ball that was being shot during the contest.

Her activities before her death had been curious, but the embarrassed reluctance of most of the Mountain Men to volunteer their involvement in those shenanigans was understandable. I had found no link between Gloria Lake's unusual persona and the shooting.

Picking up the mike, I radioed Alex to tell him that I wouldn't object if the state police and medical examiner declared the event an unfortunate and tragic accident.

CHAPTER SEVEN

In the light from the banker's lamp Angel glared at the freshly cleaned and oiled Hammer of God in its pegs on the wall. Had the ball actually struck where it was aimed? Gloria Lake had been stooping downward at the time the trigger was tripped, and from the direction of her fall it seemed that the trajectory of the projectile had dipped lower than it should have.

Was it a missed flaw on the surface of the ball that had caused it to drop ever so slightly from the expected line of aim? Or a slight miscalculation of the weight of the charge? Angel didn't think so. There had been no breeze. Everything had been perfect, or as nearly so as a human could make one of God's creations.

The range had been just over fifty yards, a bit long for a weapon whose bore probably had been worn overlarge over two centuries of use. Even when new, Daddy had said, the Hammer had not been intended for sharpshooting, but for massed fire from a company of soldiers standing in close ranks. The military strategy of the eighteenth century was simple. A hail of lead from scores of smoothbores wielded by massed lines of soldiers fell willy-nilly upon the foe, the fatal balls finding their targets solely by chance as they hammered apart the tight enemy ranks. Volley upon volley would follow in rolling curtains of fire until the surviving soldiers broke discipline and ran, cursing the luck of the Devil.

"That's why it's called 'the Hammer of God,' " Daddy had declared.

Using it for the purpose Angel intended had been a challenge. But Daddy had loved challenges. "Risk makes life more interesting," he had said, but also warning, "Risk can also be foolish." Nonetheless the Hammer had proved a success: it had admitted its latest owner to the family elect, those who through the centuries had slain evildoers. Gloria Lake had at last paid her debt to the Kingdom of God.

Perhaps it was now time to move on to a weapon more suitable for the dispatch of a single human target, perhaps a rifle. That was a long gun with twisted grooves inside the barrel that would cause the ball to spin rapidly in flight, sending it along a straighter trajectory than a smoothbore could. Rifled weapons were much more accurate than the Hammer, though not as powerful.

Angel examined the Twelve Apostles. Two were long, light and graceful Tennessee rifles, both shooting a ball smaller and lighter than that of the Hammer. One was a flintlock like the old family musket and the other ignited the powder with a more modern percussion cap. Percussion caps were more reliable than flint sparks. But the flintlock was to be preferred. Flintlocks were more challenging. There was always the risk of failure of the primer to fire. But Angel was confident that anyone who used the Hammer could spot the Devil a point and still beat him.

Angel caressed the bird's-eye maple stock of the flintlock Tennessee. The rifle was not an antique, Daddy had said, but a modern replica his own father, a skilled amateur gunsmith, had built from disparate parts. The barrel and action came from England, the maple from a tree Granddad had felled on his southern Illinois farm for the purpose and seasoned for two years in the woodshed.

Granddad, Daddy had added, had not carried it, or the Hammer, into battle on Iwo Jima. He had employed a Thompson submachine gun the Marine Corps had issued, and with it had slain the Nation's enemies.

Rather, Granddad had used the Tennessees at home for deer instead of a modern smokeless hunting rifle with five cartridges in its magazine. "Granddad said that would not have been 'sporting,' " Daddy said. "It was not fair to the deer, one of God's finest creations, an animal whose beauty lifts the heart and whose meat sustains the body. God put the deer on earth to serve mankind. God gave us dominion."

Yes, Daddy had taught Angel to love a challenge. But no, a long rifle was not really the proper weapon for the mission in mind. Angel replaced the Tennessee on the wall and took down a heavy cavalry pistol, an 1860 Remington New Model Army. This was a six-shot .44-caliber percussion revolver like the one Great-Great-Granddad had carried in the War Between the States, but of modern manufacture, a working replica. It had a rifled barrel.

A swift turn of the long lever under the barrel, and the cylinder fell free. Now for powder and ball in one of the six chambers of the cylinder, followed by a percussion cap pressed into the rear of the chamber.

The task completed, Angel replaced the cylinder in the revolver frame, lowered the hammer to half cock and returned the gun to its pegs on the barn wall.

All was ready. Let the Devil come.

CHAPTER EIGHT

"God damn it, Ginny," I said. "The motive is there somewhere. Sex, one of the holy four motives for murder, the other three being money, revenge and power. If Gloria Lake had been only a mousy young teacher from Madison it wouldn't have bothered me. But look what she was."

"Coincidence. The mere *existence* of a possible motive doesn't mean murder occurred," Ginny said equably. "You don't know that any of those Mountain Men wanted to kill Miss Lake just because they had sex with her. Be reasonable. You've turned up no evidence of that, and besides, men aren't like female praying mantises—they don't kill the mate they've just copulated with."

"Some do. Sick fucks, for instance."

"Not in my house, Steve."

"That didn't happen here!" I can be *so* dumb.

"No, your choice of words."

I leaned back in the oaken dining-room chair and gazed at the love of my life with deep skepticism. When provoked, Virginia Anttila Fitzgerald can outcuss a Marine drill sergeant so fiercely *her* choices of words raise bubbles on the wallpaper. I didn't challenge her, however. No percentage in it.

Ginny is tall, leggy, red-haired and green-eyed, with a lightly freckled complexion that needs no makeup and a buxom shapeliness that turns the heads of indifferent teenagers. Her early forties have only ripened her contours. I am, to put it bluntly, crazy about her. She is a hell of a woman.

Ginny subscribes to several other social niceties of the Upper Peninsula. She is filthy rich, thanks to her late husband's fortune, but wears her wealth so lightly almost nobody knows about it except me and the Detroit law firm that discreetly administers the big foundation she set up to help the denizens of Porcupine County without their knowing about it. She drives a ten-year-old Chevy pickup, dresses in jeans and Pendletons, and except for her sprawling log home in thick woods on the lakeshore and its discreet collection of fine art from the Middle East and Orient, lives like any other Porky. Thanks to the ambitions of her mining-engineer father, a second-generation Finnish American and native Porky who wanted the best possible education for his children, she holds a degree from Wellesley and another from the University of Michigan. She employs her intellect as the resident historian at the Porcupine County Historical Society, her tiny salary publicly paid by her own secret foundation.

As you would expect, Ginny is a smart cookie with a sharp analytical mind, and I often run professional problems, including sensitive police matters, past her during the quiet stillnesses in her king-sized oaken four-poster after we have made love. There is nothing that clears the cluttered mind better than a relaxing rumpus between the sheets. But we were in her kitchen, and I had just dried the dishes.

"You yourself said a muzzle loader would be a stupid murder weapon," she said.

She had me there. No rational person with homicide on his mind would choose a muzzle-loading rifle, musket or pistol for the deed. Smoothbore weapons like the Brown Bess are notoriously inaccurate at fifty yards and it would take an expert to hit a man-sized target at forty. All muzzle loaders are unreliable, especially flintlocks, and if you miss the first time there's no quick chance for a second shot unless you've brought another loaded weapon with you.

Most states do not even consider muzzle loaders true firearms and don't bother to regulate them—although the smarter ones do require a firearms registration card to buy the black powder those antique arms use. In fact, the statistics—I had looked them up as soon as I got back from the Mullet—said that there were fewer than a dozen deaths by muzzle loader each year in the United States, and about half of these were self-inflicted.

"Steve, it was obviously an accident," Ginny said. "Sure, it would be nice to know who's responsible for the accident and tie up everything neatly in a bow, but is justice being cheated if you don't know?"

"I guess not," I said. I had been a cop long enough to know the profession's dirtiest secret: most homicides were never solved. This one had been, officially at any rate. Further work on it was not going to bring back Gloria Lake to continue her pursuit of authenticity at Mountain Men gatherings or to instruct her Madison pupils in their letters and numbers.

I couldn't let go of the subject. "Ginny, what do you *make* of these people?"

"The Mountain Men?"

"Yes."

"Before the rendezvous, I'd always thought of people who like to reenact history as, well, oddballs," she said. "The kind of people who feel they were born in the wrong era and want to regress to a simpler time when life was black and white, not shades of gray. A few of them are true Luddites who choose to live in the woods in houses without electricity or plumbing. Others like to make noise with guns and dress up in military uniforms and get drunk at night and stuff like that. Some just want to be bigger frogs in a make-believe pond.

"But in talking with them on the Mullet I also learned that many of them do know their American history, and immersing themselves deep into it for a week or two every year just allows them to crawl out of their dull lives and be somebody else for a short while. They tell me that life in the old days was physically difficult and when they go back home they have a new appreciation for what they have. By putting down roots in the past they anchor themselves emotionally, even if they don't feel a connection to where they live in their modern lives.

"They're proud to be Americans, and not in a sentimental way, either. Sure, most of them are politically conservative, but a surprising lot are liberals. For a couple of weeks every summer they get along with each other, and when they go home they try to hold that feeling."

I wasn't persuaded—for me, there is just something too mindlessly romantic and theatrical about reenacting history.

"In other words," I said, "they're a bunch of eccentrics and misfits."

"You are so cynical, Steve. Every group has a few misfits."

Before I could rescue myself from the conversation with an indifferent shrug, a tall and skinny fourteen-year-old lad tumbled down the stairs with all the finesse of a runaway beer barrel, a big yellow Lab mix on his heels, claws drumming the oaken treads. Tommy Standing Bear, an Ojibwa from the reservation at Baraga, was Ginny's foster son of three years and Hogan his dog. Although I was not Ginny's husband, Tommy was like a son to me, partly because we were both Indians, although Tommy was thoroughly grounded in his tribal history and I hardly knew a stick of Lakota lore.

Tommy wore a canvas jacket with a buckskin fringe down the sleeves, rows of brightly colored wampum crisscrossing its lapels, and a round-crowned, flat-brimmed black felt hat with an osprey feather stuck in its finely embroidered band.

"That doesn't look Ojibwa to me," I observed. "A western tribe?"

"Cheyenne," Tommy said. The Cheyenne are cousins of the Lakota and had fought beside them in their finest hour, the Battle of the Little Bighorn in 1873. Indians know the massacre of Custer and his Seventh Cavalry troopers by Crazy Horse, Sitting Bull and Gall as the Battle of the Greasy Grass. Like any other Lakota, traditional or assimilated, I was deeply familiar with its history and could rattle off the order of battle of both sides, giving a minute-by-minute, blow-by-blow account of the action.

"Why not Ojibwa? After all, that's what you are."

"Steve," said Tommy with the know-it-all cockiness of every lad of his age I had ever encountered, "that's so *tribal*. We're long past that. We're united now."

I knew the political unity of American Indians was a sometime, off-and-on thing, and that inertia and the bureaucratic power of the Bureau of Indian Affairs kept alive the status quo of tribal separation. But young Indians, as idealistic as their white counterparts, never let the idea die. Tommy was young and eager.

"Handsome outfit, though," I said. I had seen it for sale in a dry-goods tent emporium at the Mountain Men encampment. The price was not outrageous, either.

"I'm joining the Mountain Men," Tommy said.

"I've given some thought to that, too," Ginny said. "It might be fun to dress up in those clothes and learn how to teach history from a hands-on point of view."

"As a seamstress?" I asked before I could stop myself. I can be *so* stupid.

Ginny glared, and I knew I would have to do penance. Exactly what, I didn't know, but Ginny had her ways, and they are usually painful. I kicked myself mentally.

Tommy rescued me. "I want to get a Hawken kit and build it myself."

Many muzzle-loader shooters built their replica flintlocks and percussion period pieces from commercial kits. It didn't take a lot of money, labor or skill to turn out a handsome and serviceable Plains rifle.

"Don't you have to be sixteen?" I said. Most kids in Porcupine County didn't get their first rifles until they had reached that age, although they were no strangers to shooting. Their mothers and fathers took them out back or to the local rifle range starting at about age eleven or twelve and taught them how to shoot a .22 safely. Everybody grows up with rifles and shotguns in hunting country, where harvesting birds and animals for the table is a long and honored tradition that gun-hating city dwellers who shoot their meat at the supermarket just cannot understand. Although, like many if not most police officers, I can see no sense for ordinary Joes to carry handguns and wouldn't mind if they were strictly regulated, I do not begrudge rural hunting folk their long arms. Nearly all are well trained in gun safety from an early age, and if somebody should shoot another human being in the North Woods, it's almost always with a motive, not from mindlessness. That was another reason the death of Gloria Lake irritated my consciousness.

Well into her twenties Ginny had taken a deer for the freezer every year, and she still kept her well-oiled old .30-30 Winchester saddle carbine on pegs over the mantelpiece. She had the ammunition for it, too, locked away in a kitchen drawer. It had come in handy once, against a homicidal intruder I had been chasing.

"I'll be sixteen in a couple of years," Tommy said. "Ginny, can I get a kit before then and build it so I'll be ready when my birthday comes?"

"We'll see," she said, the universal maternal code for "All right, if you keep your nose clean and do all the chores and get B-pluses or better in school."

And that was the last thought I had about muzzle loaders and manslaughter and Mountain Men for the rest of the summer.

CHAPTER NINE

It was pitch dark outside when the phone rang.

"Steve?" Joe Koski was doubling this week as night corrections officer, as we called it, or jailer, as the civilians said. "Downtown's on fire! Looks like a really bad one. Half of River Street's burning."

River Street is the main drag in Porcupine City. Just about every business in town lies on it.

Instantly I shook the sleep out of my head. "Good God!" I cried. "What's the response?"

"Artie has the pumper and the ladder on the scene already, and is calling out for help. We're gonna need a lot of it."

Art White, the village mayor of Porcupine City, is also the town's volunteer fire chief, and a good one.

"Call all hands," I said, adrenaline kicking in. "I'm on my way."

"On your way where?" Ginny said sleepily beside me.

"Bad fire downtown. Looks like an all-points call."

"Oh, shit! Coming with." She bounded out of bed and began throwing on clothes. I did not dissuade her. She was responsible for the historical museum and if the fire threatened it, she'd need to be on hand to direct evacuation of the museum's most prized possessions.

She quickly jotted a note for Tommy, still asleep in his upstairs bedroom, and left it on the kitchen table. As we raced together to the Blazer I could see an orange glow five miles east on the lakeshore, flames beginning to lick the night sky. That made me tromp the accelerator a little too hard and we fishtailed up the driveway. At the highway I had to stop while the sole fire engine of the Silverton volunteers roared and rattled by at seventy, the fastest the old pumper could go. In a few seconds I had caught up and passed it at eighty-five, hoping a deer wouldn't dash out from the forest and impale itself on my front bumper.

Two miles west of town we could see the flames leaping hundreds of feet up from the north end of River Street.

"Holy crap," Ginny said in a marvel of understatement.

I couldn't tell how many buildings were involved, but there had to be maybe half a dozen and probably more. As we tore across the bridge over the Porcupine River and headed for the junction with US 45, three more fire engines roared into town from the south.

As I skidded to a stop on River Street I saw that Gil O'Brien, my efficient undersheriff, already had three deputies shooing onlookers into side streets away from the blaze. Five buildings, all two-story wooden houses with square false fronts, were burning, shooting high into the sky fiery embers that rained down on roofs all over town.

"Gil?" I yelled over the roar of the flames.

"Troopers are helping," he shouted back. "Two so far and more coming from Wakefield."

"Anybody in those buildings?" Though one was vacant, people lived in the second floors above the shop fronts of the four other burning buildings.

"Got 'em all out as far as we know," Gil said.

"What about the other side of the street?" I shouted as the wind-driven embers arched like mortar shells over the pavement onto the buildings opposite and licked at their combustible roofs. Firemen had begun to play hoses on the roofs, wetting them down against secondary blazes. Outside the downtown area, homeowners likewise were at work with garden hoses against the rain of fire.

"Getting 'em now," Gil said, as a volunteer fireman helped an elderly couple stumble down a set of outside stairs attached to a feed store. "I think they're the last ones."

"Praise God for that," said the Reverend George Hartfelder at my elbow. "Steve, what can I do?"

"Pastor, could you see if you could settle down those folks, make them comfortable?" I said, pointing to half a dozen frightened evacuees huddled by a corner a block away. "They're scared."

"Sure thing," George said, and he was away to do his duty.

The flames leaped higher into the black sky even as the sweating and cursing firefighters brought more and more hoses into play, the roar of the flames rising and falling with the streams of water. Slowly but inexorably the arcs of water shortened and drooped, barely carrying onto the burning buildings.

"Damn! Losing hydrant pressure!" a firefighter yelled. "We're running low on water!" Too many hoses, I knew from previous fires, were sucking from the town's tap.

"Artificial ponds!" shouted Artie from his command post on a corner dangerously close to the blaze. "Silverton, Bergland, set 'em up on the north side!"

Quickly the volunteer firefighters from those towns hauled folded canvas and steel poles from their engines and assembled pickup-truck-sized containers, each holding thousands of gallons of water siphoned from the river by pumper trucks. Other pumpers in turn took deep draughts from the artificial ponds and hurled the water under high pressure onto the fire.

A two-story wooden building, completely engulfed in sixty-foot flames, suddenly collapsed in a crackling, billowing shower of cinders and flinders. Everyone on the street ducked from the lapping tongues of fire.

"We're gaining in the south, but it's getting hotter in the north and moving!" Artie yelled, mopping his soot-stained brow. "We're gonna have to knock down Algren's. That'll keep the fire from spreading to Entwhistle's."

Algren's Tax and Accounting Service occupied a small wooden building next to Entwhistle's Insurance, a three-story face-brick structure that had been expensively renovated just the previous year. Pulling down the smaller building would rob the fire of fuel and save the bigger one.

"Can't you at least let us get our computers out?" said Patti Algren, the accountant who with her husband Bill owned the place. "If it's okay with Artie," I said.

"There's time before the excavator gets here," the chief said. "I'll go in with you."

Patti, Bill and Artie—carrying a large hand extinguisher—dashed into the building, emerging a few moments later with two large computers and hard drives, loading them into the back of Bill's pickup outside the storefront.

"Bless you, Artie," Patti said. "We can lose everything else, but our lives depend on these computers."

They drove away and Artie and I returned our attention to the blaze. A big yellow excavator driven by Jack Elder, the county's biggest contractor, rolled up to the back of Algren's. At Artie's nod Jack plunged the machine's huge maw into the roof of the structure, tearing it apart in a crackling hail of splinters, and kept at the job until the entire building was destroyed, fire-fighters wetting down the wreckage and depriving the blaze of fuel.

By an hour after sunrise the flames had all but disappeared, thick clouds of smoke rising from the ruins as the firefighters sought out hot spots. Six buildings had been destroyed and two storefronts across the street were badly damaged, one of them—a hiker's outfitter—a total loss.

"Coulda been worse," Artie said. "Nobody killed. Just one fireman with a burned hand."

But the real cost to Porcupine City, I knew with a sinking heart, had yet to be calculated. Not all the buildings had been replaced after the great Diamond Match Company fire in 1896 that destroyed most of the town, and the ones that had burned today had been built on the ruins of that earlier blaze. The downtown skyline had been snaggletoothed for more than a century, and now it was missing more teeth.

I wondered how many of the buildings were insured, and if the insurance was enough to rebuild—and in some cases, I knew, there would be none. Porcupine County's population had been slowly dwindling for three quarters of a century, and so was its income.

"Artie," I said, returning to reality, "think it's time to set up the tape around the scene?"

"Ya," said the chief. "It'll be cleanup from here on in."

I called Gil and Chad over, and spoke to them briefly. The two deputies took large rolls of yellow crime-scene tape from Chad's cruiser and started blocking off the burned portions of River Street. Hoses still crisscrossed the ember-strewn pavement. Some of the volunteer fire departments, their jobs done, began packing up hoses and gear.

"Stevie boy!" It was Alex. "Exciting morning, eh?"

"I am strangely not happy to see you," I told the trooper, who had been helping control traffic at the south end of town. "Every time we get together, a corpse seems to be involved."

"Well, not this time," Alex said. "Don't seem to be any casualties."

"Thank God for that."

Not five minutes later, in the center of the burned block, at the Salad Bowl—a long-boarded-up greasy spoon with a small apartment on the second floor—a firefighter waved from where he'd been poking at the charred ruins in the basement. "Steve! Alex! You better come look!"

As we gingerly stepped over and through water-sodden debris, I said, "Alex, something tells me you spoke too soon."

"Mm. We'll see."

With a hook the firefighter pulled aside a curtain of smoldering lath and plaster. Alex and I hunkered down and peered into the basement, holding our breath against the sweet aroma of burned human flesh.

A figure sat slumped in a wooden rocker on the littered concrete floor, head thrust back, mouth agape. Though its hair had been singed away and the skin of its face deeply browned and cracked, juices dribbling down its neck, we could see immediately by the swell of her chest that it was the body of a woman. Her denim shirt and jeans lay intact though scorched brown and in spots charred. The flames had not reached into the basement, but the searing heat had broiled the corpse.

"What's she doing here?" I asked nobody in particular. "This building has been vacant and boarded up for years." For so many years that the village fathers had all but forgotten who owned it, although that information was easily available at the courthouse. There had been talk at village council meetings about contacting the owner to either spruce it up or tear it down, but the council had so much else on its mind that it never followed up.

Alex and I crouched by the body.

"She wasn't killed by the fire," Alex said. "Look here."

A ragged hole crowned the back of her splintered occiput, like a small skullcap that wasn't there.

With a small flashlight Alex peered into the corpse's mouth, careful not to brush against it.

"Her palate's gone. She was shot through the mouth."

Alex took several photographs of the corpse, then, with a

pencil and latex-gloved hands, carefully lifted charred splinters from the woman's lap, revealing an old-fashioned black-powder cap-and-ball revolver by her roasted right hand. Its grips were scorched but the brown steel untouched.

"Unless I miss my guess," Alex said, "that's a Remington New Model Army, a forty-four-caliber Civil War replica." He showed me the markings on the barrel: A. UBERTI ITALY. Uberti is a leading replica arms manufacturer.

"Suicide, you think?" I said.

"Sure looks that way," Alex said.

I held the revolver in a gloved hand and examined the cylinder.

"No balls or caps in the other chambers," I said. "Think the fire cooked off the other five shots?"

"Probably not," Alex said. "Not without caps. But forensics will tell for sure."

"That means there was probably just one slug in the gun. A suicide would need only one. Wouldn't a killer want more shots, to be sure?"

"Looks that way," Alex said.

"No note," I said. "But if there was one the fire probably got it. Look at all this newspaper ash."

Alex nodded. "Let's see if we can find out who she is." With tweezers he pried open her pockets, the fabric crumbling to the touch.

Out of a jeans pocket he fished a warped driver's license and a similarly damaged credit card, carefully dropping them into a plastic evidence sleeve. "Can still read 'em. Name's Ellen Juntunen, two-sixty-four Main Street, Bessemer."

"Chad?" I called from the wreckage. The big deputy stepped close.

"See what you can find out about Ellen Juntunen," I said, giving him the plastic bag containing her identification.

Bessemer lies an hour west of Porcupine City, a few miles east of Ironwood and a couple of miles northwest of Mason-ville.

"She was probably here for the Labor Day show," I said.

The last decade or so Porcupine City has put on a big country-style party, including a wiener roast, a downtown flea market, an antique-auto show, bake sales, foot races, a lawn-mower derby and a parade every Labor Day weekend. People come from all over Upper Michigan and northern Wisconsin to participate in the festivities and watch the parade.

"Maybe popped the padlock with a pry bar," said Alex, who already had set two uniformed troopers to sifting the wreckage. "Maybe she chose this place so her body wouldn't be discovered for a while. Maybe she chose it because she didn't want people she knew to find her body and get all upset."

"She could have gone into the woods to do that," I said.

"But she was a woman. She knew what animals would do to her face. Women don't like to be disfigured."

"But why would she eat her pistol?" I said. "That's very rare, and for the same reason."

"Yes, but it's not unheard of. This is gun country, after all. People aren't quite so delicate about that."

"Steve?" Chad called from his cruiser.

"Yeah?"

"She owned the building. Inherited it from her dad. Rented it out for a while years ago but apparently never had the dough to fix it up. Water pipes broken, stuff like that. Nobody wanted to live there."

Alex and I looked wordlessly at the corpse for long seconds.

"It does make sense," I said. "Suicides often want to be alone when they do themselves in. They decide on a place to do it, and they go there, and they do the deed. She had the key, and she knew she wouldn't be disturbed. As for the noise, it's a celebration weekend, and people set off firecrackers all the time."

One more question occurred to me. "Any connection between her and the fire?"

"Doubtful," Alex said. "It's already clear the fire started two doors south and worked its way here. Just a coincidence."

I took a deep sigh and suddenly coughed. The smoke had finally gotten to me.

"Steve, you've got enough on your plate," Alex said. "I'll send this body to Marquette and follow up in Bessemer. Okay?"

"Sure." I was happy to be relieved of the routine, especially next-of-kin notification. I set off down the smoking, cinder-strewn street to find Ginny in the next block. She was helping Horace Wright, the *Porcupine City Herald* reporter who served as president of the Historical Society, roll up the hoses they had used to wet down their building's roof.

"Everything OK?" I asked.

"No damage," said Ginny, soaked to the skin, her hair flying. "We were upwind the whole time and the embers didn't reach us."

She sighed, still quivering from her frantic labors.

"Steve, Artie's declared that the parade's still on," she said with a touch of defiance in her voice. "We're not going to let the fire spoil it."

I had suspected that Porcupine City wouldn't let the fire, devastating as it was, derail its Labor Day plans, and knew I'd have to help the city fathers plan an alternate route for the parade as well as secure the fire site for the state police fire marshal, who was already on his way to investigate.

As Alex walked by on his way to his vehicle I called to him.

"Yeah?" he said.

"Two deaths by muzzle loader in one county in one month," I said. "What do you make of that?"

He stood silent for a while. It was easy to see that the thought had occurred to him before I voiced it.

"If we find no connection between the two," he said slowly, "then it's probably an awful coincidence. A statistical sport."

"I'd like to believe that," I said.

"Don't you?"

"I guess."

CHAPTER TEN

Angel was exhilarated. Everything had gone as planned. It was too bad the revolver had to be sacrificed for the cause, but it could be replaced. It was just a tool of the trade, an easily replaced copy, not an heirloom. It had done its job and it had done it well. Another minion of the Devil had been dispatched. Neither God nor man could ask more than that of a weapon.

The task had been easier than expected. When, shortly after one in the morning, Angel suggested that they leave the bar in Ironwood where they had agreed to meet and find a secret place where nobody could see them, Ellen Juntunen had eagerly agreed. She was buzzed, but not enough to dampen her libido.

It was the whore's idea to drive to Porcupine City and use the basement room in the old building she owned. They wouldn't be noticed in the noise and lights of the Labor Day revelry.

They had just entered the room when the woman had turned and said with a lustful breathiness in her voice, "Shall we take off our clothes now?"

Fighting revulsion, Angel had replied, "Not just yet, Ellen. Sit in that rocking chair and let's talk a little."

The whore did so, coyly opening her blouse and exposing her breasts. At their sight Angel was stirred to disgust and fury.

When Angel had grasped Juntunen's hair and thrust the muzzle of the revolver into her mouth, she was too surprised to struggle. Astonishment still wreathed her dead eyes when Angel waved aside the acrid curtain of black-powder smoke and wrapped both of Juntunen's warm palms around the revolver's barrel and grip, then placed the weapon in her lap, being careful to wipe down the rest of the brown steel with the whore's shirt.

There had been a brief moment of fright in emerging from the basement almost into a horizontal wall of flames that had erupted from a back window of the building next door. A burning two-by-four fell with a crash across the doorway, forcing Angel to grasp it and hurl it aside, stifling a scream from the pain.

The fire spread quickly, and the hue and cry was bound to be raised before long. It was vital to get away immediately. Swiftly Angel raced from the burning building and dashed through the night to the railroad yard at the edge of town, ducking behind a string of boxcars and racing to the pickup left by a street corner. By the time the fire bell rang, Angel had crossed the Porcupine River bridge and was speeding west unseen, escape made good.

"Thank you, Lord," Angel said to a small portrait newly hung on the wall above the desk just below the Hammer. It was an old framed picture from the 1950s, common on Sunday-school walls of the time. Its subject had fair skin and long, flowing blond locks.

Jesus did not look Jewish at all. Jesus looked like regular people. That was pleasing.

Now it was time to select another weapon and choose another target.

With bandaged hands Angel opened the shutters, knelt before the stars and, as a wolf howled somewhere in the night, prayed for guidance.

CHAPTER ELEVEN

The autumn passed without incident, and it was a cold afternoon in December when Alex called.

"Muzzle-loader shooting in Schoolcraft County this morning," he said. "Another accident, it seems."

I looked at the calendar. It was the first day of the muzzle-loading deer season.

"What happened?"

"Stray ball. Caught a hunter square in the back."

"He wearing orange?"

"No." That was illegal, but citizens of Upper Michigan, independent almost to a fault, often followed their own personal laws.

"How long before they found the victim?"

"Right away. He was with three friends and they heard him cry out right after the shot."

"Did they find the shooter?"

"Didn't come forward."

It was anybody's guess what happened. Mistaken target? Unlikely. Muzzle-loader hunters get one chance and they want to make sure of their quarry. Maybe somebody took a long shot at a running deer and missed. It happens. Maybe it had been a hang fire and the shooter hadn't dropped his muzzle in time.

Deadly gun accidents were a dime a dozen during regular hunting season, when liquored-up yahoos from Detroit and Chicago failed to set their safeties, tripped over roots and plugged the hunter in front of them. But they were very, very rare during muzzle-loader season. Hunters who shoot flintlocks and cap locks know that they cannot afford to waste the first load. They tend to be careful, far more careful than their breech-loading brethren.

"Hmm. Glad it's not my case."

"Uh-huh," said Alex. "Thought you'd want to know."

Late that afternoon curiosity overcame me, and I picked up the phone and dialed Bob Epler's number. Bob was my opposite number in Manistique, the seat of Schoolcraft County a couple hundred miles to the east in the Upper Peninsula, a smart sheriff and a good guy. But before the call could be completed I hung up. His county's medical examiner wouldn't have had time to finish the postmortem. I'd wait until morning, just as I'd waited for the Marquette forensics fellows to finish with Ellen Juntunen the previous September. Everything we'd found, they had said, was consistent with suicide.

Juntunen, Chad had also discovered, had been a deeply troubled woman. She was fifty-three years old, divorced, no children, a rap sheet for public drunkenness and one felony possession of small amounts of crystal meth that had been pleaded down to misdemeanor and a few days in jail for the promise of getting help. She hadn't, and her habits had grown worse. She lost her job as a hardware-store cashier and the bank was preparing to foreclose on the mortgage it held on the tiny cabin outside Bessemer that she also owned.

What's more, according to witnesses, she had lately been supporting herself on the meager generosity of fellow barflies who took her home after closing hours, often soliciting what she called "monetary considerations" for the acts she performed. DNA analysis after the autopsy had revealed the presence of semen from three men, confirming that Juntunen had had multiple sexual encounters in the forty-eight hours before her death. There were no tears or bruises, indicating that there had been no assault.

Members of her little storefront church in Bessemer had tried to help, they said, but she had angrily turned them away. Her few friends said she had appeared depressed.

While there was no paper trail on the revolver that had killed her—there rarely is for muzzle loaders beyond the first owner, and those weapons change hands often at swap meets—she had owned a modern deer rifle, though she had not applied for a deer permit in years. Lots of disadvantaged people in this neck of the woods have supported themselves for years by poaching, and the problem had grown worse as the economic crisis deepened.

There was no doubt that Ellen Juntunen had possessed both means and reason to do away with herself.

Shortly after lunch at Ginny's the next day, I called Sheriff Epler. He was at his desk.

"Martinez here. Calling it an accident?" I said without preamble.

"Jeez, Steve, you're starting to sound like Alex." The trooper's work takes him all over the central and western portions of Upper Michigan, and every law-enforcement officer has been subjected to Alex's peremptory phone manners.

"Yeah, sorry, hello, Bob."

"Now what accident is that?"

"The guy who got shot yesterday."

"Ah yes. Medical examiner finished up. Yes, we're calling that shooting an accident."

"Tell me."

"No motive we can discover. That spot in the woods was full of deer and there were about a dozen hunters within an eighth of a mile of each other. A bunch of deer, maybe six or eight, had been hunkered in a copse and just exploded out of there when the hunters got close. We figured maybe six of the hunters shot their loads at almost the same moment and one of those rounds hit the guy. No way of telling who fired the shot."

"Who was the victim?"

"Dickie Atkins, a logger from Marquette, an old muzzle-loader hunter from way back."

"Anything unusual about him?"

"Not that we could find out. Upstanding citizen, devoted Presbyterian church member, active in the Democratic party, well liked and so forth. Hey, what's your interest here?"

"Had a couple of muzzle-loading deaths here in Porcupine County last summer. The circumstances were unusual. I'm just a little antsy about it."

"I heard all about that. Joe Koski's wife is a friend of my sister and they drove over for dinner a while back."

I chuckled. Joe, the department's dispatcher and chief corrections officer, is a notorious gossip. He had, however, betrayed no confidences—the facts about Gloria Lake and Ellen Juntunen were public information, even if they hadn't yet gotten out to the public. Nobody had asked. The press had better things to do. And I had nothing against Joe sharing the details of police work with a brother officer, whether in an official capacity or not. That was often useful. Two minds or more on a problem sometimes helped.

"Yeah, well, three fatal accidents involving muzzle-loading weapons in the UP in one year seems like a lot. There are no more than six or eight every year in the whole damn country."

"Probably won't be any more for five or six years," Bob said. "Let's hope so, anyway."

"What'd the medical examiner find?"

"A fifty-caliber rifled ball in the chest cavity. No markings at all. All those hunters we talked to were carrying either fifty-caliber or fifty-four-caliber. Mostly Hawkens."

"No sixty-nines or seventy-fives?" I asked.

"You think anybody would hunt with a smoothbore that weighs as much as a howitzer?" Bob said incredulously. "Why would they want to blow apart a deer—if they could even hit it?"

"Got me there." It was obvious to both of us that what had happened in the woods of Schoolcraft County could not possibly have any link with what had happened in the woods of Porcupine County. At least not where the choice of weapons was concerned.

"Okay, never mind," I said. "Except maybe could you send me a copy of the incident jacket? I'd like to have it on hand just in case."

It was a long shot, but long shots are the mother's milk of detective work. God knew what I would find in the case reports that might shed any light on the incident at the Mullet. Probably nothing.

"Sure. I'll have it faxed over in the next day or two."

"Thanks."

It actually was five days before Bob got around to the task—he is as busy as I am, his deputies as overworked as mine—and when the file came in I stuck the printed fax sheets into a folder that over the next few months worked its way to the bottom of my in-box, covered by paperwork that grew more pressing as it rolled in. A county sheriff never leaves behind a clean desk when he goes home for the night. He can't. It's impossible.

CHAPTER TWELVE

Angel folded the *Marquette Mining Journal* and, having had
nothing to do with the accident in Schoolcraft County and not
even knowing the victim, dropped the newspaper unconcernedly
on the desk.

But the meaning of numbers was clear. Three muzzle-loader
deaths in a small region in a short time is a statistical anomaly
that might whet the curiosity of law enforcement. They might
even investigate.

The Lord's work would have to be spread out, and it would
have to be executed with even more care. But anyone who was
smarter than the lawmen would easily stay ahead of them. Jesus
would make sure of that.

Angel gazed at Jesus and His tools on the wall. They would
have to be patient, too. It was time to lie low, like a mountain
lion lurking in the shadows of the forest, and wait for a good
opportunity to resume the work of the Lord.

"Don't rush into things," Daddy had often said. "Pick your
moments. No use killing three woodchucks in four weeks when
with a little patience you might kill ten times that in four
months."

That applied to human vermin, too.

CHAPTER THIRTEEN

The rest of December passed quietly, then January, February, March, April and May. The Mountain Men encampment of the previous summer had faded into memory, along with my fretting about Gloria Lake, the suicide in the fire, and the accident in Schoolcraft County.

As the year deepened, so did our ever-present budget crisis. Our crapped-out Crown Vics—all had tried harder for Avis before we bought them secondhand and had them painted, then equipped with flashers on removable bars—had reached the point of no return. But there was no money to be had. The current administration in the White House had stood for election promising more grants for rural law enforcement but when it won it cut the already meager funds we had been getting.

What's more, the economic crisis gripping the country had consumed Porcupine County's largest employer, the paper mill. Its owner had gone bankrupt and had sold the mill to a demolition company. Nearly one hundred fifty employees had been thrown out of work, and the livelihoods of at least the same number of independent loggers who cut pulpwood in the national forests and trucked them to the mill had been wrecked.

Petty crime was increasing, and so were alcohol- and drug-fueled domestic disturbances. My deputies and the state cops could no longer keep up with the calls but had to choose which ones to investigate, a kind of triage of crime.

There was also Ginny to placate. She was beginning to drop

hints that maybe our relationship should be made official and permanent. We had been keeping company, as the old ladies put it, for four years. Most Porkies aren't judgmental about these things, but every once in a while at a church supper or Elks or American Legion hoedown, when the hour was growing late and people started running out of better things to talk about, someone would say, "When you gonna get hitched?"

I just didn't want to deal with it. My future seemed cloudy. I'd thought I wouldn't mind being sheriff for another term or two, but given the ever-growing hard times Porcupine County faced, I wasn't sure I was up to coping with tighter and tighter budgets. I could see the job getting harder and harder, and maybe I'd accept the Michigan State Police's standing offer of a job—or leave law enforcement entirely and do something else.

Of course, if I wed Ginny, my financial future would be assured. But I was not ever going to marry anybody for money. I'd sooner end up a pauper on the dole than do that. I could get a good job as a town cop in Marquette or Ironwood, but I didn't want to leave Porcupine County. Maybe I would have to.

"Why are you so prideful, Steve?" Ginny always replied to that argument. "If the tables were turned and you had the money and I didn't, I wouldn't hesitate to take the step. I love you and that's what counts most of all."

At that point I always changed the subject, and Ginny had the grace not to press it.

But life otherwise was good. Tommy had lost interest in the Mountain Men. I was not surprised. Boys of his age flit through enthusiasms like houseflies from pie to pie. But he was still captivated by muzzle loaders, and had finally persuaded Ginny into letting him mail-order a kit for a Kentucky rifle, .50-caliber percussion. It had taken months for him to make the breakthrough, but he agreed to shoot it only under adult supervision until he turned sixteen in the fall of the next year.

I watched as Tommy carefully filed the rough edges off the white steel of his kit rifle's barrel, lovingly polishing the metal and immersing it in a tank made of plastic drainpipe and filled with chemical bluing to preserve it against rust. I believe in letting a youngster learn by his mistakes, but it's not a good idea to make errors with something that uses gunpowder, so I hovered over him like a papa eagle on the nest as a fledgling spread his wings. Not once did I need to correct him. He knew exactly what he was doing. He had consulted not only the best books on the subject but also had visited local gunsmiths to ask their advice. He knew a lot more about muzzle loaders than I did. But I was only a cop, not a bright lad with an obsession.

And with a wisdom far beyond his age, he asked me to sand and finish the roughly carved maple gunstock that came with the kit. He knew that like most men I suffered from the Pinewood Derby syndrome, that I wanted to help but if I helped I might take over the whole damned thing. Having me do a small but important part of the job would keep me out of trouble. I enjoyed working along with Tommy far more than I'd have admitted to Ginny.

When it came time to test the finished rifle, he and I drove out to the range at the Porcupine City Rod and Gun Club deep in the woods near Silverton. Tommy knew exactly what to do. He was not a virgin with muzzle loaders, for he had joined his friends in the club's informal lessons for youngsters. I did not worry at all.

First Tommy tied a string around his new rifle's trigger, then wedged the stock in a large truck tire used to test weapons, its barrel pointing toward the backstop. Then he placed a copper percussion cap on the nipple, and levered back the hammer. He crept behind a log-and-sand safety wall ten feet away and hunkered down with me.

"Fire in the hole!" he called, although nobody else was out

on the range that morning. There was no answer, so he yanked the string.

The rifle coughed discreetly and a puff of vapor emerged from the muzzle.

"Standard chamber test to make sure there's no powder and ball already in there," Tommy said, sounding like a very young professor of engineering. "It prevents accidentally putting a second charge on top of another you forgot was there."

Now Tommy got down to business. With a cleaning rod and a couple of patches he swabbed out the residue left by the fired percussion cap. He stood the rifle on its stock and tipped into the muzzle a carefully measured charge of black powder. Then he placed a lubricated patch on the muzzle, crowning it with a lead ball. Next he used the sphere of his short starter to roll the ball into the muzzle, then the ferruled peg to drive it in a couple of inches. He followed up with the ramrod, shoving the ball and patch all the way home into the chamber.

"All set," Tommy said. He carefully nestled the rifle back into the tire, placed a cap on the nipple and crept back behind the wall with me. "Fire in the hole!"

With a mighty "WHAM!" the rifle bucked against its restraint, and the ball gouged a crater of dirt out of the backstop.

"It works!" Tommy shouted. "It's safe!"

Then the lad grew serious. "Better try two more, just to be sure."

With three oiled patches he swabbed and dried the inside of the barrel, then he repeated the test firing twice, both with slightly more than full charges of powder to test the limits of the chamber. It held.

Tommy smiled at me as the breeze finally carried away the sulfurous clouds of black-powder smoke. "Ready for sighting in, I think."

For the next hour he worked at the test bench, the rifle snugly resting in an immovable wooden cradle as he fired it, while he adjusted the open rear sight with taps from a maple mallet.

"Fires a bit low," he said, examining the paper target he had used at the twenty-five-yard mark. "I'll file a little metal off the top of the front sight."

Finally the job was done.

"I've got me a good rifle," Tommy said proudly. "Can't wait for my birthday!"

As we drove home the thought occurred to me for the first time in six months that a muzzle-loading rifle makes a very poor murder weapon. Too much time and too much fuss and too much care and too much expertise. Way, way too much.

CHAPTER FOURTEEN

The rest of the summer passed swiftly, then most of the fall. The hard times grew worse, especially after the plant at Lone Pine that refined copper from Canada shut down and threw scores more out of work. There was a small but significant uptick in the number of felonies, mainly theft and burglary. Summer people returning to their cottages for deer season reported break-ins, fortunately not many, and in any case they had had the sense not to leave valuables behind. And, of course, domestic disturbances, usually fueled by alcohol, had increased.

The most memorable call we fielded at the sheriff's department during that time was from a woman who wanted to know if her teenage son and daughter had committed attempted murder. They hated the woman's second husband and, mindful of his weak heart, persuaded the grandmother who lived with the family to use lard instead of margarine in the molasses cookies their stepfather loved. Eagerly the husband—a cookie freak of monstrous proportions—scarfed the result, and after several months suffered a heart attack that resulted in a quadruple bypass.

"Can't you arrest them, Sheriff?" the wife had said. "Put a little fear of God into them?"

"I'm afraid no prosecutor or judge would go for that," I had replied. "After all, the victim participated in his own attempted homicide, didn't he?"

When I suggested family counseling she hung up in a fury.

I chuckled at that memory late the first week in December as I headed on Highway M64 to Silverton in the west of the county on a chilly morning. Snow had fallen early in Upper Michigan. The county plows had already been out, carving foot-high ridges of snow on both sides of the road. By February those ridges would be a good eight feet high. Maybe that would happen earlier, because the air had turned noticeably damp and the western sky had grown heavy with dark clouds washed with red by the sun as it rose in the clear eastern sky.

Last night's snow had dusted and hidden whatever roadkill remained on the verges. In hard times, deer, groundhogs and even raccoons struck by cars are swiftly scooped up and dispatched to the freezer by less fortunate Porkies. Dead skunks, foxes and coyotes are pulled to the side of the roads and left to the eagles, vultures and crows.

I tootled along at the official speed limit, constantly watching for suicidal deer in the tree lines, in the department's best Crown Vic cruiser—the one with the fewest miles on its odometer and the fewest dings and dents as well, making it the sheriff's official vehicle—on my way in official gold-braid uniform to Silverton for official ceremonial duties at the official dedication of the new firehouse. I hated official.

Upper Michigan sheriffs often dress casually, though their deputies wear full uniform, and I gratefully took advantage of those loose sartorial standards, except to wear a six-pointed star and official departmental ball cap over Pendleton woolen shirt and jeans, my favorite attire of the season. The star and cap immediately established that I was law enforcement when I arrived on a scene or pinched a speeder, but it was easy to go plainclothes simply by taking off the star and replacing the cap with a souvenir from a long-ago Cubs game at Wrigley Field. Just by looking at my head, everybody in the county knew when I was on the job or not.

Suddenly I spotted a lone wild turkey gobbling to herself as she strolled down the snowy verge. That caught my interest. Wild turkeys were recent immigrants to the county, having waddled up from Wisconsin only during the last couple of years as winters grew warmer. The big birds were still fairly rare in these parts, but people increasingly had been reporting sightings of small flocks to the game wardens. I tapped the brake to slow slightly, and at that very moment the turkey—biologists consider the species smart and wily, but to me it is always a few feathers short of a headdress—chose to launch herself across the road at me in a perfect deflection shot.

Whang! I ducked but kept control of the Crown Vic as the turkey smashed into the left outside mirror and ripped it off the mount in a cloud of feathers. Good thing the driver's window was closed, or I'd have had a faceful of turkey and mirror and maybe lost my grip on the wheel as well as a few teeth.

I whirled the cruiser around and drove back to the scene of the crime. As I stood on the road by the turkey's carcass, the shattered pieces of mirror in my hands, I thanked my stars that not only I but also the sheriff's budget was uninjured. In a collision with an animal there is no five-hundred-dollar deductible for a broken mirror. Insurance would pay the entire bill.

Just then a dilapidated pickup stopped across the road in a squeak of brakes.

"Everybody okay?" called the middle-aged driver, a freshly unemployed mill worker I knew slightly. He had been an overnight guest in the lockup once or twice after a long evening's toot, but we often don't bring misdemeanor charges if people and property remain uninjured. Saves time and court costs.

"Yup, thanks," I replied.

"You gonna eat that?" said his wife from the passenger seat.

"Nope."

"Can we?"

"Sure."

With that, she dismounted, crossed the road, and scooped up the turkey by its legs.

"Dinner tonight!" she said with a toothless smile, immediately returning to the pickup. "Bye!"

"Bye!" I said with a wave.

As I drove on to Silverton, I smiled to myself. I was starting to talk like a native Yooper, employing severe economy of expression. Yoopers do not waste words. Nor do they waste roadkill. Especially when times are harder than normal, and up here normal times are always hard.

But then a barely suppressed emotion bubbled to the surface. I was beginning to feel a little like roadkill on the highway of my relationship with Ginny. She had not yet mounted a frontal challenge of my reluctance to make things legal and permanent, but she was subtly cooling toward me. The official adoption papers had made their way through the warrens of reservation bureaucracy and needed only a brief trip to Baraga for signing, and she was impatiently waiting for me to pop the question so that I could put my name next to hers and Tommy's. In the last week or so she hadn't invited me to spend the night, and Tommy was barely hiding his embarrassment and concern over the unexpressed but palpable tension between the two adults in his life.

"I'm Lakota," I had confessed to Alex the evening before over a burger at Merle's. "The Lakota need to be free."

"You're just a guy," he retorted. "You just can't commit. Lakota, phooey."

"I don't want to marry money," I said. "I can't stand the idea of a prenup."

I stopped. Had I inadvertently spilled the beans about Ginny's wealth?

"Does she want one?"

I stared at Alex. Did he know she had money? Maybe not her propensity to share it with the needy in Porcupine County. He is a detective, after all. Not much escapes the notice of detectives like him. But once in a while a lot does. I decided to trust Alex, a discreet as well as trustworthy man.

"She hasn't said anything. But I'm sure her lawyers would demand one. After all, she's their meal ticket. They would want to protect the franchise."

"Franchise?" Alex said, his eyebrows rising. I relaxed. He didn't know as much as I did.

"When you have money, you have lawyers and accountants," I said.

"Yes, well, would she go along with your not signing a prenup?"

"I don't know."

"Why don't you ask her?"

"That's impossible!"

"Why?"

I had no answer. But Alex did, and said with his usual disconcerting directness, "Crazy Horse would have been ashamed of you."

The mention of the Lakota hero who may just possibly have been my ancestor caused me to rise, put on my hat and coat, nod good night to Alex and stalk wordlessly out of Merle's. Not because Alex had made a gratuitous reference to my biological roots but because I knew he was right, and I had no defense. I hate that.

The truth is that I was afraid of being burned again. During the height of Desert Storm my fiancée back home, a young woman with whom I had grown up, wrote and confessed that she had fallen in love with one of my best buddies, was pregnant by him, and had married him. Besides, she said, her father—a

Chamber of Commerce stalwart but a closet bigot—had told her I may have been a nice guy and all that, but he really didn't want brown-skinned half-breed grandchildren.

That news was so devastating that I resigned my commission as soon as I could and took the first law-enforcement job I could find, a deputy's post in a tiny sheriff's department in the boonies as far from urban civilization as you can get. It was a rash act born of disappointment and despair.

But I almost immediately fell in love with Porcupine County, its sturdy people, and its gorgeous wilderness. The salary was low—barely subsistence level—but the intangible benefits were glorious. One of them was my relationship with Ginny. No strings had been attached to it. Both of us had our freedom, and an important part of that was our choice to be together in a strong but loose alliance of love and affection. But now Ginny wanted more, and that brought back a painful memory. I just did not think I could handle it.

I was trying to sweep the blues from my head and concentrate on the official task at hand when, just outside Silverton, the radio crackled.

"Steve?" Joe Koski said without preamble. "Bill Koons called. Geoff Armstrong's missing in the Wolverines. Didn't come back from hunting yesterday morning."

I winced. Geoffrey Armstrong, an uncle of Garner Armstrong, the Porcupine County prosecuting attorney, was the former Democratic congressman for northern Michigan. He had been out of office for six years, having tacked through the political storms a port or two too far. His socially conservative constituency had tolerated his contrariness on hot-button social issues so long as he brought home the bacon, and he was one of Washington's most eminent pork producers, skilled at trading votes for projects. His election victories had all been cliffhangers, however, and he had been swept out of office in a landslide when his womanizing—some of it with other politicians' wives, some of it with girls barely of legal age—became public knowledge. His constituency had been willing to overlook certain of his beliefs but finally could not abide his actions. The many men he had cuckolded, as well as the fathers of the young women, had issued dark threats of revenge.

Geoffrey Armstrong also had become an embarrassing alcoholic, and in his cups he liked to phone political columnists and tell them what he really believed about the controversy of the day. The next day he'd deny everything the reporters printed. He was a colorful rogue, always good for an amusing story or column on a slow news day, and he was nationally known, but not in a very flattering way—you might say it was the way an errant alcoholic congressman of an earlier day, Wilbur Mills, got caught in drunken high jinks with the stripper Fanne Foxe near the Capitol.

I was not surprised Armstrong was in the Wolverines. He was an avid hunter, always good for a quote in gun and game magazines, and it was the second day of the Michigan muzzle-loading deer season.

"Details?" I asked Joe. "What'd Bill have to say?"

Bill Koons is the second-in-command at the park, the operations chief who usually takes charge of search-and-rescue operations for lost hikers, children and hunters. According to protocol the sheriff, who holds jurisdiction in the Wolverines, was nominally the boss, but I always deferred to the experts and let them do their thing. If I got involved, it was to assist Koons, the incident commander.

"Bill said the three hunters with Armstrong said they went out at dawn yesterday in the Summit Peak area," Joe said. "They split up and planned to meet at noon with their snowmobiles at the lot near the Union Bay campgrounds ranger station.

Armstrong didn't show up, and this morning they checked with the rangers and other hunters, and nobody's seen him."

"Was he equipped?"

"The hunters said he was dressed warmly and had plenty of jerky and a full canteen when they left. Maps, compass and GPS, too."

This didn't surprise me. Armstrong had grown up in the woods and knew how to survive a cold night as well as to make his way out of the forest to civilization. He was no tenderfoot.

"Probably got hurt somewhere," I said. "Joe, this is gonna be a hairball. If Armstrong doesn't walk out of the woods sometime today, the press is going to get hold of it and they'll be all over us. Call Bill back and tell him I'm coming to see him right now. I'm sure he'll call out the troops for this one."

Normally Koons would mount an initial search with park rangers, who usually would locate the missing person within a few hours. At this time of year, I knew, he had only eight full-timers, including himself, to call on. But he had immediate access to sheriff's police, state troopers and fire departments from neighboring counties as well as forest rangers and the skilled civilian volunteers of the Porcupine County Search and Rescue Team. If a hiker had been reported missing for forty-eight hours, the word would go out, and a systematic search involving scores and even hundreds of rescuers would be mounted. Almost always, however, the missing person walked out of the woods within twenty-four hours of the report, cold, hungry, tired and scared but otherwise unhurt.

I swept past Silverton without stopping and pointed the cruiser to the Wolverines Wilderness State Park three miles west.

CHAPTER FIFTEEN

"Maybe I better be the front man for this circus," I told Bill Koons in his office at park headquarters. "But you run the show. Okay with you?"

I did not need to tell the ranger, a short, wiry and mustachioed former Army sergeant in his late thirties, that the heavens and earth would open and dump the media, the governor, the family and all kinds of hangers-on, official and unofficial, on the Wolverines once word got out that a celebrity was missing in the woods. Being the figurehead meant that they would fasten on me as the putative boss and leave Bill alone to do his job as the real incident commander.

"Fine with me," Bill said. He did not have the prickly ego of a lower-echelon bureaucrat who hungered for public recognition.

"Of course this means you do all the work and I get all the credit," I said, and I wasn't kidding. The press likes things to be simple and easy to understand. One man, one hero.

"If we find him," Bill said. "If we don't, you get all the blame."

"That's true."

"You do look the part," Bill said. "You're irresistible with all that gold braid."

I grunted and peered through the glass of his office door to the three hunters sitting on hard metal chairs in the anteroom. "Permission to talk to them?"

Bill snorted. "You're the big chief. You can do what you

106

want." He knew, however, that I meant what I said. He was in charge and I would back up every decision and move he made.

"Did Armstrong have a snootful?" I asked the three hunters as Bill stood in the doorway and listened. When I talk to witnesses who are good friends of the subject, my first question often comes out of left field and is designed to derail a story carefully prepared to hide or fudge important facts in order to protect the subject. Had I done this in the beginning with the Gloria Lake case, a lot of time might have been saved—although I probably would have been no closer to the truth about what happened on the Mullet.

Of course, all three hunters had separately filled out incident forms for Koons, and none of the details they had given clashed. Still, witnesses usually want to make themselves look good, even unconsciously. Of course, this was not an interrogation—if it had been, it would have been held with one subject alone in a small room without windows. This was just a little quick fact-finding before a rescue mission, and I treated the hunters accordingly. They were not suspects, and I made sure they knew that.

"He did like to take a swig of Jack at breakfast, and he carried a flask," replied the tallest of the three men, all in their late sixties or early seventies and clad in stained Carhartt canvas pants and thick, well-used parkas, goose down popping from the seams, over heavy wool shirts. All were shod in battered high-top leather boots. Blaze-orange vests and hats completed the ensembles. All three looked leathery, tough and competent, not at all like the dewy sportsmen in expensive big-city outfitters' equipage we often had to deal with in lost-in-the-woods situations.

The other two nodded. They knew I knew all about Geoffrey Armstrong. They wanted to save their friend's life, not to protect his reputation, not that he had much of one to protect. I decided they were not trying to yank my hat over my eyes.

"Good man in the woods, though," one volunteered. In these parts, that is the highest mark of respect one can give to another.

"Yep, I know," I said. We all left unspoken the certain knowledge that something must have happened, something that had slowed down or even immobilized Armstrong.

"Where'd you last see him?"

"We left our snowmobiles at the Summit Peak lot and split up there," said the tall fellow, who had identified himself as Fred and seemingly appointed himself spokesman with the quiet assent of the other two. "I headed for the Little Carp River trail, Jack went out on the Mirror Lake trail, Jim on the Beaver Creek trail and Geoff down the Lily Pond trail. We kind of divided up the area in quadrants."

That is rugged country, some of the most difficult in the Wolverines. This was not going to be an easy search.

"You've hunted together before?" I said.

"Years and years, forty years maybe," said Fred. "Each of us usually gets a deer."

"How'd you come to know each other?" Relationships sometimes are revealing.

"High-school buddies in Petoskey." That town lay on Lake Michigan in northern lower Michigan, and was Armstrong's home as well as the population center of his old constituency. "We get together every year to go deer hunting. We go all over the state and this year it was the Wolverines."

"Anything bothering him? Was he behaving in unusual ways? Worried about anything?"

All three shook their heads. "Same old happy asshole we always knew," Fred said affectionately. "He was talking about going to a niece's wedding next week."

"Armstrong is getting on in years," I said. "Any sign of dementia, forgetfulness?"

Three slow headshakes.

"Think he was under the influence?" I asked, pressing my original question.

"Sometimes he is," Fred said quickly. "But not this time. It's always under control."

Having dealt all my professional life with alcoholics, I doubted that. People who are friends with or live with boozers tend to deny facts hanging like wet underwear on a clothesline in front of their faces.

We all sat silent for a long moment. "Well, then, it sounds like he might have had some kind of accident," I said. In the doorway Koons nodded slightly, although he wasn't going to agree publicly. It is better not to draw conclusions before a search operation has been mounted.

Then I had another idea. "Is he carrying?"

The three hunters blinked. "Well, of course," Fred said, "we're hunting. He has a rifle, a custom-made Hawken percussion."

Simple and reliable, like Tommy's rifle, a popular design with muzzle-loader enthusiasts.

"I mean a cartridge handgun," I said.

The three looked at each other and hesitated. Michigan hunting laws forbid carrying of cartridge weapons into the field during muzzle-loader season, unless the hunter has a concealed-pistol permit. The pistol may be used only for protection, not for hunting—it cannot legally perform a quick *coup de grace* on wounded deer.

Having been a controversial congressman, Geoffrey Armstrong most likely held a concealed-pistol permit just in case some former constituent with a long memory decided to get revenge. Even a tiny possibility of that can justify packing heat wherever one goes, for the Secret Service doesn't protect current congressmen, let alone former ones. It would be easy to find out in a call to state police headquarters in Lansing if Armstrong had such a permit.

"If Armstrong has a pistol, he could use it to signal his position," I said.

Slowly each of them nodded. "Yeah, he has one," Fred finally said. "A short-barreled five-shot .32 Smith & Wesson."

"Holster?" I asked.

"Stuck it in an outside pocket," Fred said. "Liked to keep it ready."

That made sense. Either a belt holster or a shoulder holster underneath a hunter's parka would make drawing the weapon slow and clumsy.

But nobody, so far as I knew, had heard the distinctive sound of a cartridge weapon anywhere in the woods yesterday. That was not a good sign.

"Okay," I said. "Thanks for your cooperation."

"Please don't go anywhere for a while," Koons said. "We'll need you here to show us on the maps where you went, so we can plan our search."

The three men nodded quietly. They, too, knew the implications of the silence of that Smith & Wesson.

"Yes, gentlemen," I said, "maybe you ought to stick around until Armstrong turns up."

They nodded in unison and left the room.

"If it's a congressman we're looking for," Koons said with a straight face, "maybe he shouldn't be found."

I chuckled at the ranger's dry humor. People in the Upper Peninsula generally don't like politicians and think of them as necessary nuisances, and Bill Koons was no different. But I knew he would search just as hard for a missing pol as he would a lost child.

I walked outside, where a few rangers from the park and the US Forest Service had joined several troopers and deputies in the parking lot. Search and Rescue volunteers were arriving, some of them in pickup trucks pulling flatbed trailers hauling snowmobiles. The noisy machines would enable searchers to cover more wilderness ground than they could on foot, so long as the terrain was not too rocky and the brush too deep. As they penetrated deeper into the park, I knew, they'd have to switch to snowshoes.

Before I could catch my breath, Gil arrived in the department's Blazer from Porcupine City thirteen miles to the east, Chad with him. Neither wore uniforms, for as volunteer members of Search and Rescue they were officially civilians. Gil, however, knew the park nearly as well as Koons did, and being a former Marine sergeant who kept in shape he had the chops to direct men in the wilds. In fact, Gil would be the tactical leader of the searchers at Summit Peak under Bill's command.

"Sit rep?" Gil asked briskly and without a shred of deference. Quickly I gave him the situation report on what the hunters had told me and what they had said in their questionnaires.

Koons handed Gil a huge topographical map of the Wolverines, trails marked on it as well as hills and dales and brooks and rivulets. Gil studied it wordlessly for a while.

"The command post will be here at headquarters," Bill said, "but you'll set up a forward post at Summit Peak Tower where the guys can bivouac for the night. It's gonna be dark in an hour and the forecast is for heavy snow tonight, so they'll have to stay there till morning and begin the search right at dawn. If they can. Tomorrow's forecast is lousy."

We would lose some time, but it couldn't be helped. The first rule about search and rescue in the wilderness is never to create another victim.

"Visibility's not so bad right now," Bill added, "but we might have a whiteout in the morning."

By the first of December all deciduous trees and bushes had shed their leaves, and only clumps of evergreens and ridges of rock would block sight lines. It would not be hard to spot blaze orange against the snow—if it wasn't snowing.

It was obvious to every Yooper that the winter was going to be unusually hard. On Thanksgiving Day the temperatures over Upper Michigan had suddenly dropped into the low teens and remained there for four consecutive days, sending the entire county into a deep freeze. Such Arctic conditions don't normally appear until January.

"Plane?" I said. In lake searches for lost boaters I flew the sheriff's aircraft, a veteran but airworthy Cessna 182, having earned a pilot's certificate in the Army.

"Not yet," Bill said. "We'll spot any smudge fires from Summit Peak. Let's wait until tomorrow before launching the air force." He spoke without irony. He and I both knew that the oncoming weather probably would reduce visibility to zero and render an air search useless as well as dangerous.

"Yessir," I said, just to keep things light and to remind Bill, who was capable of the most outrageous poker-faced *lese majeste,* that even though he was running things I was the official boss.

He chuckled. He knew his place. He knew he was king.

Quickly Gil counted off his troops and snowmobiles in the parking lot as if they were small companies of mechanized infantry and in a calm but commanding voice gave them their orders.

"Packs and chow?" Gil asked. Each searcher checked his kit, including down sleeping bags, bivouac covers and trail rations. Four women, two of them veteran members of law enforcement, were among the twenty-three that would set out into the forest.

Koons directed half a dozen searchers—two troopers, another ranger, a deputy and two Search and Rescue volunteers—to stay behind with their snowmobiles and the rescue sled to await the call. The rest would go with Gil to Summit Peak, some of them to snowmobile almost four miles further down to Mirror Lake, where they'd bivouac for the night in summer cabins closed for the winter and in the morning fan out along the warren of foot trails that began at the lake. If they could.

"Mount up!" Gil barked, like a cavalry sergeant, and they were off into a snowy dusk.

I stayed behind. Even though it was a good fifteen miles from Summit Peak Tower, the highest point in the park, the best place for the command post for a search in the Wolverines is the park headquarters itself. With the new state police radio tower atop the long escarpment a few miles away, we'd be in easy contact with searchers wherever they might be.

I may be an Indian, but I am not an expert woodsman, having grown up in the city rather than the forest. Compared to the others I am a rank tenderfoot. The best I can do is find my way out of the woods, which is not a bad accomplishment but hardly worth crowing about in these parts.

And as sheriff of Porcupine County I had wider responsibilities. They would, I knew, fall upon me like an avalanche the next morning.

Several times before darkness enveloped the mountains, the crew at Summit Peak heard, faintly, the heavy whumps of muzzle-loading rifles from hunters who hadn't yet had word of the search or the oncoming storm and were still stalking deer. In the first hour on the peak the crew had encountered four hunters, three men and one woman, and all had immediately volunteered to join the search for Armstrong, although their offer was politely declined because they had not undergone S&R training. One said he had seen Armstrong the previous day heading west on the Correction Line Trail near Mirror Lake.

"Good place to start your ops in the morning," Bill told Gil on the radio. He leaned back in his swivel chair and looked at me. "Going home for the night?"

Home was ten miles east on the lakeshore. My own warm bed sounded good to me.

"I'm already here," I said. "Might as well stay. Besides, you might need me a lot sooner than you think."

Bill shrugged. "And you're dressed to kill. You look like something out of *HMS Pinafore.*"

The reference was not obscure. The year before, the Porcupine City Players had staged the Gilbert and Sullivan comic opera to thunderous cheers. Amateur theatrical groups in the most remote boondocks can be surprisingly accomplished, and ours was no exception. My dress uniform, dripping with stars and gold braid, would not have looked out of place on that stage.

"I'll get Chad to bring me my jeans and ball cap in the morning," I said. "No need for me to look like Captain Corcoran when I meet the press." Captain Corcoran was the brass-bedecked master of the *Pinafore.*

"Nah, you'll look like Dick Deadeye instead."

"I'm the monarch of the sea," I sang, "the ruler of the Queen's Navee . . ."

"Good luck, Admiral," said Bill. "You'll need it."

I had just fallen asleep in full uniform on a couch in Bill's office when his landline phone rang.

"For you," Bill said. He was still awake and communicating via radio with Gil deep in the forest.

"Hold for the governor," an officious bureaucratic voice said.

She came on the line. "Sheriff?" she said, letting her distinctive contralto do the introduction.

"Yes, Governor?" I said.

"What's the story so far?"

I told her all I knew. How Geoffrey Armstrong had been reported missing, how he was an expert woodsman, how his companions had described his deportment, including his having taken a drink that morning. And how he was said to have carried a handgun, illegal for muzzle-loading hunters without a concealed carry permit, but not at all uncommon in the circumstances.

"That pistol worries me," the unsurprised governor said. "You know Armstrong has lots of enemies. He probably carried the weapon for protection from them. This could be sticky."

"All the same, ma'am, there's no evidence, absolutely none at all, of foul play."

"Let's hope it stays that way," she said. "Anyway, good luck on the search tomorrow." She knew how rescue teams operated. More than once on her watch a VIP had gone missing in the woods or in a boat on the Great Lakes.

"Let's hope you find him quickly and alive," she added. "Michigan doesn't need more bad news."

She sighed deeply. "The press will be all over you in the morning. Get some sleep."

"We'll do our best, ma'am," I said.

"I know you will, Sheriff," she said. "Thank you."

And she hung up.

Bill gazed thoughtfully at me across his desk as I replaced the receiver.

"Better you than me," he said.

CHAPTER SIXTEEN

At five in the morning Chad pulled up in his cruiser and honked. I awoke with a start on Koons's office couch and peered out the frost-encrusted window. In December this far north—and this far west in the Eastern time zone—first light does not arrive until well after seven-thirty, and darkness still enveloped the parking lot, now covered with nine new inches of wet and heavy snow that blew in with increasing velocity as the storm moved in off Lake Superior. This was not going to make tracking easy or even possible. And it would not improve the dispositions of the news crews at the briefing scheduled for nine, more than an hour after the searchers had been scheduled to depart their bases at Summit Peak.

Just as Chad handed me a package containing my uniform ball cap, a fresh shirt and fresh jeans, another set of headlights arrived in the lot. Behind them was a pickup and still another snowmobile trailer. Two men got out of the pickup. One strode to the park headquarters with a large cardboard box. I met him at the door.

The smiling face of the Reverend George Hartfelder, wreathed in the irresistible aroma of bacon and eggs, greeted me.

"Morning, Steve," he said. "We brought breakfast."

"Who's the other guy?"

"Father Jim."

I chuckled. The evangelicals and the Catholics had not always gotten along well in these parts, beginning hundreds of years ago with a bitter rivalry for the souls of Indians. But this was the twenty-first century, and despite the theological chasm between them and the Catholics, Pastor George and other Protestant churchmen now threw benefit pancake suppers for the local Saint Vincent de Paul charity store, which served everyone, Catholic or not. Now they were allies in support of Porcupine County Search & Rescue.

In the parking lot Father Jim Sweet dragged a tandem snowmobile and sled from the trailer. "We'll take a hot breakfast to the searchers, too," George said. "They're gonna need it after a night like this." The snow was gaining in intensity, the temperature nudging ten above zero.

George and Father Jim lashed breakfast to the sled, hooked it to their snowmobile, and tore off down the South Boundary Road in a rooster tail of snow.

"The Men in Black have arrived and are on their way with hot grub," Bill told Gil over the radio. The undersheriff had already risen and roused his troops to be ready to move out at first light, if it ever appeared through the storm.

"Ah, good," Gil responded. "Better than the goddam MREs we had for supper." Search and Rescue personnel in the field carried military Meals, Ready to Eat, which as any former grunt will tell you, are all right for survival but are not exactly Culinary Institute quality.

As we ate, the door opened again.

"We could set our watches by you," I said as Horace Wright strode in, smelled the bacon and made a beeline for the breakfast box.

"Be that as it may," said the retired Milwaukee newspaperman, who now wrote part-time for the weekly *Porcupine City Herald*, was a stringer for the daily *Marquette Mining Journal*, helped Ginny run the Historical Society and was invariably the first to sample free feeds, "you'd better get ready for the hostiles."

"Hostiles?" I said, but I knew what he meant. I like Horace. He is an old pro and a crackerjack reporter, although his fiery letters to the editor in the *Herald,* which serve as much of that paper's political commentary, are a little too Tea Partyish for my taste.

"Yup. They're all bunking at the Americinn." That was the big chain hostelry in Silverton three miles east of the Wolverines. "CNN, Fox, ABC, NBC and CBS all sent camera crews. Stringers from the *Free Press,* the *New York Times,* the *Milwaukee Journal Sentinel* and the *Chicago Tribune* will be here this morning. Local bloggers, too," he said with a sneer. He took a dim view of Web commentators, even though some of them were laid-off professional journalists.

"And they're all out for blood," I said.

"Not gonna be easy to handle," Horace said, delicately helping himself to another rasher of bacon. "You gonna feed them?"

"Hell no," said Bill. "Our budget's too tight."

"So it goes," Horace said. "I'll have another Danish."

At the stroke of nine I brushed the lint off my shoulders and glanced into the mirror in the office bathroom.

"Pass muster?" I asked Bill.

"Uh-huh. You done this before?"

"Couple times in the service," I said. Most of the reporters I had dealt with during Desert Storm were embedded individuals, but several times I had had to help in the daily briefing in Riyadh. That had taught me how to respond to questions without actually answering them.

"Better you than me."

"Would you stop saying that?" I retorted. "That's an order from the official incident commander."

Bill snorted.

The door to the conference room opened and a low mosquito-like buzz wafted through.

"Showtime," Chad called from the door.

I got up and followed the big deputy to the podium through a bedlam of questions.

"Did you find him yet?"

"Do you suspect foul play?"

"Is he still alive?"

"Where are the doughnuts and coffee?" yelled a soundman plugged into the CNN camera.

Horace Wright stifled a chuckle in the front row. I suppressed a smile and affixed my best stone-faced Indian stare on the soundman.

He settled down grumpily. So did the rest of the yammering pack.

I felt a little sorry for them. The sardine-packed conference room was too small—way too small—for five camera crews and half a dozen print journalists. The heat from the camera lights was beginning to mount.

"I apologize for the lack of victuals," I said, "but government entities in the Upper Peninsula have no spare change during hard times. Those of you who missed breakfast at the Americinn can go back later and have some. It's free, you know."

A couple of veteran journalists chuckled at the dig. Newspeople are notorious freeloaders, and they know it.

Then one of the television reporters shouted, "How long have they been searching? What time did the search start yesterday?"

No presidential press-conference protocol for these people, not even identifying themselves and the news outlets they worked for. They evidently thought rudeness would shake the nervous rube's tree and apples of facts would shower to the ground.

I threw up my palms. "Please, ladies and gentlemen, I have a statement to make. After that I will take questions."

They settled down, muttering, and for the next five minutes I told them what we knew, which wasn't much, following up with "Finally, sixty-seven highly trained searchers are camped at Summit Peak and Mirror Lake and when the storm abates will set off down these trails," pointing to a large wall map of the Porcupines. "They consist of park rangers, conservation officers, the civilian Porcupine County Search and Rescue, US Forest Service personnel, Tribal Police officers, and Gogebic County and Porcupine County law enforcement. We are confident that if Geoffrey Armstrong is to be found, he will be found."

I did withhold a few facts—that Armstrong had had a drink or two before setting out and that he had carried a revolver with him—but I emphasized his skill in the woods, his preparation for the hunt, and our confidence that he had the knowledge and supplies to pass a cold and snowy night safely while waiting for rescue.

But the press wasn't fooled. It knew all about Geoffrey Armstrong and his peccadilloes.

"Armstrong's an alcoholic," said the CNN reporter. "Do you think that played a part in his getting lost?"

"I can't answer that question," I said. "And we don't know that he's lost. Maybe he knows where he is, but is injured. We do not, however, have that information."

"Was he armed?" a *Chicago Tribune* reporter said. Everyone chuckled.

"Well, yes," I said. "He was hunting, after all. He carried a muzzle-loading rifle."

"What's muzzle-loading?" the reporter said. Her ignorance

spurred a low groan from the rest of the press.

That gave me a delicious opportunity to string out things, answering the question at length and with dry academic detail as the audience squirmed in impatience. This wasn't what their news bosses wanted—especially the cable-television ones, back in the city control rooms. They wanted blood and guts. Disappearing ex-congressmen weren't as dramatic as vanished blondes or kidnapped children, but there hadn't been a new case of either of those for a week or so and Geoffrey Armstrong seemed to be the next best story.

Just as I was about to explain how a ball was seated in the muzzle a reporter with the Fox News camera crew lost his patience and shouted, "But was he carrying a pistol?"

"Please do not interrupt," I said politely but firmly. "I am not finished yet."

Notebooks rustled impatiently as I came to the end of my lecture and glanced down at Horace. He was dozing, catching a few winks until I answered the next question, the sly old fox.

"Next?" I said, and Horace's hand shot up with the same speed as his eyelids. I pointed to him.

"Horace Wright, *Porcupine County Herald* and *Marquette Mining Journal*," he said. "Was Armstrong indeed carrying a handgun?"

"I can't answer that question," I said, "but I can say that carrying a cartridge weapon while hunting during muzzle-loading season is an infraction of the Michigan fish and game statutes. Michigan conservation officers issue quite a few citations every year for that."

I said nothing about concealed-weapon permits. Armstrong did have one—Chad had checked the day before—but there was no point in fueling speculation.

"But don't a lot of muzzle-loading hunters carry a pistol anyway?" Horace said. "For finishing off a wounded animal, protection against grizzlies and the like?"

"Yes," I said. "It's permissible for them to carry black-powder pistols during muzzle-loading season." I let the bit about the grizzlies pass unanswered. Horace knew perfectly well that the only bears in the Wolverines were black bears, smaller and much less dangerous than their Western and Alaskan brethren. The old troublemaker was setting up gullible reporters to make fools of themselves.

But the *Detroit Free Press* reporter wasn't biting. "*Did* Armstrong carry a handgun?" he insisted.

"Again, I can't answer that question," I said. Eventually I would, but that insistent hunch I had stifled so long told me to withhold the information, at least for a while. Cops never release all the details of an incident at first, just in case they need one to trap a perpetrator or trip up a false confession. "Can't answer that question" is a time-honored cover-up, especially if it's often used in place of "I don't know."

"Diane Mehaffey, CBS News," said the next reporter I called upon. At last they were showing some respect. "Some of us rented snowmobiles. Can we go up that South Boundary Road to that Summit Peak and get video?"

"I'm afraid not," I said. "The road is now closed to everyone except those involved with rescue operations. And we really shouldn't have untrained civilians in the deep woods at this time of year, especially in a heavy snowstorm. That can be dangerous." I looked out the window. Last night one of my deputies had parked the department's Blazer across the entry to the South Boundary Road and sat watchfully in the driver's seat, checking everyone who passed to make sure he had legitimate business at Summit Peak.

The camera crews muttered in disappointment.

"Okay, this press conference is over," I said, causing some of the reporters to grumble. They hadn't had a chance to ask their leading and impertinent questions. "We'll keep you up to speed throughout the day after the search begins."

It didn't. Snow fell all day and the next, hurled horizontally by the kind of vicious howling wind that turns winter searches into white hells, snapping branches and stinging eyes. The searchers stayed holed up where they had bivouacked, their rations replenished from time to time by Pastor George and Father Jim in their snowmobiles. The clergymen, both of them natives of Upper Michigan, knew the roads and the woods as well as any of the searchers and could find their way to Summit Peak blindfolded.

Geoffrey Armstrong, I thought, probably had survived the night, but whether he could live through more than a couple of days of this kind of storm I didn't know. Not until the third day—seventy-two hours after he had been reported lost—did the sun emerge. Almost fifty inches of new snow, a December record for these parts, had fallen. In the bright sunlight the temperatures dropped into the single digits as northerly chill rolled in behind the storm, and fell below zero after sundown.

Over the next two days, snowshoe-wearing searchers and the Coast Guard helicopter from Traverse City scoured the western end of the park all the way along the lake and inland. I spent a morning in the sheriff's Cessna with Joe Koski riding shotgun, assisting the crew of the Coast Guard chopper by flying at slowest controllable speed low but above the helicopter, hoping to spot something its crew might have missed. But all trace of Geoffrey Armstrong had been lost under the snow, and it was too cold for the cadaver dogs to do their work even if they could have managed the deep snow.

Finally, at nightfall five days after the congressman's disappearance, Bill turned to me and said, "Time to call it off."

I nodded. No point in expending men and money on what

had slowly changed from a rescue mission to a recovery of remains. We were not going to find Armstrong, or whatever was left of him, until spring.

I opened the door to the press room. Only Horace and a two-person camera crew from the Fox station in Marquette remained of the couple of dozen journalists who had arrived for the hunt. Most of the rest had left during the middle of the storm, reassigned to more promising stories.

Horace had spent the last couple of nights at home in Porcupine City—and the Fox crew at the Americinn—waiting for word. All three looked somberly at me, knowing exactly what I was going to say. They were all Yoopers and knew how things worked.

"We're calling it off," I said. "When the spring thaw comes, we'll go looking."

"What do you suppose happened?" Horace said, even though he knew what I would answer.

"Don't know," I said. "Maybe he ran out of food and shelter and just froze."

Horace left unsaid the alternative, being the kind of gentleman who does not put a public official on an unnecessary spot, and we all walked out to the parking lot and mounted up for the trip back to Porcupine City.

CHAPTER SEVENTEEN

Angel gazed at the Hammer of God on the wall. For months it had lain idle on its pegs, its Apostles instead taking up the burden of the Lord's work. The Hammer had needed blooding once again. This time, Angel had very nearly perished in the endeavor.

Angel had lacked a deserving target, so had decided to go into the woods and find one. The Hammer of God demanded it. So what if the particular sins of a target were unknown? All men sinned. All men deserved death. The Hammer and its Apostles simply helped the Lord with the inevitable.

Two years ago Angel had been given a bootleg copy of the key to the padlock on Little Carp Cabin at the mouth of the Little Carp River and the trail of the same name on the lakeshore of the Wolverines. During cartridge deer season, hunters rented the park's cabins, but before the beginning of muzzleloader season the cabins were locked and the keys returned to park headquarters. Little Carp Cabin would make an excellent base of operations, especially since the cold December snap had frozen the mouth of the river, making it easy to proceed east on the lakeshore. The plan was to hunt by day, hole up by night and stay unseen, making an escape along the shore to the west in the old snowmobile purchased with cash, no questions asked, from an elderly man in southern Wisconsin. Quick in, quick shot, quick out. It hadn't quite worked out that way.

Hiding behind a hemlock just off the Big Carp River Trail a

mile and a half east of the Little Carp Cabin and two miles inland from the shore, snowmobile tucked out of sight under a bough, Angel had seen the hunter slowly approaching through the woods, carefully picking his way over roots and rocks as he peered for deer through the trees. Spotting a large buck in a copse of spruce saplings, the hunter raised his rifle as Angel placed the Hammer's front sight on the center of the hunter's body forty yards away.

The hunter's rifle boomed a millisecond before the Hammer, the unexpected thunder causing Angel's trigger finger to jerk slightly, spoiling the aim. The Brown Bess's heavy ball dropped low and struck the hunter in his left thigh, kicking up a gout of blood as it tore through tissue and femoral artery. The hunter screamed and toppled into a snowdrift. Blood fountained from his wound, splattering the snow for six feet around him.

Angel rose and snowshoed to the hunter, who had struggled to a sitting position and clawed a snub-nosed revolver out of his belt, trying to lift it and point it at his assailant. Angel had prepared a brief apology to recite over the quarry, telling the hunter that the shooting was not personal but had to be done if a tool of the Lord was to do its duty. The Will of God was sometimes unfathomable.

As his adversary emerged from the trees Geoffrey Armstrong raised his head, and Angel instantly recognized the old congressman. Sudden exaltation flooded Angel's heart, for the work of the Hammer indeed had continued under God's unseen guidance. Armstrong, the whole world knew, was driven by creatures from Hell, and justice had been exacted for his transgressions. This was not a random encounter, but God's unerring plan.

"Why . . . ?" Armstrong said incredulously as Angel silently gazed down at him, the flow from the hunter's ruined artery now subsiding. Slowly the hand grasping the revolver drooped, the weapon tumbling deep into a snowdrift. Quietly Angel stood by as Armstrong at last bled out and collapsed into himself, eyes gazing emptily into the darkening sky.

Quickly Angel returned to the hemlock that had served as a sniper's lair and retrieved the snowmobile. It took considerable sweating and grunting, but Armstrong's corpulent body at last lay lashed on the rear seat of the machine, ready for the two-mile trip over a steep and rocky trail south to the lake, then a mile and a third west to a hiding place already chosen.

Slowly and carefully Angel picked the way along the trail, twice nearly losing control of the snowmobile as it slipped down icy slopes and caromed off trees. At a low cliff too steep for the snowmobile Armstrong's body had to be untied from the machine, then shoved over the rocks. Angel then manhandled the snowmobile around the cliff and downhill through dense thickets of yellow birch a hundred yards from the trail, finally returning upslope to retrieve the body and lash it down once again.

Angel's goal lay just a few yards east of the Little Carp Cabin. It was a pile of slash and logs park rangers had piled as a windbreak to protect the cabin from gales howling in off the lake. Snow had drifted against the windbreak, and Angel scooped away enough so that Armstrong's body could be stuffed loosely under a couple of logs, making sure to place the rifle underneath the corpse as if he had hunkered over it to protect it from the elements. With luck, time and animals would take care of the soft tissue and most of the bones before the body was found in the spring.

It would be the next day before Armstrong was reported missing. Angel had plenty of time to escape to the west along the shore on the snowmobile before the oncoming storm arrived and covered Armstrong's body.

For all the careful planning, Angel had not allowed for the speed of the storm's arrival, or its intensity, or of the possibility of accident. Setting off right away for the west instead of holing up one more night in the Little Carp Cabin would have averted near disaster.

Instead Angel woke up the next day in the midst of howling wind and snow. Scarcely half a mile west of the cabin the snowmobile collided with hidden rocks under a drift, shattering the machine's right ski and tearing its track off the bogies. Angel was thrown into the sharp rocks and broke the fall with outstretched arms. The rocks left deep gouges in the skin, but Angel wrapped the wounds with bandages from the snowmobile's first-aid kit, stuffing the paper wrappings into a knapsack.

Shortly before going into the woods, Angel had scraped the Wisconsin vehicle stickers off the machine and had also ground the serial number off its frame so that the snowmobile's ownership could not be traced. Always plan for the unexpected, Daddy had said.

Angel had done so, and successfully. Leaving the heavy machine on the rocks where snow would cover it for the winter, Angel slipped back into snowshoes and started the long trek west to the deserted campground at the mouth of the Presque Isle River. It had been closed for the winter after regular deer season and there would be a long hike down the equally lonely highway to Wakefield carrying the heavy Hammer of God. But trust in the Lord, and a little tenacity would see things through. If there were witnesses along the way, the excuse of being a stranded muzzle-loader deer hunter would serve. A hunting license Angel had lawfully obtained from a sporting-goods store a few days before would bolster the statement.

It took three days of steady snowshoeing, sheltering under spruce boughs while the small supply of beef jerky shrank, and a couple of times Angel thought the Lord had other plans than a safe return. When the Hammer of God was finally returned to its pegs on the wall in the barn, a deep sense of satisfaction warmed Angel's heart. The Lord had posed a difficult test, and Angel had passed it.

CHAPTER EIGHTEEN

It was the end of March, the spring thaw had begun, and I had nearly forgotten all about Geoffrey Armstrong when the phone in my office rang.

"Steve? Bill Koons. We found Armstrong, or what's left of him."

"Where?"

"Windbreak at Little Carp Cabin. Looks like something happened and he took shelter inside a pile of slash, probably during the big storm. Most of his bones were picked and scattered in a hundred-yard radius, but so far we've found a pack, a muzzle-loading rifle, a hat, one boot, and a coat with ID inside. The rifle had been fired and the spent percussion cap was still under the hammer. No .32 revolver, though."

"No indication exactly what happened?"

"None. It's still a preliminary search. But we've called the troopers, and Alex is on his way."

"His bones were already scattered?" I said. "This early in the spring?"

"Yeah," Bill said. "Remember, there was that long warm spell in January." There had been a ten-day period of temperatures in the high forties, melting much of the snow cover.

I nodded to myself. "Yeah, that would give enough time for the body to thaw and the predators to do their work." Eagles, vultures, wolves, and coyotes would have made a quick buffet of the newly exposed corpse.

"We're still searching for clues along the trails and the lake-shore," Bill said.

"If you find any, mark the spots and leave 'em alone for Alex, will ya?" I said.

"You think I fell off the paddy wagon yesterday?" Bill said indignantly, and hung up. I laughed.

That night Alex called.

"Tell me you've solved the mystery," I said.

"Nope. We don't know what happened to Armstrong. We've bagged the few other remains we could find, but nothing stands out. Don't think the forensics guys at Marquette will come up with anything, if they ever get around to it."

If Alex didn't think so, they wouldn't. He had far more experience than any white-coated scientist in the Michigan State Police and knew almost as much as they did. In any case, the state police forensics department was overworked and un-dermanned, like us all, and I doubted that even the remains of an important congressman would fetch more than a cursory glance from the white coats in the absence of hard evidence pointing to homicide rather than ill fortune.

"One thing, though," Alex added. "We found Armstrong's .32 on the Correction Line Trail a little more than two miles south of the lakeshore. It hadn't been fired, either. A full five rounds in the chambers."

"Could have fallen out of his pocket," I said. "That spot on the trail would be a logical place for a hunter to set up a stand in the trees and to field-dress a deer before carrying the carcass back to base on his shoulders. But the lakeshore is awfully far from that spot. Way too far to hump a hundred-pound load back to Summit Peak, if you ask me."

"Bill said Armstrong's rifle had been fired. Any deer bones on the trail?"

"We found no deer carcass anywhere near it. Maybe Armstrong became disoriented in the snowstorm and walked toward the lake instead of back to Summit Peak. We didn't find a compass in his pack. If he had one it coulda got lost, like the pistol. From everything we've been able to find, that seems to be the story. Pure and simple, he got lost in the storm and froze to death."

"No slug near the bones?" I said, grasping for straws and knowing it.

"None at all."

"Okay. Guess that's it."

"Close the case?"

"We'll put it on ice for the moment," I said. "I'll call the governor."

In December she had been unhappy that the search had been called off, but was too smart to make a stink about it. We had done our best, and she knew it.

"No foul play?" she immediately asked after I got through two officious underlings who wanted me to give them the message for relay to the governor. I told them I would have their scalps on a lance if they didn't put me through right away. I think they knew who I was.

"No evidence of that. No evidence at all," I said, and that was perfectly true, although the unease that had been gnawing at me for almost two years was telling me otherwise.

"Thank you, Sheriff," she said after a moment's hesitation. Clearly she shared my discomfort, although she wasn't privy to all that I knew—and suspected. "That's all I can ask."

We ended with a few polite noises and hung up.

Later in the afternoon Alex called again.

"We found a wrecked snowmobile on the lake half a mile west of Little Carp River. Looks like it's been there all winter. It's old, about twenty years old, and wasn't in good shape to begin with."

"What else?"

"Whoever it was drove it right into a low rock wall and busted a ski and the track."

"That's rare but not unheard of." Snowmobiling on the shore of the Wolverines is illegal, except for on the thick ice way out in the lake in the winter, but people do it anyway, because the park is undermanned and they're rarely caught. It was understandable that the driver didn't report either accident or abandonment. Nobody wants to own up to an offense that carries a heavy fine.

"Gonna trace it?" I asked.

"That's the thing," Alex said. "All the tags have been scraped off, and . . ."

Alex was silent for a moment, but I wasn't fooled. He likes to build up suspense before delivering the most important goods. I waited.

"The vehicle serial number has been ground off the frame."

"Anything to connect the snowmobile to Armstrong?"

"No. It's been out there so long that snow and rain have washed it clean."

"Your thoughts?"

"If anybody used that snowmobile to get at Armstrong, how would he know in the first place where the congressman was going to hunt?"

Alex was right. Hunters generally do not broadcast where they plan to go, except to tell a few companions who'd either go looking for a missing buddy or report his absence. Hunters don't want others horning in on their favorite hunting spots. No one bent on revenge could have foreseen the trails where Armstrong was going to hunt. Possibly he didn't know himself until he got to the Wolverines.

"Yeah," I said, but without conviction.

Another hunch was building up in the far recesses of my

weary brain, jumping up and waving for attention even as I tried to stifle it while rooting around in the sheriff's budget for another line item to cut. Fresh rumor out of Washington had it that Porcupine City's population had dropped by a staggering fifteen percent in the last ten years—as jobs disappeared, hundreds of Porkies had chosen to move rather than starve. Fewer people would mean steep cuts in federal and state money for law enforcement as well as just about everything else. We would have to sell the Cessna, expensive to maintain and expensive to fly, and I doubted that the county board would let the sheriff's department use the money to buy replacement vehicles. I could see layoffs coming in my department before long.

I snapped back to the more immediate problem. Why would anyone remove all identifying marks from a vehicle? I could think of only two reasons. Because it was stolen or because it was to be used in the commission of a crime. Or maybe both. Either way, the machine could not be traced. Weather had washed away any fingerprints that had been left. Still, its existence and Geoffrey Armstrong's death could be somehow connected. The simple possibility that they were was reason enough for me to keep on stewing.

My mood momentarily brightened when Ginny swept into my office and plunked herself into a chair across from my desk. Despite my fretting about our relationship, the simple sight of her always sends my heart soaring. She is that lovely and she is that wonderful.

My heart sank again when she said, "Steve, I have something to tell you."

From Ginny, that phrase always precedes a portentous announcement, one that often is inconveniencing if not disturbing. Was she going to end our relationship now?

"Mm." I steeled myself.

"I'm going to Finland next month and will stay until Christmas. I didn't want to tell anybody because I thought I didn't have a chance, but the University of Turku has accepted my proposal to be a visiting scholar in its humanities department. I can do some research I've always wanted to do, and I'll be able to teach, too."

I was dumbfounded, and my mouth fell open. I had had no idea.

"Aren't you going to congratulate me?"

"Uh . . . oh . . . yes, yes, yes. That's wonderful. You deserve it!"

I got up to hug her but she stopped me with a raised hand and a cocked eyebrow.

"There's more."

My heart hit bottom.

"What?"

"I'm taking Tommy with me. It'll be good for him to be exposed to another culture and maybe learn a bit of Finnish. So Hogan's going to live with you while we're gone," she said. "That is, if it's okay with you."

Keeping the dog was fine with me, and I was glad not to be Tommy's minder in Ginny's absence. The last time he had been left in my care, he was twelve years old and wandered off into the woods while I wasn't looking, resulting in a major search-and-rescue operation that cost the county and the state police a bundle, but its happy result persuaded them to chalk up the cost to a training operation.

Ginny had about flayed me alive for my carelessness and then taken me back into her heart, but I had never felt really forgiven.

"Sounds like a plan," I said, finally gathering my wits and putting some enthusiasm into my voice. "This is going to be wonderful for you!"

As an historian Ginny had long wanted to trace the European

roots of the Finns who had settled in Porcupine County more than a hundred years before, and to measure the depth and breadth of the national culture that had remained in the immigrants and their descendants. We had had long conversations about third- and fourth-generation "Finlanders," as Ginny and her comrades called themselves, and the remarkable connection they felt to their forebears, even after a century in the United States and Canada. I had often confessed my envy for their rootedness, for I had none. Being born Lakota and raised white had given me a foot in both camps, but without a secure place to stand on. In short, I fell between two stools, as the saying goes.

"You're okay with it?" Ginny said.

"Yes, of course," I said, hoping Ginny could not tell that I was hardly okay with it. "When are you and Tommy leaving?"

"April third." That was just three weeks away. I was not exactly okay with that, either, but there was little I could do or say, except to support Ginny's decision. Even if in her long absence she made another decision, as I knew she would. Or, rather, was afraid she would.

I had not been spending much time at her home or she at mine, in a kind of unspoken agreement not to press matters while we each sorted them out for ourselves. I had been missing her and hoped she was missing me, too.

CHAPTER NINETEEN

It was the middle of June when Joe Koski called to me as I walked into the squad room with Hogan, who in the absence of Ginny and Tommy had appointed himself my partner and rode shotgun everywhere with me. "Interesting item just came in from the Soo."

"Yeah?"

"Muzzle-loader killing on a highway just outside Sault Ste. Marie on the American side. They're saying it's probably murder."

"They get the shooter?" I already knew the answer.

"Not yet."

I picked up the phone, consulted the Rolodex and called the Chippewa County Sheriff's Department at Sault Ste. Marie, two hundred eighty miles east from Porcupine City on the far northeastern edge of the Upper Peninsula.

"Sheriff in?" I asked the dispatcher as he answered. "This is Steve Martinez at Porcupine City."

"He's out."

"Heard you had a drive-by homicide," I said. "Got any details?"

"Not many," said the dispatcher, "but I can tell you what we've got."

"Shoot."

"Shoot?" said the dispatcher, amusement in his voice.

"Figure of speech."

136

"I know. Okay, here's what we know."

The day before, Marilyn Schneider, thirty-five years of age, a resident of St. Ignace on the Straits of Mackinac between Lake Michigan and Lake Huron fifty miles south of the Soo, had been sitting at a picnic bench eating a ham sandwich in a roadside rest stop where her old Corolla was parked near I-75 just south of Sault Ste. Marie on the US side of the Canadian border. Suddenly, witnesses said, her head exploded, showering brains on half a dozen fellow picnickers at the next table. Two witnesses said they had quickly looked up and spotted a small cloud of smoke behind a rocky ridge on a forested hillside deputies later measured as one hundred and twelve yards from the point of impact. They also had seen a white van, age and make unidentified, departing at high speed on a gravel road that ran from the ridge to another track a quarter of a mile away.

Deputies had discovered scorched fragments of muzzle-loader patch just in front of the ridge, and a bloody, misshapen lump of lead easily identifiable as a muzzle-loader ball had been found thirty yards from the body on a direct line from the ridge. The case was being treated as one of murder, although it was still in the early stages of investigation. The medical examiner had not yet finished the autopsy.

So far, the dispatcher said, no one knew why Miss Schneider had driven up from St. Ignace, nor if she had had any enemies who would have caused harm to come to her. She was unmarried, lived alone, was a faithful churchgoer according to witnesses, worked as a cleaner for a motel, and had no law-enforcement record except for a parking ticket she had successfully contested. So far it appeared that she just had the bad luck to be in the wrong place at the wrong time, that she was a victim of chance and circumstance. The deputies and the troopers were searching for the white van, but white vans being as common as Canada geese in the Upper Peninsula, they didn't have much hope of finding the right one any time soon.

"Checking out the owners of muzzle-loading weapons?" I said. "Maybe one of them has a white van."

The dispatcher harrumphed. "You teaching us grandmas how to suck eggs, Sheriff?"

"Just thinking out loud. Say, would you tell Sheriff Champion that I called? I've got some information about muzzle-loader shootings he might be interested in."

"Sure thing."

Not five minutes after we hung up, the phone rang.

"Sheriff Champion here," the voice said. It was cool and curt. Wayne Champion, the sheriff of Chippewa County, did not like me. He had had run-ins with Indians from local reservations, and like many small-town bigots, thought all members of minorities were troublemakers. At sheriffs' conventions he went out of his way to avoid shaking my hand or speaking to me. In matters of law enforcement he communicated information, but always had a deputy do the talking. Not this time. That told me he was stumped and had to forget his dislike.

"Just got back from the field," he said peremptorily. "My guy said you called. What do you want?"

Quickly I filled Champion in on the three previous muzzle-loader shootings in the Upper Peninsula during the last year— the accident and the suicide in Porcupine County and the hunting mishap in Schoolcraft County. "That just seems like a lot to me, and now there's a fourth," I said. "Then there was the disappearance of Geoffrey Armstrong in the Wolverines during muzzle-loading season."

"Yeah, I recall those," Champion said. "But taken together they sound merely like a statistical anomaly to me." Champion, for all his unreasoning hatred, was a smart and tough-minded sheriff, one who did not follow will-o'-the-wisp evidence without good reason, but by-the-book law-enforcement officers are not terribly imaginative. They don't waste time chasing wild hunches. They don't solve a huge number of crimes, either, just the cases that are open and shut.

"There don't seem to be any connections in the shootings," Champion said. "Three women, one man. Two accidents, one suicide, one possible murder. Did any of them know any of the others?"

"Not to my knowledge," I admitted.

"So there it is, Martinez. Hang on. Got another call."

Two minutes later he returned to the line. "That was the medical examiner," he said. "The victim was killed by a fifty-four-caliber ball. The blood on the ball we found matched hers. Surprise."

"Your man said the range was a hundred twelve yards, quite a bit downhill," I said. "A head shot at that range is a hell of a good one for a muzzle loader that shoots balls, not bullets. You're looking for an expert rifleman."

"He coulda been aiming for her body," Champion said. "If he was. Mighta been an accident and the shooter got scared and run off."

His tone had subtly changed. Now he was not talking to an Indian but a fellow law-enforcement officer, reminding him— and himself—that without further evidence the nature of the homicide was still an open question. This happens a lot. Prejudice can often take a brief backseat to self-interest.

"We're checking out all the local muzzle-loader shooters we can find, from hunting-license records and members of shooting organizations who've won contests," he said.

"Do me a favor," I said. "Send me the list of names you've checked out. I'll compare them with a list we made after our Mountain Men encampment accident."

"All right," said Champion, the chill returning to his voice. It was clear he thought he was chasing a dead end, but a dead end that had to be investigated and eliminated.

"Calling in the state police?" I asked.

"Don't need to," Champion said with a growl. "Can't go running to your old man every time there's a problem."

That was a clear reference to my relationship with Sergeant Alex Kolehmainen, but I kept my temper. "Might help," I said.

He hung up without a "good-bye," and it suddenly occurred to me that Champion had addressed me as "Martinez" throughout our conversation. Sheriffs habitually call each other "Sheriff," the same professional courtesy physicians extend to their colleagues by calling them "Doctor." Wayne Champion was a tough nut who held on to his wrongheadedness.

Two weeks later—a few days longer than necessary, I thought—the sheriff did send me the list of local muzzle-loader experts he had amassed, as well as an admission that his investigation had turned up nothing except the discovery of an abandoned white 1993 Ford van near Munising, a hundred twenty miles west of Sault Ste. Marie. It had been reported stolen in Houghton, another hundred forty miles to the northwest, the day before the shooting at the Soo. Investigators had found no black-powder residue or any other clue to either the theft or the shooting. The prints the police had lifted were not on file anywhere, nor was the DNA that had been extracted from dried semen on the backseat. It was not even certain the van had been the one that witnesses to the shooting had seen. It looked as if Sheriff Champion indeed had struck a blank wall.

None of the names on Champion's list matched those on mine. The trouble, I saw right away, was that Champion's shooters were all locals, eastern Upper Peninsula residents. Mine came from all over the Midwestern map. I should have pointed that out, but I didn't want to offend a brother officer of equal rank by suggesting he had been less than thorough. It wasn't my case, anyway. It wasn't even my jurisdiction. Let him

compare my list against his, if he felt like it. I doubted that he
would.

The hunch that had knocked at the door of my mind last
summer was now jumping up and down and waving its arms
frantically. If only I had been more assertive with Champion.
Anthropologists will tell you that Indians don't like to make a
fuss—it's part of our cultural heritage—but the truth probably
lies in my upbringing. The Methodist missionaries who had
adopted me as an infant from the Lakota reservation at Pine
Ridge in South Dakota had raised me to be polite and
deferential, never to challenge authority. I have always needed
practice in stirring up the hornets, at pounding my desk and
yelling.

CHAPTER TWENTY

For ten minutes Angel prayed for the soul of Marilyn Schneider. She had not been chosen in advance to meet the Lord, but she had appeared on the scene as a perfect target—not too close, not too far, and right out in the open. What's more, she had been surrounded by others, so that they could behold the work of the Lord, although they may not have known at the time that they were bearing witness.

Angel had not known Marilyn Schneider, but in life she had deserved death, as every sinner does. After a few millennia in purgatory her sins might be sufficiently cleansed for her to be elevated to sit in heaven with the Lord. Otherwise there was no point in ending her life.

It would have been best if a year had passed before the Lord issued the order to resume His work, but after a few months the call to ride again had grown insistent. This time Angel would not make the deed look like accident or suicide, but let it appear to be what it was, a deliberate sacrifice. It would be an execution sanctioned by God, but the lawmen would not know that. It would be different from the others. There would be no common similarity other than the choice of weapons, but this would be the first action of the calendar year, and perhaps it could take place far enough away from the others—hundreds of miles away—so that the police were not likely to deduce that the events were definitely linked.

Angel was pleased with the performance of the flintlock Tennessee. The shot had been a difficult one, at least a hundred yards downhill and with a fifteen-mile-an-hour crosswind. On the first attempt the flint failed to strike a spark, and the stone had to be removed from its vise on the hammer and a new edge knapped into it in the hope that the target would remain at the picnic bench eating her lunch.

But the second shot was straight and true, and Angel's heart lifted as the ball struck the woman's head and she fell back over the bench.

Angel had sprinted to the stolen van and driven away, knowing that the onlookers below could see its departure. They would report the vehicle and its color to the police, but Angel knew there was plenty of time for a getaway. It had not rained for many days, and the police would have extreme difficulty tracking the van's tires through the loose dry sand of a warren of mostly abandoned logging roads between the rest stop and the shore of Lake Superior. They would have to scour the area carefully and on foot, and that might take a week or more. By then Angel would be long gone.

For twenty minutes the van bounced through the woods, then stopped at a deserted beachfront lookout often used as a Saturday-night lover's lane. The site, hidden by a screen of trees, lay well away from the logging track. There the van was abandoned, keys in the ignition, all surfaces carefully wiped down even though there was little reason to worry about fingerprints. Angel's had never been taken and there would be none on file to process through computer databases to identify the person who had last driven the truck.

And someone, probably filthy, sex-obsessed teenagers looking for a place to copulate, would find the van and make off with it before the police found it. They'd leave their disgusting prints all over it, and if the prints were on file the police would waste valuable time hunting down their owners and interrogating them. *If* the prints were on file. Few teenagers' are.

For ten minutes Angel trotted west along the beach, careful to stay close to the tree line in order not to leave tracks in the sand, and loped through the woods on deer trails with smooth-soled moccasins whose imprints would be so indistinct that they would be impossible to identify.

Angel loved it when a plan fell into place.

Now it was time for a new challenge, the biggest one yet.

Chapter Twenty-One

Since April, Ginny's e-mails from Turku had been long, enthusiastic and detailed narratives about her studies and lectures as well as Tommy's delight in his new surroundings, but ominously lacking in passion. Sure, she always signed off affectionately, but she made no reference to our relationship other than a terse "Miss you." Was she preparing me for something, perhaps an ending? Or was I reading too much into what she wasn't saying? Maybe she was just being discreet, knowing that e-mails could end up in the wrong hands. Or maybe she was just being circumspect and modest in the way of the native-born Yooper. Perhaps she simply valued her privacy as I did mine.

I responded in kind. Maybe I was worried about nothing. But I stewed anyway.

I was stewing a lot because I had a lot to stew about. Not all of it was about Ginny.

Finally one morning in mid-September, just as the sugar-maple leaves began to burst into red and yellow, I decided to stick my neck out.

I picked up the phone and dialed Alex.

"Do ya for?" said Alex in his customary way, without identifying himself and before I could speak. I frequently remonstrated mildly with him about this habit, suggesting that it was only helpful if he'd give his name when he picked up the phone.

"Waste of time," he had replied. "Anybody who calls this

number is looking for me, not Groucho Marx."

I decided to get even.

"OK if I call Sue?" I began without identifying myself.

"Sure, why not?" was the airy answer. He had recognized my voice.

Then his own took on a serious note. "Is this professional or is this personal?"

"What do you care?" I said. "You've broken up, haven't you?"

"Just wondering," Alex said, but a hint of pique colored his voice.

Alex Kolehmainen and Susan Hemb of the Michigan State Police had been an item, off and on, for all the years I had known him. It was off and on because the two rarely had occasion to see each other—Alex was based in Wakefield an hour southwest of Porcupine City and Susan, a forensic psychologist, many hours away downstate at headquarters in Lansing. During each of the few cases that they had worked together, Alex had once told me, Sue had put their relationship on firm hold while the investigation progressed. She was so single-minded about the job that "it was like a high-school football coach telling us to keep our hands off our girls—or ourselves—until the big game was over," he groused with a wry smile.

I had met Sue two years before when Alex called her as a consultant into a case we were both investigating, an unholy game involving GPS receivers and geocached corpses. As usually happens with the work of criminal profilers, her insights had explained the whys of the case better than it had led to discovery of the whats, whos and whens. It's damned near impossible to track down a perp on the basis of motive, although that helps the case a lot when he's finally arrested and charged.

Sue and Alex had drifted apart the previous autumn when she was promoted to lieutenant and put in charge of her department. The news had unhinged Sergeant Kolehmainen, who could not stand the idea of sleeping with an officer of higher rank. That offended his sense of protocol, for despite his preternatural affability Alex occasionally can be ridiculously stiff-necked. Sue pointed out quite reasonably that she wasn't his superior, that they worked for different departments and that it was highly unlikely a criminal profiler would be ordering around a detective sergeant anyway, even if she outranked him on the charts.

Alex was unmoved and inconsolable at the same time. I think he was just upset she'd made lieutenant and he hadn't. The truth is that his superiors had hinted more than once that he take the exam for a lieutenancy, and he had replied in no uncertain terms that he preferred to detect in the field than direct from a desk and they could just forget all about that. The state police brass refused to let the matter alone, for everyone on the force knew that Sergeant Kolehmainen had the makings of a first-rate departmental boss. Regularly they brought it up and just as regularly Alex said no. I often wondered who would cave in first.

In other circumstances—if he had not had Sue and I had not had Ginny—I'd have thought about exploring a relationship with the lieutenant. She was pleasant to work with, pleasant to be with and pleasant to look upon. Her rank as a state worker and mine as a county employee would have posed absolutely no problem so far as I was concerned.

But that had been far from my mind when I called Alex.

"Professional," I finally said after a long moment, just to torment Alex. "Purely professional. I'm not a poacher."

"Be that as it may," Alex said with a touch of skepticism, "why?"

"Don't be so disingenuous," I replied. "You know perfectly well why."

"Do I?"

"You do."

Alex sighed and surrendered. "What have we got? A bunch of muzzle-loader shootings that don't seem to be related in any way. One obvious homicide in Chippewa County, but it's not your jurisdiction and it's way too far east for me, too. What's more, the guy in charge of the jurisdiction is being an asshole. You don't have the money or the manpower to help him anyway. What can we do even if we could?"

"I don't know," I said. "But I can't stand not doing anything anymore."

"That's my boy!" Alex said. He loved hunting bad guys, too. "But what can Sue do for you?"

"Maybe help me find a motive, if there's a motive to be found."

"Fair enough. You have my express permission to call her. Would you like it in writing?" Now Alex's tone was mock offi-cious.

That made me laugh, the first time in weeks I'd laughed.

The next morning I telephoned Lieutenant Hemb in Lansing.

She listened quietly and without interruption as I laid out the meager ragbag of facts we had and confided my suspicion that they were all somehow related as well as my frustration that I did not have the resources to try to find out why.

For a long moment, just as Alex does, she did not reply. But I could hear the faint drumming of her delicate fingertips on her desk. She was thinking, absorbing everything I had told her and listening to what it might suggest.

"I'm coming up to Porcupine City," she finally said. "No, no, that is if you want me to."

Like Alex, she was sensitive to jurisdictional protocol. She did not usually step on toes. Unless, like Alex, she felt it absolutely necessary. When she did, she came down hard and with sharp spike heels.

"Would you?" I said. "Can you?"

"Sure," she said. "We've got a light caseload at the moment and I can let one of my sergeants run the store."

"Shall I make a reservation at the Americinn?"

"I'll bunk in your spare room if I may," she said. "We have the same budget problems you do. Our per diem is minuscule. And this isn't an official consultation. Not just yet."

I knew she'd have a tough time persuading her tightfisted superiors that a trip to the Upper Peninsula on what might turn out to be a wild-goose chase was worth the state's money. But she clearly saw something in what I had said.

She did not mention staying with Alex, as she had the time she had business in Porcupine County. Nor did I mention it. But she knew I knew, and I knew she knew I knew. Knowing in the Biblical sense did not cross my mind then, although it would later.

CHAPTER TWENTY-TWO

When Lieutenant Susan Hemb arrived at my cabin on the lake early that evening in her own car, a ten-year-old Camry instead of an unmarked Crown Vic from the state police pool in Lansing, she was still wearing the usual civilian business ensemble of a downstate female commissioned officer, a form-fitting blue jacket over a knee-length sheath of the same color, with sheer hose and low dress pumps. A golden brooch on her lapel matched her hair, and so did the state police badge she wore on a leather tab around her neck. She is a tall and willowy killer blonde with eyes so blue and features so delicate that men dream of protecting as well as sleeping with her, but despite her forensic specialty she is also a trained cop capable of taking down a maddened killer twice her size, if not blowing a hole or two through him.

I knew all that already. I can appreciate feminine beauty without lustful thoughts—most of the time, anyway. Besides, so far as I was concerned Sue belonged with Alex, although maybe he didn't at the moment know that.

In my spare room Sue quickly changed into Yooper cloth-ing—jeans, Nike hikers and woolen shirt. She looked as trim in such fashions as Ginny did—both women filled their denims nicely—and I shook my head again at Alex's folly.

I grilled us both a steak that night. Alex having huffily declined my invitation to dinner, Sue and I ate alone, making desultory conversation about celebrated old cases. We didn't talk about what had been on my mind the last two years, for Sue preferred to approach case documents and reports with a fresh and uncluttered mind—and we turned in early. I slept the sleep of the virtuous, untroubled and untempted by the presence of a hell of a woman in my spare room.

On the way to Porcupine City the next morning I turned to Sue in the passenger seat of the sheriff's Blazer and said, "Anyone ever tell you that you snore?"

"Yes," she said with a smile, gazing out the window. "Apologies for that."

"Oh, it wasn't bothersome," I said with a chuckle. "Yours is a *polite* snore."

Lightly she slapped my arm with the back of her hand. "I can't stand it when people know my secrets!" she said with a tinkling laugh.

At the sheriff's department I told Sue to use the undersheriff's office, Gil being away on a week's vacation, and spread out on his desk the thin files of the case that was not yet a case, if ever it would be.

She took things chronologically, beginning with the death of Gloria Lake on the Mullet. She read my case notes carefully, then the coroner's report. Twice she put down the document she was reading and picked up another she had already read. She made no comment, although from time to time a graceful eyebrow arched. She had nice eyebrows.

"Steve," she said after an hour, "would you take me out to the Mullet?"

This was unsurprising. Good cops don't draw conclusions just by the observations of other cops. They like to view the scene of the crime for themselves, even if a lot of time might have passed. Sometimes a fresh set of eyes leads to a fresh new observation.

I drove Sue out to the site where the Mountain Men had set up their encampment and where they had fashioned a shooting range. We climbed the earthen berm that had served as a backstop and surveyed the long eddy of the Mullet.

"Yes, a shooter could have hidden here," she said at the same copse that had given me the same thought. "Maybe one did. But as you said in your report, too many people had trampled too much grass for a conclusion to be drawn."

I waited while Sue waded in the shallows where Gloria Lake had died and quietly surveyed the scene. After a few minutes she nodded and said, "I've seen enough. Let's go."

Back at the department she sat in the same wooden chair Ginny had occupied just a couple of weeks before and crossed her legs with a soft sigh of denim.

"It does seem to me that the medical examiner drew the most likely conclusion," she said. "An accident. But some of the facts indeed are very curious, quite suggestive of a different conclusion."

"And those are?" I said helpfully.

"Exactly what you think. Who Gloria Lake was. What she was. And what she did. Steve, if the accident scene wasn't what it was, I'd spend a lot more time investigating the sex angle. Somebody might have killed her for revenge. Or to keep her mouth shut. Or maybe something else that isn't immediately obvious. Sex can be a subtle thing where homicide is concerned."

"Maybe I'd better take another run at the Mountain Men we interviewed," I said. "If I can find the time."

"Good idea. If you can."

After lunch at Merle's, one of the two remaining cafes in town—a third had closed shortly after the paper mill was shut—Sue and I took a walk past the site of the River Street fire. Just a few months ago, the village had finally scraped together enough money to demolish the charred ruins, carry away the debris and grade the bare ground, planting it with donated grass seed.

"The building where Ellen Juntunen died was right here," I said. "Odd that she killed herself in a place she owned but that wasn't her home."

"Suicides are often odd," Sue said. "It's sometimes hard to follow the meanderings of a troubled mind. Even us shrink types don't always understand how they work."

"Just for the sake of argument," I said, "what if it wasn't a suicide? What if somebody set it up to look that way?"

"That could have been more easily done somewhere deep in the woods where witnesses would be unlikely. To kill somebody here would have been taking an enormous risk."

Sue fell silent for a while. "No connections between Gloria Lake and Ellen Juntunen, are there? One a vigorous, life-loving woman with a good job and the other one impoverished, alcoholic and mentally ill. Let me go through the paperwork again."

I left Sue to her devices in Gil's office. At my own desk I desultorily chased the budget around and around, hoping to find something somewhere to save money and knowing I wouldn't.

Half an hour later Sue reappeared in my office door.

"There might be something," she said. "Religion."

"How?" I said. "One lived in Madison, the other in Bessemer, and so far as I know they didn't belong to the same denomination."

"They're not really denominations. Many of these little evangelical churches are independent and follow the individual beliefs of their pastors, who often are not full-time but hold other jobs. Most are Pentecostal in nature, and many can be extreme in their theologies. Both Gloria Lake's church and Ellen Juntunen's may have been of this kind. Let me see if I can find out if so, and exactly how."

"How are you going to do that?" I said.

"Cop shrinks have networks, too," Sue said with a smile. "I'll make a few phone calls."

Two hours later she reappeared in my doorway.

"What wondrous new knowledge do you bring me?" I asked.

"Not a lot. As I suspected, both the preachers at the churches in question are hellfire-and-damnation types. They picket abortion clinics and point public fingers at sinners. They haven't done anything illegal, at least not yet, but they've made large enough nuisances of themselves that the local sheriffs are keeping an eye on them just in case."

"In case of what?"

"In case a suggestible member of the congregation decides to carry his overdeveloped sense of moral judgment too far. It happens. Look at Eric Rudolph."

In the 1990s Rudolph, a white supremacist and anti-abortion terrorist, killed two people and injured hundreds with bombs, including one at the Atlanta Olympics, then disappeared into the Appalachian wilderness, where he eluded the authorities for years before a North Carolina cop caught him. He is now serving five consecutive life sentences in a Colorado federal supermax while managing to publish screeds against abortion, homosexuality and other hot-button culture-wars issues on an Army of God Web site.

"Yeah," I said. "Judge and jury. But I'm not aware that Lake and Juntunen ever marched against abortion, let alone for choice."

"No," Sue said. "But they were both willing to sell themselves for sex."

"One for fun, the other out of sick desperation. I don't see a connection in that. Everybody has sex one way or another.

Besides, does the world's oldest profession unhinge people the way abortion does?"

"There's that," Sue said. Sighing, she returned to Gil's office.

An hour later she was back. "Just looked at the Dickie Atkins material. Nothing there."

"Just a poor hunter who found himself in the wrong place at the wrong time," I said.

"And he was a churchgoer, but a Presbyterian," she said. "Presbyterians are pretty conventional and civilized about sex."

"It's naughty, but they do it anyway, huh?"

"I think we can rule out this case as being connected with the rest, except for the means of death. Which brings us to Geoffrey Armstrong."

I looked at the clock on the wall. "Let's call it a day and dig up the congressman tomorrow."

CHAPTER TWENTY-THREE

"Well, if anybody killed Geoffrey Armstrong," Sue said late in the morning, "sex had to be a good reason. I never heard of such a wick-dipper."

"Wick-dipper?" I said.

"Shrink jargon for sexual adventurer," she said.

"Serial swordsman," I said. "Sheriff jargon."

"Be that as it may," she said, stifling a giggle, "there's your motive."

"Doesn't give us the murderer. That is, if he was murdered."

"You have doubts?" Sue said.

I explained about hunters and their obsession with discretion about their hunting grounds.

"It's probable that Armstrong wasn't even certain where he was going to go until he got there," I added. "They tend to arrive at their hunting grounds with a general idea, then refine it to specific sites. Some of them have no idea where they're going and that's when they get lost."

"That didn't happen to him."

"Doubt it," I said. "Armstrong was just too experienced in the woods."

"So what happened?"

"I don't know. He should have been able to survive a two-night storm by cutting boughs and sheltering under a wide spruce. That windbreak where his body was found also could have been a decent shelter. His buddies said he had food and a canteen. And he could melt snow for more water."

"So what happened?" Sue said again.

"I don't know," I said again. "But look. His bones turned up on the lakeshore, where a hunter starting from Summit Peak Road would have been unlikely to go, and his revolver was found two miles inland, at about the farthest point a hunter would want to carry a deer carcass from. Something happened to make him lose his revolver, and something else happened to get him to the beach. I do not—repeat, *not*—think he got lost."

"Maybe the Unsub met him on the trail." Sue had unconsciously fallen into the FBI jargon we in law enforcement were all starting to use, probably because we watched all those television mysteries, too. "Unsub" means "unidentified subject." It's easier to say than "unknown bad guy" when you don't know his name.

"But how would an Unsub with a reason to kill Armstrong know where he was going that day?"

"Could he have been one of Armstrong's hunting buddies?" Sue asked.

"I don't think so. Every one of them has an alibi. Other hunters saw them where they said they had been. Besides, Armstrong never slept with their wives or daughters. We checked."

"Assuming Armstrong was murdered, could this have been random?"

"It could," I said. "But a random murder wouldn't have involved revenge for a sexual transgression. So what's the motive?"

Sue shook her head. "This is a puzzle indeed. But I agree with you about one thing. Something happened, and I think it was probably criminal. The pistol, the location of the body, and that abandoned snowmobile that can't be traced. Three big fat clues. But together they sure don't tell us much. Even the fact that Armstrong was carrying a muzzle-loading rifle does not necessarily link his misadventure to those that befell Gloria Lake and the others."

"Including Marilyn Schneider," I said. "But she was murdered, that's almost certain, judging from what we know. Or what Sheriff Champion is letting us know."

"He's jealous of you, Steve," Sue said. "He wants to solve a celebrated case like you and get his name in the papers nationwide, and he wants to do it without outside help."

She had discreetly asked Champion, through the chain of command in Lansing, if the services of the state police would be helpful, and had been just as discreetly rebuffed.

"How do you know that?"

"Forensic psychologist intuition," Sue said. "Also known as a wild-ass guess."

In all our consultations during the last two days, Lieutenant Hemb had not pooh-poohed my hunch that something big was going on in the Upper Peninsula of Michigan, something big that might even be a case of serial murder, and that the weapon or weapons of choice were muzzle loaders. She had listened quietly, echoed my insights and doubts, pointed out where the holes lay, and generally strengthened my resolve to do something. Asking her help had been a good idea. A very good one.

But now something else was gnawing at me. I had to admit it: I was attracted to her. Sue Hemb could be strictly professional one moment, warm and sisterly the next, and even funny and mildly flirtatious.

Damn it, I missed having a woman in my life.

"Let's go get lunch," Sue said, puncturing my reverie. "All this talk about sex is making me hungry."

"Hungry?"

"In a 'Tom Jones' sort of way. Better wear a bib."

At Merle's I tried hard not to look her in the eye as we ate, and I tried hard not to spill sandwich crumbs in my lap. But Sue smiled and even giggled all the way through the meal.

Sergeant Alex Kolehmainen, I was now certain, was a damned fool. The question was whether I was on my way to becoming one, too.

CHAPTER TWENTY-FOUR

It wasn't long—ten days—before the damned fool called again.

His former girlfriend had returned to Lansing. "Something indeed is going on," she had told me, "but we need one more piece of evidence to shape this case. Something that will tell us its nature. Once we know that, we can start searching for the killer."

If nothing else, I was grateful for her support, happy to have had her company, and kept thinking about her speculatively. How could I not? She was a very good criminal profiler and a hell of a woman besides, as I said.

To my utter surprise the damned fool was calling with that one more piece of evidence I needed.

"Ready for this, Steve?" Alex said. "The forensics lab finally got around to Geoffrey Armstrong's remains yesterday. And they found something."

"God damn it, what?" I almost shouted. Alex can be *so* annoying.

"Armstrong's right femur, the one that was found two hundred feet inland from the body. It's a DNA match to the rest. And it's slightly chipped, with a tiny smear of lead from a projectile on it. The lead is the same alloy used in muzzle-loader balls."

"So Armstrong was shot?" I said stupidly.

"So Armstrong was shot," Alex echoed. "Probably took out one or more branches of the femoral artery. Forensics is calling it the likely cause of death."

"Jesus," I said. "What now?"

"We're opening an investigation," Alex said. "That is, I am opening an official investigation. That is, if it's okay with you. It's your jurisdiction and your case."

Relief flooded through my bones. My old hunch was finally panning out.

"I think we should call in Lieutenant Hemb," I said.

"You already did. Remember, you asked. You hung out a lot after work, too. In fact, she stayed with you."

"You knew?" That was a silly question. Sue was well known in Porcupine City, having assisted in a previous investigation that made headlines, and nobody comes to town without Alex knowing about it. His sources are that good. And Sue is that good-looking. Nobody that good-looking appears in a restaurant or outside a sheriff's cabin without tongues wagging.

On the phone I could almost hear Alex shrug. He kept his voice neutral. "We've talked. The lieutenant thinks you're on to something, and she said so before forensics told us about the femur."

"Let's get this going," I said.

The next day a conference call was held from my squad room. Gil took notes, and Alex dropped by. Chad Garrow listened in at his desk. Lieutenant Sue Hemb participated from Lansing. The sheriffs of all the Upper Michigan counties where muzzle-loading deaths had occurred in the last few years also came on the line. So did Bill Koons from the Wolverines State Park and a couple of Department of Natural Resources colleagues, including the conservation officer—or game warden—in whose district Porcupine County lay. I'd also asked Camilo Hernandez, Tribal Police chief for the Lac Vieux Desert Ojibwa reservation at Watersmeet in neighboring Gogebic County, to participate. Camilo, a mostly Apache *mestizo* from El Paso who has bounced around several reservations during his long career, is a smart cop. Hogan was also in attendance, but he was snoring under my desk.

This late in the game we needed all the help we could get, and it was coming from everywhere.

Except for Chippewa County. Sheriff Wayne Champion couldn't be bothered, and delegated his undersheriff, Howie Markowitz, a fat, wisecracking good-old-boy type happier at the poker table than out in the field doing his job. I had met Howie at law-enforcement seminars and had pegged him as a trouble-maker and time waster, the kind that embarrassed the profession.

"We've all reviewed what we know so far," I said, "and it isn't a hell of a lot. All we know for sure is the basic modus operandi—death by muzzle-loading rifle. Which suggests that our killer is an expert with that kind of weapon. But we're looking at a lot of people who are experts, or close to it. The first killing was at a gathering of muzzle-loader enthusiasts, so it's logical to consider that our perp may have been one of those enthusiasts, probably one we already interviewed. It appears we're going to have to solve this case by a process of elimination."

"I'm all for eliminating bad guys," Howie chortled.

"Good-bye to you then, Howie," Chad growled.

"Chad! Dammit!" I said, but wiggled my eyebrows across the squad room at my big deputy. "You know I meant eliminating suspects, Mr. Markowitz."

I carefully omitted his official title, a subtle insult. Probably too subtle for Howie.

Before I could proceed, Lieutenant Susan Hemb extinguished the sparks of rebellion, her voice stern and flat as a disgusted schoolmarm's.

"*Under*sheriff Markowitz," Sue said, emphasizing the first part of his title, "it seems that in this possible case of serial murder Chippewa County wants to go it alone. It would be the state police's great pleasure to cooperate with that intention. It's up to you. Do you want to stay or go?"

A long moment passed during which I imagined Sue's eyes flashing between sky blue and steel gray, then Markowitz spoke.

"Yes'm," he said quietly, like a chastened schoolboy who had finally realized the consequences of spitballing the teacher when her back was turned. "Sorry. I'll stay."

"Very well, then," I said. "Let's go back to the beginning and make everything clear. This case started two years ago at the Mountain Men rendezvous in Porcupine County with a muzzle-loading death that was ruled an accident but may not have been one. If the shooting was murder, then the murderer most likely was an expert with a muzzle-loading rifle, as seems apparent in all the other cases.

"At that time my department interviewed several subjects who were participants in the rendezvous and crack shots as well. Let's start with these people and build complete dossiers on them all. If one of them is the shooter at the rendezvous, five gets you ten he's the shooter in all the others."

Paper rustled as the lawmen consulted their notes.

"The most obvious suspect seems to me to be Richard Trenary, the aviation mechanic from Indiana," I said. "I think he's a real piece of work. He's a crack shot by his own claim. He's clearly antisocial and a woman-hater, and if Gloria Lake humiliated him by charging him five times the going rate for sex, there's a motive right there. Revenge for humiliation."

"And he wasn't at the rifle range when Miss Lake died," Chad said. "He was out near the Mullet, almost at the scene. Practically in the perfect place to pick off Miss Lake."

I don't know if the others noticed, but Chad's use of "Miss" struck me. He was thinking of her as a human being, not as a nameless victim. That meant he cared. That in turn meant I could count on him to go the extra mile to catch her killer.

"Almost too obvious," Alex said, "but Trenary *is* a good place to start."

"Right. We'll begin with him. Chad, please take care of that. Call the La Porte police and ask what they know. Ask them to keep the lid on."

"On it," the deputy said, like an eager-beaver young agent on *NCIS*. We all watch too much television.

"I'll get back to the rest of you as soon as we find out anything definite on Trenary," I said. "Now let's go over the other possibilities among the subjects we interviewed after the killing of Gloria Lake."

"If I may," Sue interjected.

"Go ahead."

"As we've said, it's pretty clear that the Unsub is a crack shot with a muzzle loader. Maybe we ought to look at ability alone rather than motive, at least for now, in winnowing down our list of suspects. It might make things go faster."

"Who's the best shooter on the list of people who had sex with Lake?" Alex said.

"Ray Mitchell," Gil said.

"Pretty prominent businessman in the Detroit area," I said. "I don't think he's our guy, but he'll be easy to eliminate. People like him are out in public all the time and their movements are recorded. We could subpoena his credit-card and phone records and, if it comes to that, we could get a warrant for his appointments book."

"Why don't you think he's our guy?" Alex said.

"Two things," I said. "First, witnesses put him on the rifle range about the time Lake was shot. If the bullet that hit her came from his weapon, it had to be an accident. Second, he just didn't strike me as a killer. His manner was open and forthright. He didn't behave as if he had anything to conceal."

"Intuition isn't proof," Sue said, donning the cloak of devil's advocate. "Besides, Steve, you know as well as I do that serial killers often are consummate con men, able to divert suspicion solely by force of personality. Some of them are superb actors."

"No argument there," I said. "Mitchell very well could have pulled the wool over my eyes. And the time line isn't rigid. We don't know the exact minute Lake died—maybe there's room on either side for someone to have gone from the firing line to the Mullet and get back to it without being missed. Yeah, we'll have to go back to the Mullet and treat it as a crime scene, taking time and motion measurements. Even after all this time we might find something out."

"That's my thing," Alex said. "I'll take a crew out and we'll do our job."

It occurred to me that if that had been done at the time Gloria Lake was killed, we might not be here today. But I didn't say so. No use beating myself up now or implying that my brother officer hadn't done his job. Everything on the scene had pointed to an accident.

"Want me to check Mitchell out?" said Sue, who was an experienced field investigator as well a psychologist. Lansing was close to Detroit, and she would not need to ask cooperation from Detroit area police to investigate there. The whole state of Michigan was her bailiwick. "I can start as soon as Chad reports in on Trenary."

"Excellent," I said. "Now who's next on the list?"

"I nominate Dale Suppelsa," Sue said.

I snorted. "Suppelsa? I don't think he's smart enough to be a killer."

"Actors, Steve, actors," Sue snapped. On the job she is all cop, as Alex said. For a fleeting moment I imagined her blue eyes and blonde hair next to mine on a pillow, then slapped my hand mentally and wrenched myself back to reality.

"Putting first impressions aside," I said, "Suppelsa does know how to shoot, even though he wasn't on the rifle range at the time of Lake's death. Like Trenary, he was on the river near the Mullet. And, like Trenary and Mitchell, he admitted to having sex with Lake."

"Maybe he was lying about the competitive skills," Sue said. "Maybe he dogged it on the range so nobody would think him a crack shot."

"But it might have taken only an adequate shooter to kill Gloria from the other bank of the Mullet," I said, encouraging Sue in her skepticism. "The range of the shot might have been only twenty, maybe thirty yards. Even a smoothbore like a Brown Bess is accurate enough for that."

"My team and I will check that out as well," Alex said.

"Okay, we'll keep Suppelsa on the suspect list," I said. "Now who's next? Ah, Bill Du Bois, the professor and ex-priest in Ann Arbor. He's a good possibility. He struck me as a pretty slippery guy, a bit of a phony. But he said he was in town talking to kids at the historical society at the time of the shooting. That would have been easy to check at the time, but I didn't."

"Why not?" said Alex.

"Too much else to do, and that would have been so easy to follow up if he were lying, so I just assumed I'd do that if it seemed like a good idea. Goddam it."

We all knew that in an investigation assumption is always a mistake, but there wasn't one of us present who hadn't cut that corner from time to time. And we all knew that memories are short. Enough time had passed since the killing that the kids and the adults who were there might not remember anything about the event at the historical society.

"I'll take Du Bois into my ever-growing caseload," said Sue with a surprising touch of humor in her voice. "Ann Arbor is close to Lansing."

"Thank you," I said. "Be sure to put in for overtime."

We all laughed. We all worked overtime, and we never got paid for it. No money in the till.

"Now then," I said again. "Fredericka Barnes."

"Big Freddie," Chad said. "My kinda gal."

I tried hard to keep from laughing, and barely succeeded. "Yes. The high-school lunchroom director from Waunakee, Wisconsin. There's a good possibility here. She's a champion with a muzzle loader. She said she had sex with Gloria Lake. She didn't seem at all bitter and judgmental about it, but maybe she was being an actress."

Bill Koons cut in. "Come to think of it," said the park ranger, "from your description, Steve, she's big and strong enough to have humped Geoffrey Armstrong's body halfway across the Wolverines from the place where we found his pistol to the lakeshore."

"Could Armstrong's killer have used that snowmobile your guys found wrecked on the lakeshore?" I said.

"Not sure," Bill said. "That's pretty rugged and rocked country. It's possible, but even with a couple of feet of snow there would be a lot of places on the trail where a snowmobile would hang up or fall through."

"Something else," said Sheriff Dan Roane of Gogebic County, "Waunakee is just north of Madison. Barnes lived only a few miles from Gloria Lake."

"Then she's most definitely on our suspect list. Dan, would you take her on?"

"Yup. I've got both kin and old friends in law enforcement down by Madison and can make time to snoop around in the next week or so."

We all sat silent for a moment, then I said, "Let's keep all this as quiet as we can. If and when the press finds out what happened with Armstrong, it'll be a media circus. And it will do us no good if our perp knows we're hunting for him."

Murmurs of assent all around. Then Alex said, "At some point, if we don't have any luck with our list of muzzle-loader shooters, we need to take a hard look at the others interviewed after the Mullet killing. Richard Crockett and Sheila Bodey, for instance."

"Don't think Crockett is a shooter," Chad said. "And even if Bodey is, she strikes me as way too small to have dragged Armstrong through the woods."

"Be that as it may," I said, "we can't rule them out at this moment."

"No," Sue said. "And Bodey does have a strong connection to Lake in that they were schoolteachers together in Madison and were also friends."

"Yes. Bodey struck me as a caring person, too," I said.

For a moment we all considered the angles. Then Chad spoke.

"What about Miss Lake's boyfriend, Teddy Gillson? The one Bodey told us about. We never called him, did we?"

"Good catch," I said ruefully. "Always suspect a lover or former lover. Would you check him out, too, Chad?"

"Yup."

Finally Alex said, "Given our resources, it's probably best to start with what we've got so far. Even with an official investigation going, we can't throw manpower around the way we used to be able to do."

"I just hope the Unsub doesn't hit again while we're looking for him," Sue said.

As we all signed off that thought hung heavy in the air.

One more call.

"Governor?" I said after ten minutes of drumming my fingers on the desktop waiting for the call to go through. "Sheriff Martinez, Porcupine County."

"I hope you have good news for me."

"I'm afraid not."

"What is it, then?"

"We think Geoffrey Armstrong was murdered. So were three other people. We think it's the work of a serial killer using muzzle-loading weapons."

"Good Lord. Explain, please."

I did and at length. The governor listened quietly, asking a brief question from time to time.

"I'll be damned," she said when I finished.

"So there it is. We've started an official investigation. The Michigan State Police is assisting. So are the sheriff's departments of three counties, the Tribal Police and the DNR."

"Are you confident you'll find the killer?" the governor said.

"Not at all."

"Thank you for being honest."

"But we'll do our damnedest."

"That's all I can ask, Sheriff. Thank you for calling."

CHAPTER TWENTY-FIVE

The next morning, as if to mock us, chance delivered two unsettling bits of news to my desk within the space of half an hour.

Hogan and I had arrived to behold Chad in the squad room, phone in his massive fist, an hour before his shift officially began. Before I could sit down in my office I heard him sigh and mutter, "Shit."

"Shit?" I called.

"Just talked to the Indiana troopers. Dick Trenary could have killed Gloria Lake," Chad said wearily, "but not the others."

"Why?"

"He's been in prison for the last eighteen months," Chad said. "He's doing ten years in the max security unit at Michigan City for assault with intent to do great bodily harm. Beat a hooker nearly to death outside a bar in Gary. She wouldn't go home with him."

I whistled. Michigan City is Indiana's toughest prison. John Dillinger did time behind its bars. Condemned inmates are executed there.

"We shoulda taken a harder look at Trenary in the beginning," Chad said. "He has a long record of abuse against women. He was married twice and arrested several times for domestic assault, but his wives wouldn't press charges. He did a year for aggravated assault after a bar fight."

"That wouldn't have done us much good," I said, "if Trenary's not the guy who did the others. I'm now pretty sure he didn't kill Miss Lake, either."

"Why?"

"If he actually did," I said, "with that kind of record, he'd never have admitted to having sex with her, let alone offered any details about the encounter. He would've clammed up tight or played stupid. He's a bad guy, but he's not dumb."

"So we can write him off the list," Chad said.

"Well, no, not yet," I said. "There's still that thin possibility he shot Gloria Lake. But he isn't going anywhere. We can leave him on ice for the time being. Now what about Teddy Gillson?"

"On it."

I chuckled.

Half an hour later Chad returned. "Gillson's clean. I tracked him down in Mexico City. He's been teaching at an American school there for two years. Said he hasn't been back in the States all that time, and his credit-card records back him up. He's married now and has a kid."

"Ah. That's all we need to know about him."

Chad nodded. "Now what?"

"Inform the others. I'll call Lieutenant Hemb. If she hasn't already, she'd better get moving on Ray Mitchell."

Sue wasn't at her office. "Gone to Detroit this morning," said her sergeant at the shrink desk. "Said to tell you she's checking out a guy named Mitchell."

I tried her cell but either she was out of range or had turned it off.

Grass doesn't grow under the feet of Lieutenant Susan Hemb, I thought. *She knows what she needs, then goes and gets it.*

But I worried that time was running out.

For several minutes I played desk hockey with budget projections Gil had put together for the county commission meeting in the evening. All of us needed to qualify on the shooting range before the end of the month, and we didn't have a dime for the ammunition. These days the commissioners approved all extra expenditures over a hundred dollars, and I'd have to plead and beg and whine and generally abase myself to get every cartridge we needed.

Suddenly the squad-room door flew open as Cheryl Waite trundled in with her mailbag. "Sheriff!" she called, waving a thick white envelope. "Mail from Finland!"

Every head in the squad room snapped to attention. As a professional United States Postal Service mail carrier, Cheryl was expected to be discreet and circumspect, but being Cheryl and knowing all her customers in Porcupine City, she believed in being friendly rather than official. Her bosses put up with her mild indiscretions because she was such a good salesperson for Priority Mail packages that both the UPS and FedEx drivers complained she was cutting into their business. And because she was so sweet and likable.

I took the envelope, shut the door and pulled the blind in its window.

I was not surprised that the envelope, covered with small-denomination Finnish stamps and bearing a Turku postmark, was addressed to me at the sheriff's department rather than my mailbox out on State Highway M64. I habitually forget to check the mailbox when I come home—in my private life, few people write letters to me, so I just let the junk mail build up inside the box. Cheryl, who often rides the rural circuit when the regular driver-carriers are off, sometimes empties the mailbox when it gets full, drives into my yard and dumps the contents inside my screen door. I might not see an important letter for three weeks after it is delivered to the mailbox.

I slit open the envelope with a Buck knife confiscated years ago from a teenager who had used it to cut the screen in a hunting-camp window and break in, not to steal anything but to fool around with his girlfriend. As a deputy then I had acted on a tip and caught them in flagrante. Rather than making an official arrest and creating a police record, I chose to read both the riot act and, after making sure the boy would repair the screen, let them go. The knife should have been inventoried, but that would have meant opening a file on the boy, so it just seemed better to slip it into my desk and employ it in official police work, such as opening unexpected letters from my own girlfriend.

Thinking about all this was just a way to drag out the clock. The truth is that I didn't want to open the letter. It was the first paper-and-ink communication I'd received from Ginny since she'd gone off to Finland with Tommy. Up to then she'd sent frequent and chatty e-mails, full of news about her teaching, her learning and her visits to tourist attractions all over the country. But she'd attached no photographs. Ginny always has been a latecomer to electronic technology, and she still carries a little plastic point-and-shoot film camera rather than the digital models everybody else in the whole damn world uses. Not until they stop making thirty-five-millimeter film will she change.

All this filled and churned the empty corners of my mind as I shook out the contents of the envelope—two densely typed and printed pages on lightweight paper and half a dozen glossy four-by-six snapshots. The photographs fell on the desk facedown, so I decided for no good reason to read the letter first.

But I waited for a few more seconds, eyes closed. Was this going to be bad news? Another Dear John letter? I was certain everybody else outside in the squad room was thinking the same thing.

Damn Cheryl, I thought. *Dear, sweet Cheryl.*

"Dear Steve," the letter began. Not "Dearest" or "Steve honey." *That doesn't mean anything,* I thought. *Ginny, who can be private to a fault, has always been reticent about endearments on paper and especially in e-mail. She prefers to whisper them in my ear in person.*

I forced myself to read the next line.

"The weather in Finland all summer reminded me of the UP," it said, and went on like that, meaningless social twaddle, for an entire paragraph. *The long softening up for the decisive blow.*

Then followed several paragraphs about Tommy. He was thriving in school, soaking up Finnish—a difficult language related to Hungarian—and helping his classmates perfect their English. "That reminds me how my dad said everybody spoke at least two languages, sometimes three, growing up in Porcupine County during the 1890s and early 1900s," she wrote. "In school everybody spoke English. At home it was their parents' native language—English, Croatian, Finnish or Canadian French. And on the playground it was 'Finn,' because that was the most common tongue of the times."

As for Ginny, she had not only thrown herself happily into her studies but was also developing a textbook on the Finns in America with her department chairman.

"Lauri Nissinen is one of the nicest guys I've ever known," she wrote, an ominous sentence that raised my hackles. "He's been such a brick, not only helping me choose my studies and find a school for Tommy, but also finding us a good apartment near downtown Turku. He's taken us all over Finland to see the sights, and even drove us to Pudasjarvi, the little town in the north my grandparents emigrated from in 1896. I met some distant cousins, and oh, Steve, it was like old home week again."

It was a happy, chatty letter, full of homely detail important mostly to writer and recipient and nobody else. But the name "Lauri" kept cropping up. He's one of the most prominent historians in Finland and the European Union, Ginny wrote, the author of several important books in his field, the history of Northern Europe since the First World War. He has a palatial home in Turku and a sprawling summer place near Oulu far up on the Gulf of Bothnia. Of course Ginny had visited it several times. And she never mentioned a Mrs. Nissinen.

When I took a look at the photos, two things struck me. First, so much of Finland looks like the Upper Peninsula of Michigan—thick hardwood and evergreen forests, rolling cutover meadows full of cattle—that it's unsurprising the immigrants of a century ago thought the UP their particular land of milk and honey.

Maybe Ginny thinks Finland is hers. For, judging from the photographs, Lauri Nissinen is tall and sandy-haired, with chiseled features that likely will be handsomest when their owner reaches the age of fifty. He drives not only a late-model BMW but also a brand-new Land Rover. The photos of his homes showed a taste in art and furnishing both impeccable and unimpoverished. This is a man who would be sweetly untroubled by Ginny's immense wealth, because he has his own.

I folded the letter and slipped it and the photos back into the envelope. *She's telling me something,* I thought. *She's telling me she's found someone else. She's preparing me for the bad news when she gets home.*

For the rest of the day I sat in my chair festering under a damp blanket of inadequacy. How could I, a lowly and underpaid county sheriff, ever compete with a man like that? The corners of my despair were lifted only by Hogan's nudges and Gil's soft reminders—he was uncharacteristically gentle because he sensed what was in that letter—that I needed to prepare the budget request for the county board.

That evening the commissioners quickly rubber-stamped my line-item request for fourteen boxes of nine-millimeter cartridges for the deputies' Glocks and two of target wadcutters for my personal sidearm, an old-fashioned Smith & Wesson .357 Combat Magnum revolver. The brusque truculence with which I demanded—not asked for—the money for the ammo clearly shocked them. It startled me, too. Maybe I've been in this job too long.

Chapter Twenty-Six

"Can't get a thing on Mitchell," Sue said, her voice fading in and out on the cell phone as she drove through, under and over the spaghetti expressways of Detroit. "His record is squeaky, squeaky clean."

"Credit cards? Phone?" I asked.

"No luck there, either. Visa and MasterCard don't put him anywhere near the murder sites at the right times. Nor do his cell or landline records suggest anything."

"What *has* he been doing all this time?"

"The usual prominent businessman stuff. He *is* on the road a lot, but as near as we can find out it's mostly to his far-flung auto-repair empire around central Michigan. He's a hands-on guy, a micromanager, always checking up on his people. A couple of his employees groused a little about that—we engaged them in casual conversation when we brought two of our personal cars in for oil changes and checkups—but it's also clear they like and respect him."

"Does his entire life revolve around work?" I asked.

"Oh, no," Sue said. "He's a Shriner—drives one of those little magic carpet cars in local parades—and also is a vice president of his Rotary chapter. He ran for alderman in Grosse Pointe Fields a few years ago and lost by just a handful of votes."

"Republican or Democrat?"

"For alderman, neither," Sue said. "That town's government

is nonpartisan. But he's a registered Democrat. Gives lots of money to the party."

"Unusual for a small businessman."

"Not so small. His repair shops are worth millions and so is he."

"Education?"

"MBA from Northwestern."

I whistled. That's a top business school. "Before that?"

"Patchwork and part-time—a couple of courses here and there in community colleges while he was working as an auto mechanic, then Ferris State and Eastern Michigan, where he finally got his bachelor's. His GPA and bootstraps story got him into Northwestern."

"Industrious fellow."

"Indeed. He came up from the streets of Flint. Both mother and father were auto workers at GM. He was an Eagle Scout. After high school—his grades were only average—he enlisted in the Marines and did a year in the Middle East during the Gulf War. He saw combat and won a Bronze Star. Made lance corporal. Honorably discharged after three years."

"What was his MOS?" I asked. Military occupation specialties can sometimes be revealing if their talents are transferred to civilian life.

"Zero-three-one-seven. Scout sniper."

"No surprise, that."

"He still is a champion shooter," Sue said. "After the service he competed in rifle matches at Camp Perry and won many if not most of the long-range events. I found an article in the National Rifle Association magazine about him that said he was quitting cartridge weapons and taking up muzzle loaders because it was a greater challenge."

"Quite a guy. Doesn't seem like a murderer, does he?"

"Absolutely no evidence for that."

I thought a moment. "Do you think there's a possibility that he could be leading a secret life on the side? Maybe he's one of those smart cookies who fools everybody around him and then disappears into another dimension. Like Lindbergh."

"Lindbergh?"

"The aviator. He had maybe seven children by not one but perhaps three secret mistresses in Germany and nobody found out about that until after more than a quarter of a century after his death."

"Lindbergh wasn't a killer."

"Certain conspiracy theorists might disagree with that," I said. "There are some who swear he accidentally killed his own son and framed Bruno Hauptmann for the crime."

"Far-fetched," Sue said.

"But not impossible. Lindy knew how to cover his tracks."

"Not impossible doesn't mean it actually happened."

"Nope. But if there's a wee possibility, just a tiny one, doesn't that mean the case of Charles Lindbergh Jr. might still be open, at least technically?"

"Ah, I see what you mean, Sheriff," Sue said. "You don't want to write Ray Mitchell off just yet."

"Nope. He may have been a Boy Scout, but Boy Scouts have their dark side, too."

"Such as?" Sue asked.

"Arthur Gary Bishop. Utah Eagle scout and pedophile. Murdered five small boys. Executed in, I think, 1988."

"Ugh."

"There were others, too."

"Be that as it may," Sue said, "there's not much else we can do without letting Mitchell know we're investigating him. Getting a warrant for his appointments book, as you suggested, would tip him off—and maybe everybody else, too. He'd call his lawyer and his lawyer would call the press."

"Okay," I said. "We'll put him on ice with Dick Trenary for now. We'll shake Dale Suppelsa's tree and see what falls out."

"He's from Mount Pleasant, Iowa," Sue said. "What about asking Jack Seymour, that Dog Soldier cop, to have a look? He's from Des Moines, isn't he? Might have contacts at Mount Pleasant."

"I don't think so," I said. "Seymour was a participant in the rendezvous. He knew what Gloria Lake was up to and looked the other way. He could be up to his ears in this."

"But he's gay, isn't he? There wouldn't be a sex motive, and I don't see anything about his relationship to religion in these reports."

"I thought you were a shrink who knows everything," I said. "Think of Big Freddie. Maybe Seymour swings from both sides of the plate, too. He'd be an awfully long shot, though."

Sue did not bristle but chuckled at my choice of words.

"You know what I mean, dammit."

"Yes, I do," she said quietly, all cop again.

"Okay, I'll call the sheriff in Mount Pleasant."

"Henry County Sheriff's Department."

"This is Steve Martinez, sheriff of Porcupine County in Michigan. May I speak to the boss?"

"Speaking. This is Sheriff Ed White." Gruff and low-pitched, both businesslike and friendly.

"You answer your own phone?"

"Secretary's on vacation. Nobody to cover. Budget."

"Tell me about it."

"You got all day?"

I chuckled ruefully. "No," I said, "for the same reason you don't. But I've got a situation here, and thought you might be able to help."

"Go ahead."

For the next five minutes I filled White in about the Upper Michigan muzzle-loader shootings, giving brief descriptions of our persons of interest and finishing with Dale Suppelsa.

"I know the kid and his family," White said. "Good family, good lad. I'd be surprised, too, if he was able to hold more than one idea in his head at a time. Doesn't seem that he's mentally capable of serial murder. But you never know, do you?"

"Right. I'd appreciate it mightily if you could see if you could find out where Suppelsa was during the other killings so that we could eliminate him from our list."

"Glad to."

"I'll fax you the reports."

"Okay," White said. "I'll get back to you as soon as I can."

"We're keeping the lid on," I said.

"As well you should," he said. "I will, too."

"Thanks."

CHAPTER TWENTY-SEVEN

Two days later Sheriff White called back instead of faxing. Just by chatting with Suppelsa's friends and the boy himself in the local café where just about everybody in Mount Pleasant had breakfast, the sheriff had been able to nail his whereabouts during two of the deaths.

"Both the afternoon before and the morning after that fire in Porcupine City," White said, "Dale was coaching his Pony League team to the county championship. In fact, I remembered that I saw him at the ballpark both times myself. And in that Wolverine Mountains thing, he was in Costa Rica, kayaking with friends. Only place I haven't been able to put him is during the sniper shooting near the Soo. Want me to keep at it? I really don't think he's your man."

"Thanks, Sheriff," I said. "I don't think so, either. But I'll just move him to the bottom of the list."

"There's something else you might be interested in."

"What's that?"

"Just heard that three days ago a guy was found shot to death in the woods near a rifle range just outside La Crosse, Wisconsin. Shooter unknown."

"Tell me."

"It was during a NRA long-range rifle contest at the local rod-and-gun club. Nowhere near the firing range, but in the deep woods a quarter mile or so away. Don't know any more details. Thought you might want to know."

"I sure do. Thanks, Ed."

"No problem. Hope you catch your bad guy."

Quickly I phoned La Crosse, a town on the Mississippi more than three hundred miles southwest of Porcupine City, and immediately the dispatcher on duty handed me over to Jack Clarke, sheriff of La Crosse County. I explained at length.

"Maybe my shooter is your guy," I finished.

"I would call that preposterous," Sheriff Clarke said, "if it were not for one thing."

"What's that?"

"Medical examiner's report landed on my desk this morning. Huge hole in the guy's back. The bullet was recovered from a tree a few feet in front of him. Large-caliber muzzle-loading ball, a seventy-five by the weight of it."

I let out a long breath. "Brown Bess," I said.

"Yeah," Clarke said. "Weird choice for a murder weapon. Anyway, that proves the shot couldn't have come from the range. All the shooters were using .30 caliber scoped rifles. And the body was way too far into the woods for a ricochet."

"The time line?" I said.

"Coroner puts time of death almost exactly at the start of the competition."

"Killer was using the noise on the range to mask the sound of his gun."

"Sure seems that way."

"Find anything at the crime scene?"

"Not much. But we were able to place the shooter. He came from the nearby road, probably from a parked vehicle, followed the vic down the trail all the way from the entry point, then stepped off it and rested his piece on a tree limb to shoot. We found shreds of burnt patching in front of it, and the grass by the tree had been trampled. There's a distinct footprint, absolutely no tread or heel mark, at that spot."

"Sounds like a moccasin."

"*Is* a moccasin, our tracker said."

"Tracker?"

"Ojibwa from the Bad River reservation," Sheriff Clarke said. "Professional tracker. Ex-military. All over Wisconsin we call him in to help us find the bad guys."

"Lucky fellows. Wish we had one like him."

"Sheriff Martinez, what about you?"

"Me?"

"You're Native American, aren't you?"

News travels widely.

"Yes. But I'm not much good at Indian skills," I said. "I'm a complete babe in the woods. I would get lost if I didn't have my GPS, and would be eaten by wild animals if I didn't have my .357. What's more, I'm not good enough with it to be sure of taking small game for survival. Peculiar, huh?"

"I don't believe you," Sheriff Clarke said.

"Why not?"

"Your reputation precedes you."

I snorted.

"There's something even more peculiar," Sheriff Clarke said, returning to the subject.

"What?"

"Our victim's a Hmong. His name is Chu Lo Vue."

I whistled. "Hate crime?"

"Yeah. The feds're on my ass already."

After Saigon fell in 1975, hundreds of thousands of Hmong, mountain tribesmen from Vietnam, Laos, Cambodia and Thailand who had served as anticommunist guerrillas in American employ, were granted refugee status in the United States to protect them from North Vietnamese reprisals. Today some 40,000 Hmong live in various Wisconsin cities, many of them around La Crosse.

Their absorption into American culture has been rocky. In 2005 a Hmong, Chai Soua Vang, murdered six white hunters in Wisconsin, claiming they had harassed him, and is now serving six life terms. In 2007 another Hmong, Cha Vang, was shot to death while hunting squirrels in the woods. James Nichols, a hunter from Peshtigo, Wisconsin, is doing sixty-nine years in prison for second-degree intentional homicide. A large number of people think Cha Vang was killed in retaliation for the six earlier murders.

And, as has happened so often with immigrants plunged into an alien culture, intense poverty combined with majority disdain has spurred the formation of violent criminal gangs, and many cities throughout the United States are plagued by Hmong bands that rape, rob, kill and peddle drugs. Some white Americans hate Hmongs more than they despise Mexicans.

"You *sure* it's a hate crime?" I asked.

" 'Course not. But it's the first thing we're looking at. That Hmong was carrying a Winchester .270. It's not hunting season in Wisconsin yet. He might have been poaching, and maybe that gave the shooter a motive."

"On the face of it that doesn't sound as if it's related to mine. So far our best guesses for a motive are sex and religion."

"Mine could have been just random," Sheriff Clarke said. "Maybe our vic just happened to be a Hmong in the wrong place at the wrong time." His tone suggested he didn't believe that for a moment.

"Hope you can avoid anything worse," I said.

"One more thing," Sheriff Clarke said, over gentle noises of rustling paper. "There's a prelim report from state police forensics."

"Already?" I envied my Wisconsin counterpart. That was quick.

"Yeah. The hate-crime possibility put it on the front burner. Forensics found a short-starter mark on the ball. The ball is well mushroomed and misshapen. But the mark is perfectly centered, with distinctive nicks around its edge."

"That's just about enough to convict," I said. "Find the owner of that short starter, and we've got our man."

"*Our* man?" Sheriff Clarke said, doubt in his voice.

"I'm sure of it," I said. "Well, almost."

"Come to think of it," Sheriff Clarke said, "you could damn well be right. Share our files?"

"Absolutely. Fire up your fax machine."

We made a few more polite noises of commiseration, during which we agreed to keep in touch, then we hung up.

CHAPTER TWENTY-EIGHT

Putting down the *Milwaukee Journal Sentinel,* Angel felt both exultation and relief. The man chosen to sacrifice his life for the Lord the previous day had turned out to be a pagan, an unbeliever, maybe even a Devil worshipper—a creature that did not deserve to live.

He had also been a poacher, as Angel had immediately concluded when the short and dark-skinned man with Asian features strode into view near the entry of the trail into the woods. Why else would someone be carrying a scoped rifle out of season in a place like that?

If the man were stopped and questioned on the way in, he could claim to have intended to participate in the shooting competition at the nearby gun club. But if nobody challenged him the man could disappear into the woods and drop a deer, then drag it safely away from the trail for field dressing. If anyone had heard the crack of his rifle, they would think it was an echo from the range.

Sweet. But evil.

Angel had followed fifty paces behind the man, moccasins noiseless on the trail, keeping a screen of trees and branches between them. Twice the man had stopped, turned and looked back, but failed to spot his tracker, clad in forest-camouflage fatigues. In the deep woods Angel had practiced and practiced, as Daddy had preached, until placing one foot quietly in front of another and staying out of sight had become second nature.

When the man halted for the third time and raised his rifle to his shoulder, Angel followed the direction of his aim and spotted a doe slowly stepping through the trees, searching for browse. Swiftly Angel ducked behind a stout oak and rested the maple forestock of the Hammer of God on a branch. The shot would be a little more than fifty yards through the open, an easy one for a skilled shooter.

A heavy-caliber *crack!* resounded from the nearby rifle range, almost blanketing the *whump!* of the Hammer of God. The man's chest exploded in a gout of gore as the ball tore through his torso, guillotined a three-inch birch sapling, and embedded itself in a thigh-thick hemlock. He died instantly.

God is merciful, Angel thought as the smoke cleared. *God is just.* It was a swift death, as Angel always tried to administer, and in the scheme of God's will a deserved one.

Now, as Angel contemplated the Hammer of God, now nestling on its cradle of pegs under the portrait of Christ, these words came to mind: "And Jesus answering said unto them, Render to Caesar the things that are Caesar's, and to God the things that are God's. And they marveled at him." The hunter who had turned out to be a heathen had been twice a sinner, once against God and once against man. He had broken God's law by rejecting Jesus and Caesar's law by disobeying game regulations.

Now it was time to be ever more careful. The police, if they were not stupid, would be searching.

But Angel was smarter than any cop.

CHAPTER TWENTY-NINE

"Damn near a slam-dunk that it's connected to the UP kill-ings," I told Lieutenant Hemb on the phone, having relayed to her the details of the Hmong shooting. "That seventy-five-caliber ball can't be a coincidence."

"I agree," Sue said.

"You think it's a hate crime?"

"Sure. Not necessarily in the way that other murders of Hmongs were hate crimes. The hate could be religious in nature rather than simply from cultural differences. Hmongs tradition-ally are animists, spirit worshippers of the forest. I can see some evangelicals taking issue with that. Most of them would just shake their heads and some might point and preach, but the unbalanced could take things a step further."

"But how would the shooter know that the vic was Hmong and that he was going to be there at that particular time? Most Americans can't tell one Asian from another."

"Right," Sue said. "That victim could have been a random choice. Serial killers sometimes shoot first and rationalize later."

"Random doesn't fit the MO we've been looking at," I said. "Serial killers have a more or less clear motive, don't they?"

"Yes, but the smart ones sometimes vary that MO to deflect suspicion, just to keep us tied up in knots. The Armstrong kill-ing could have been random, too."

"Sure has our number, doesn't the Unsub?"

"So far," Sue said, and we fell silent for a moment. "Now

then. Trenary's clearly not our boy. Neither is Gillson. Ray Mitchell almost certainly isn't, though he's not quite home free yet. Suppelsa just hasn't got the brains, and he has an ironclad alibi for two of the shootings. Who's next?"

"William Evans Du Bois," I said, consulting my files. "The guy who played an Anglican missionary at the rendezvous. He's a shooter, and a good one by his own admission. He also had sex with Gloria Lake."

"My bailiwick," Sue said.

"Sex with Gloria Lake?"

"No, you impossible oaf. Du Bois teaches at the university in Ann Arbor. That's not far from Lansing. I'll make a few calls."

We hung up, and for most of the rest of the day I resumed my dispiriting game of budget lacrosse.

Just before suppertime Sue called back.

"We may be getting nowhere fast," she said, "or we may be getting nowhere slowly."

"Explain, please," I said.

"First, Du Bois is a highly regarded tenure-track assistant professor in the University of Michigan history department. Gets top marks from both his students and his colleagues. A couple of them have even become fellow members of the Mountain Men, thanks to his influence.

"Second," Sue said, "he is an excellent marksman with both rifle and pistol. He has won a lot of medals in national competition."

"Is there a third?"

"Don't rush me," Sue said. "You're as impatient as Alex."

"I'm listening. I'm listening."

"No police record that I can find, except for one thing. Du Bois grew up in Lansing, and a detective I know remembers there was a juvenile arrest at fifteen for sex with a girl of the same age. They got caught going at it in an alley. There was no court disposition and the arrest file was expunged. The parents took responsibility and there it ended."

"No surprise," I said. Kids will be kids, the juvenile laws protect them, and cops have bigger fish to fry anyway.

"He went through high school in Lansing and graduated with honors from Michigan. Good athlete, lettered in basketball and baseball at both places."

"Boy Scout like Mitchell, eh?" I said.

"That too," Sue said. "Almost made Eagle Scout. But there is one thing. I talked to a former professor at Seabury-Western Seminary in Evanston, Illinois, and he told me that Du Bois was never an ordained priest. He was asked to leave the seminary in his first year because of repeated and, the professor said, 'somewhat aggressive' sexual adventures, some with faculty wives, some with students. He was warned about harassment."

"No charges, no criminal record," I said. "But he did lie to me about being a priest."

"Technically he did," Sue said, "but these role players sometimes go so deeply into their personae that they forget what's real and what isn't. It's possible that Du Bois was a pretend priest for so long that he started believing his own story."

"Should we scratch him from our list, then?" I asked.

"Well," Sue said, "I also talked to a shrink colleague of mine who happened to have taken one of his courses as an under-graduate a decade ago. She said there have been and still are stories of the professor having affairs with his female students."

"That's a matter for the university," I said, "not for law enforcement. But it does suggest that where there's smoke there might be fire."

"Exactly," Sue said. "So I got a subpoena for his credit-card and phone records and compared them with the dates of the shootings."

"And?"

"Nothing," Sue said. "A big fat zero. Not a single thing to put Du Bois at the crime scenes or anywhere near them when things went down. There's just nothing to go on either to incriminate him or eliminate him from our list."

"Maybe there is," I said. "Let me make a phone call."

Horace Wright was in the *Herald* office and answered with a cheery "Hello, Steve. How can I be of assistance to law enforcement today?"

"I've got a question," I said. "If I ask it, you're going to know what's happening. Will you promise to hold the story until we're ready? In return I'll give you an exclusive."

Going to Horace meant that the press would at last get wind of our investigation. There was no way to ask the question I had in mind without Horace guessing what we were up to. Fortunately he was a journalist of ironclad ethics—if wing-nut opinions—and I knew I could trust him. I had known him a long time.

"You have my word."

"Remember the rendezvous on the Mullet a couple of years ago?" I said.

"Sure. Is this about the Gloria Lake shooting?"

I paused. Horace had not used the word "accident." That meant he had had his own doubts about the event and the others that ensued. He was a smart reporter and knew how to put two and two together.

"Yes."

"Mm. Wondered about that. Been a bunch of muzzle-loader killings recently, haven't there?"

I didn't answer. That was all Horace needed.

"I'll do what I can to help. Just give me the story first, okay?"

"Sure thing."

"What's the question?"

"Remember Bill Du Bois, the guy who played a priest? Historian from the University of Michigan?"

"Oh yes," Horace said. "Interesting guy. Intelligent, too."

"On the morning Gloria Lake was shot," I said, "he claimed to have been at the Historical Society talking to a bunch of high schoolers."

"Indeed he was," Horace immediately said, "for most of the day, beginning in the early morning. I was there. I had invited him to speak. He had those kids wrapped around his finger talking about the voyageurs in the Upper Peninsula. He knew his subject, and he knew how to keep the attention of his audience."

I sighed. That just about eliminated Du Bois as a suspect, at least in Gloria Lake's death.

"He couldn't have done it," Horace said.

Again I didn't answer. I didn't have to.

"Steve, whatever I can do," said Horace, "just ask. Meanwhile, I'll keep mum."

"Thanks."

"You got another suspect?"

"Can't answer that."

"Think whoever it was did Armstrong too?"

"No comment." I didn't resent the question. Horace was just going through the motions of his job.

"All right," he said. "No problem. Hope you catch the bastard."

"We will." I was hardly certain of that. "Thanks, Horace. You've been helpful."

I hung up and immediately called Dan Roane at his house outside Bessemer.

"Roane. Working late, Steve?" he said as he picked up,

without even asking who was calling and before I could say a word. Dan is uncanny that way. I often wondered what a conversation between Dan and Alex was like.

"Some of us are conscientious police officers," I said. "We leave no stone unturned."

That was a deliberately ironic remark. Sheriff Roane, a red-bearded oak of a man I have known ever since I was a green deputy and he the Gogebic County animal control officer, was famous among our brethren for his painstaking investigative work. "Takes forever," Alex once said, "but he always gets his bear."

Dan just chuckled at my dig. "Go on," he said over the shouting from the television. The Brewers were playing, and somebody had hit a home run.

I told Dan of the day's events, sparing no details, and voiced my frustration over finding a viable suspect among those we had considered the best possibilities.

"Know how you feel," Dan said. "Last few days I've been spending a lot of time checking out Freddie Barnes and not getting very far."

"Tell me."

"As we know from your reports, she's a shooter and a good one. She had a go in bed with Gloria Lake. She works in Waunakee not far from Madison. She's big enough to have humped Geoffrey Armstrong's carcass all the way down the Correction Line Trail in the Wolverines."

"And?"

"Nothing. Absolutely nothing. My honored colleagues in the Wisconsin State Police checked her whereabouts for the last two years. When she wasn't cooking at a rendezvous somewhere, she was in her school kitchen practically twenty-four slash seven. Her alibis are ironclad."

"Thanks for sharing this valuable intelligence so quickly," I said, a little annoyed. "When were you going to pass it to me?"

"I was about to get around to it after supper but then the Brewers came on and . . ."

"I know, I know. Never mind."

"But I'm having a eureka moment just this minute," Dan said.

"What?"

"Who found Gloria Lake's body?"

"That's impossible!" The Reverend George Hartfelder, for all his low-rent, high-octane Elmer Gantrying, was no murderer. I would have staked my life on that. The man sometimes could be pulpit-pounding angry, hurling lightning bolts from altar to narthex and nave to choir, but I doubted that he harbored a shred of malevolence for anyone.

"Hartfelder was in the Wolverines the day we went searching for Armstrong, wasn't he?" Dan said. "And he was present during the Porcupine City fire, wasn't he?"

Dan was reminding me that serial killers sometimes like to hang around the scenes of their crimes and watch the cops clean up the mess.

"Long shot. A very long shot," I said. "But I'll put Chad on it tomorrow."

Chad Garrow would, I thought, be less likely to cut Pastor Hartfelder any slack. Chad was friendly with everyone, but like all good cops he understood that every human being has a dark side. He was no sentimentalist, unlike me. I get almost teary when firemen rescue kittens from trees. I want to see good in everybody. I want Porcupine County to be a land of sweetness and saintliness and light and caring. It never was and never is and never will be, but what the hell, I can hope, can't I?

I sighed as I reached down and tousled the big yellow dog's ears. I was missing Ginny, her beautiful face, her warm body and her wise mind. She has a way of spotting things everybody else misses. I felt terribly alone.

★ ★ ★ ★ ★

Chad lumbered into the squad room at eight the next morning, and by ten he had persuaded the prosecuting attorney to issue subpoenas for Hartfelder's credit-card and phone records. Despite the usual comings and goings of deputies and arrestees and jail trusties and police equipment salesmen all around him, Chad stayed locked to his phone most of the day. He had grown into one of the best telephone investigators Porcupine County ever had.

My office clock had just passed three in the afternoon when Chad arose from his desk and strode in. Gil followed closely behind, and shut the door to the squad room.

"So far as I can tell," Chad said, "Pastor Hartfelder's white as a swan in a snowstorm."

Gil hoisted one eyebrow at Chad's unexpected simile. Cops don't do similes, unless they're Joe Wambaugh.

I leaned back in relief. "Proceed," I said.

"According to his credit-card records," Chad said, "Pastor Hartfelder traveled almost entirely on church business. He used a Visa card belonging to the church to charge meals and lodging for conferences and the like. He used a MasterCard for personal stuff and kept the two strictly separate. Couple times he did use the Visa for ordering clothes from L.L. Bean on the Internet, but the charges were small, one forty-one bucks and the other fifty-two bucks. They were sale items. I think he may have been getting the stuff for one of his flock or something like that. That would be church business, wouldn't it?"

"Sounds like it," Gil said.

"What about the lodging and gas charges?" I said. "They tell where he was when our victims were killed?"

"Just once. On June fourteen, when Marilyn Schneider was shot at the Soo, Hartfelder was in Butte, Montana, at a church conference. Visa receipts put him there for three days."

"What about Geoffrey Armstrong?" Gil said.

"Far as I can tell," Chad said, "Hartfelder would have been at home preparing his Sunday sermon the day Armstrong disappeared last year. It would be easy to check church records to see if he was in the pulpit the following day, when the disappearance was reported. I don't think he would have had time to do Armstrong, make his way back to Porcupine City, write that sermon and deliver it the next day. One way or the other, people would have seen him in town."

"Where was he the night before the fire when Ellen Juntunen died?" I asked.

"That I don't know," Chad said. "We know he was there the morning of the fire, helping with stuff, but before then, there's nothing to go on."

"The only thing we can do is canvass the town about him—or ask him where he was," I said. "And we can't do that just yet. With him or anyone else on our list. Not if we don't want to spook the perp and cause him to fly the coop."

"We may have to," Gil said.

"Let's give it forty-eight more hours before we go public," I said. "During that time let's go over everything once more and see if something turns up. Thanks, guys."

With that I called Alex and Sue and Dan and told them what Chad had found. They all listened silently and agreed that to move the investigation along, sooner or later we'd have to talk to our possible suspects, they'd lawyer up, and word would get out, as it always does when defense counsel is involved. Then the press would be upon us like moths unto a candle, as Chad might say.

I was hoping against hope that our killer would not strike again.

CHAPTER THIRTY

On the next to last day of November, three names from the rendezvous were left on the list. Richard Crockett, the old booshway and Chicago businessman. Jack Seymour, the Dog Soldier and motorcycle cop from Des Moines. Sheila Bodey, the quilter from Masonville.

As much to save time as to save labor for the other investigators, I decided to do some preliminary spadework on all three. Turning to my computer, I did a Google search for "Richard Crockett" and "Chicago."

At the top of the hundred and two citations was an obituary from the *Chicago Tribune* dated a month before Geoffrey Armstrong disappeared in the Wolverines.

"Richard Crockett, 74, founder of Crockett Electrical Supply Company, died after a short illness October 27 at his home on the North Side . . ."

I skimmed the usual stuff about his career, his wife and his survivors and fastened on his interests: "golf, the Chamber of Commerce and the Society of Mountain Men of the United States of America."

That was all I needed. Richard Crockett, bless his crusty old Ben Franklin heart, was no longer on our list.

Now for Jack Seymour. This would be a little tricky. Cops hate being investigated, just as newspapermen loathe criticism. Even a whiff of suspicion, if it gets out, can be enough to derail a career. Facts may be suppressed, but rumors live forever.

Fortunately the Des Moines Police Department is large enough to have an officer assigned to internal affairs. After a little phone tennis, I reached the lieutenant on that job.

"Calling about one of your traffic officers," I said after identifying myself.

"Who? What's he done?" the lieutenant said in a bored tone.

"Jack Seymour. And he probably hasn't done a damn thing. I'm just trying to eliminate him from a list of possible serial killers."

"Jack Seymour," the lieutenant said, his voice suddenly alert. "We do roster a cop of that name."

"It's a long story."

"Shoot."

I shot, for ten minutes, the lieutenant interrupting me from time to time to skritch a few words on a notepad. I told him the whole story, holding nothing back.

"Jesus H. Christ on a crutch," he said when I finished, adding unnecessarily, "I'll be damned."

"And so you have it," I said. "All I really need to know is where Seymour was when Ellen Juntunen died during our fire, when Geoffrey Armstrong went missing, when Dickie Atkins was shot, when Marilyn Schneider was picked off by a sniper, and when that Hmong got himself killed."

I gave the lieutenant the dates.

"Probably the duty rosters will tell where Seymour was when the shootings went down," the lieutenant said. "Hold on a minute while I call up the rosters on the computer."

It took him less than two minutes, but to me it felt like two centuries.

"Seymour was on duty in Des Moines every single one of those dates," the lieutenant said. "There's a complete record for each of his tours, with numbers of tickets, the time they were issued and so on. He just cannot be your man."

"Thanks, Lieutenant," I said. "I'm glad. I liked Jack. He seemed like a good cop."

"Oh, he is. I know him, too. He's our liaison to the LGBT community. One of the most effective street cops we've ever had."

We hung up.

I hung my head wearily. Just one name left. Sheila Bodey. I shook my head. How could an inoffensive little quilt maker be a murderer at all, let alone a vicious serial killer who employed an obscure and unlikely weapon?

But she had to be checked out. I called Dan Roane. She lived in his bailiwick.

"I've been wondering about her, too," Dan said. "Sometimes it's the least likely person who turns out to be a perp. Maybe not our particular perp, but a perp all the same."

"Find out what you can," I said, "and let me know. Right away, okay?"

"Sure."

Within the hour Dan called back, excitement in his voice.

"She's a strange one," he said. "She uses no credit cards. Pays only in cash or checks. No phone, either. Not even a cell. Her credit record is clean but thin. She seems to pay all her bills on time. She owns a ninety-three Ford pickup—got her plates from the DMV—but there's no way to trace her movements without talking to folks or to her personally."

"Anyone you can reach out to?" I said. "Someone who knows her but won't tip her off?"

Two possibilities, we both knew, were preachers and local physicians. They were unlikely to tell us much, though. Privileged information. But what they wouldn't say—and *how* they wouldn't say it—might suggest something. "If she's been in local hospitals there ought to be public records."

"There are," Dan said. "The day after the Porcupine City fire she sought treatment for second-degree burns on her hands. Four days after Geoffrey Armstrong went missing she showed up at the emergency room at Grand View Hospital to get a couple of shallow cuts on her arms stitched and incipient frostbite treated."

Slowly I let out a deep breath. "When were you going to let me know?" I could barely keep my voice calm. This might be the break we needed. Maybe the burns and the cuts had nothing to do with our case, but maybe it did.

That hunch born on the banks of the Mullet so long ago again loomed large in my mind. *You were right the first time, Steve,* it said. *You should have acted on it. But it's not too late to get going.*

"I *am* letting you know," Dan said. "I like to save the best for last."

"Did you talk to the ER doctors?"

"The one who treated her for the burns doesn't remember the case at all, but the hospital record says she said she forgot to use hot pads when she grabbed a cast-iron skillet from the stove. The nurse practitioner who sewed up the cuts has gone to South America and left no forwarding address. That record says Bodey claimed to have sustained the lacerations trying to drag a deer out of the woods and fell down a rocky slope. She blamed the frostbite on a long hike home through the snow because her truck broke down."

"Are you thinking what I am thinking?"

"I am thinking what you are thinking."

If we could have high-fived over the phone, we would have.

"I'm not through yet," Dan said.

"Full of surprises, aren't you?"

"Miss Sheila Bodey is a member of the same little rural church near Bessemer that Ellen Juntunen attended. I called a friend in the Madison PD and asked her to see if Bodey ever worshipped at the Wisconsin church where Gloria Lake was a member. And . . ."

"She did!" I all but shouted.

"Yep. Now you have it all," Dan said. "What now, Sheriff?"

"It is time," I said, "that we pay Miss Bodey a visit."

I hung up and looked down at the dog at my feet. "Time to saddle up, Hogan."

Sheila Bodey lived in the middle of the most extreme nowhere five miles southeast of Masonville near Wakefield, at the end of a winding nine-mile single-lane gravel track through forest so thick, buggy and brambly that the State of Michigan had in an unusual burst of wisdom parked a medium-security prison in the center of it.

Few inmates attempted to escape from the Ojibway Correctional Facility, and those who managed to slip out of its double-fenced, razor-wire perimeter during the summer never got far before stumbling into nearby houses and taverns screaming for relief from the fierce mosquitoes and deerflies that inhabited the forest, their victims practically begging to go back behind bars. In the winter no prisoner with half a brain would try to brave the numbing cold and driving snow that built impenetrable drifts atop impossible thickets.

Weeks before the official start of winter, a blue norther howling through the trees ripped through our down parkas and canvas Carhartts, the heater in Dan's official Suburban barely keeping the chill at bay. As Dan, Hogan and I drove past the prison on the way to Bodey's, I tried to imagine the small woman peering from the barred windows of a cell and failed.

Her two-story, cedar-shaked frame house sat at the end of a long straight clearing roughly a hundred feet wide and eight hundred feet long. New stumps and fresh slash thickly blanketed the clearing, making it look as if a matchstick factory had exploded a week or two before. Two outbuildings, a garage and a small barn, stood to one side of the main house.

"Perfect sight lines," Dan said, speaking for us both. "Nobody can approach those buildings without the occupants knowing about it. Nobody could get up close to them through those woods."

"Perfect field of fire, too," I said, unclipping the holster sheltering the Combat Magnum, which normally resided in my desk drawer or glove compartment. I rarely wore the revolver in the field, although I made sure my deputies were always armed with their Glocks and a generous supply of nine-millimeter cartridges. At least for me, a show of unarmed authority encourages most harmless local miscreants, such as drunks and speeders, to cooperate with the wheels of justice. But Sheila Bodey, I felt in my bones, was not one of these.

Before I left the Porcupine County Sheriff's Department to drive to Bessemer and join Dan for the ride into the forest, I had belted the Magnum to my waist, prompting Gil to ask from his office, "Are we going into action?"

"Maybe yes, maybe no," I said. "Get everyone on alert and wait for my call."

"Against whom?"

"Sheila Bodey. Dan dug up some stuff on her. It looks like maybe she's our killer. Can't be sure just yet, but we're going out to interview her now."

Through the door as I left I could hear Gil telling Joe Koski at the communications desk, "Send a heads-up to the deputies, troopers and rangers . . ."

At Bodey's place Dan stopped the Suburban in the driveway a good thirty yards from the house, parking it right side to the front door, not facing toward it. That would make the big SUV a better shield against gunfire.

Dan honked the horn twice.

No response.

I told Hogan to stay, emerged from the passenger side of the door and walked to the house, keeping my gun hand close to the unclipped holster. Many if not most police officers would have drawn their firearms and pointed the muzzles to the ground as they approached a potential shooter. I felt that needlessly provocative. A subject is more likely to parley with a cop if the cop doesn't have a gun in hand. But it was a risk.

I knocked twice. "Miss Bodey?"

No answer. I knocked and called again.

Still no answer.

I turned to Dan, standing with Beretta in hand at the open driver's door of the Suburban, its bulk between him and the house, and called loudly, "Not home."

Dan remained at the Suburban, still watching the house, as I strode over to the garage and peered through the window of its side door.

"Truck's not here," I called.

"Neither is she," Dan said. That far out in the thick forest one absolutely needs a vehicle to get from place to place, unless one is an Indian who knows his woodcraft.

"Let's check the barn," I said.

Together Dan and I walked over to the single-story barn, roughly clad with cheap asphalt roofing shingles, fifty yards from the garage and slightly behind the house. The property had also been cleared a hundred yards from the rear of the house, we saw, but long ago. Instead of stumps and slash the remnants of a large summer garden occupied most of the place, chopped cornstalks still standing in one corner. Several apple trees stood at one side, a few bits of dried fruit still hanging from the bare high branches.

"That's a big garden," Dan observed. "Probably puts up

tomatoes and potatoes for the winter. Wouldn't be surprised if she poached a bit of meat, too."

"Probably," I said. "Nobody gets rich quilting for a living."

"Keeps her out of sight and out of mind. Paranoid, maybe."

Many people live deep in the woods for just that reason, so others don't observe their comings and goings. Meth-lab operators and fur poachers like their privacy. So do murderous sociopaths.

"Wonder where she is," I said.

"Day after tomorrow's the start of muzzle-loader deer season. Maybe she's on her way somewhere to do her thing again."

We looked at each other and took deep breaths.

"Wonder what she's after," I said unnecessarily. "Or who."

We arrived at the barn.

"Miss Bodey?" I called again.

No answer. I knocked hard on the side door, sending small animals scrabbling within and causing bats to screech.

Still no answer.

Dan glanced by me into the window on the side door.

"Look at that," he said.

Through the weak light of the dusty window I saw rakes, scythes, axes and an old Sears garden tractor.

And in one corner a sight that electrified me.

On the wall surrounding an old-fashioned lithograph of Christ, palms together in prayer and eyes upthrust to the sky, hung eleven muzzle-loading weapons on pegs in a loose circle.

Two Tennessees. Three Hawkens. Two Kentuckys. Three cap-and-ball revolvers, two of them Colts and one a Remington. One small set of pegs was missing the weapon it had held. *Most likely a New Model Army,* I thought, *probably the one that had killed Ellen Juntunen.*

At the top of the circle, just under the portrait of Jesus, rested a big Brown Bess.

Below the rifles, like an impromptu altar, stood a huge oak rolltop desk, open for business. On it lay a carefully arranged assemblage of muzzle-loading paraphernalia. There were cardboard boxes containing lead balls, with carefully calligraphed labels proclaiming their calibers. In one corner was a freezer bag containing flints. In another stood plastic jars of black powder. In precise ranks, like massed Continental soldiers, lay an oil can, two powder measures, boxes of percussion nipples and caps, patches and wads, cleaning jags and fouling scrapers.

And a short starter.

"Bingo," I whispered. "If that starter-peg ferrule matches the impression on the ball in the Hmong homicide, we've got her."

"Gotta get a warrant," Dan replied.

He was right. Sometimes, if a cop sees possible evidence in plain view through a window, he can use it as probable cause to get a warrant—but not for breaking in to examine that evidence. For a long moment I wrestled with the idea of just punching in the window and taking a wax impression of the starter peg's metal business end with the crime kit from Dan's Suburban. Sometimes, to prevent further homicides, a detective has to take matters into hand.

If we did that, though, we'd never be able to enter the short starter as evidence at trial. A defense lawyer would quickly move to suppress it, and we'd have to try to convict using other evidence, evidence whose existence we had no way of knowing. In any case, we were unlikely to find it, given the facts of muzzle-loading weaponry. The best evidence we could hope for was a full confession, but we also had no way of knowing if we could get one. Of course, if the perp was killed in a lawful shootout, there would be no trial.

And the legal rule of exigent circumstances, the one that allowed cops to break in if they thought someone on the premises was in immediate danger, just didn't apply here.

I was already ninety-nine percent certain, however, that Sheila Bodey was our killer. I doubted that breaking in would give any clues to her whereabouts anyway.

It would be late afternoon before we could get back with the warrant and seize the contents of the barn. Ordinarily, we'd freeze the scene by setting up roadblocks to prevent anyone from going in or out while we waited for the warrant, but there were only two of us—and Bodey lived far enough out of town so that it'd be at least another hour before we had more deputies in place. If I stayed while Dan went to town, I'd have to wait a long time for backup. No cop wants to be without armed fellow officers if gunplay is a potential event. Been there, done that, never again.

It was Dan's decision. We were in his jurisdiction.

"Steve," he said, "we'll get a warrant, but maybe now's not the time to freeze the scene anyway. That'll tip her off. We don't have the manpower right now to be sure of catching her on her way home—whenever that might be. Why don't we just leave things be and get our warrant and get back here as soon as we can?"

"Works for me," I said. "Meanwhile, let's put out a BOLO for her and for her truck."

Dan picked up his mike and did so.

As things turned out, we should have dug in and waited for her to show up, but cops aren't clairvoyant. Just lucky or unlucky.

CHAPTER THIRTY-ONE

Crouching behind the pumps at the gas station on the highway near the entrance to the gravel road that ended at her house, Angel watched as the Gogebic County Sheriff's Suburban, two men inside, emerged from the track and headed at high speed toward Masonville. As the Suburban sped past, she recognized the occupants. Sheriff Dan Roane and Sheriff Steve Martinez from Porcupine County.

Now Angel was sure they were on to her. She cursed softly as she ran for her pickup behind the station where she had been pumping up a soft front tire, simultaneously asking Jesus' forgiveness for her blasphemy. Swiftly she steered onto the track and drove as fast as she could without bottoming out the truck's creaky suspension and smashing an axle. In fifteen minutes she reached her house.

Had the cops been there? Someone had. Angel opened the door to her truck and spotted a sandy rut in the driveway. Immediately she knew that the tire tread it revealed did not belong to her Ford. They had been here.

What had they seen? Angel tried the front door. It was still locked. A shoe print in bare soil by the front stoop bespoke a size-twelve boot. One set of faint tracks in the still-dewy grass circumnavigated the house.

Angel ran to the garage. Now there were two sets of tracks in the grass leading to faint wet spots on the concrete at the garage door. There the tracks diverged, each running around one side of the garage, and merged at the rear. She followed them, now faint, over the gravel path to the barn. They stopped at the window in the barn's side door.

Angel cursed again. She had forgotten to pull the heavy sackcloth drapes over the window the day before, after she had reloaded the rifles and pistols. The police had seen everything. They were on their way to get reinforcements—and the official paper that would allow them to come in and take away the Lord's tools.

Angel had very little time. Quickly she wrapped the long guns in an Army blanket and stuffed the pistols into her waistband. There wasn't time for the rest, except for two powder horns, a couple of bags of flints, nipples and percussion caps, and several small boxes of leaden balls, all of which she threw into a musette bag.

She ran to her truck and thrust the rifles, pistols and musette bag into the pickup bed, blanketing them with an old tarpaulin. Then she was away down the road, driving as fast as she dared, tires spinning and slipping in the ruts, branches clawing at the truck as it lurched from side to side.

A mile before the narrow gravel track reached the highway she spotted oncoming blue and red lights flashing through the screen of trees. Swiftly she wrenched the truck into an even narrower dirt driveway she knew led to an abandoned cabin a quarter of a mile away, and when she was out of sight, stopped the truck and looked back. Three sets of flashing lights sped by the driveway entrance.

Angel counted to ten, reversed her truck down the driveway, and emerged onto the gravel road. Just before she reached the county highway she forced herself to slow to a normal speed. She drove past the gas station, hoping the attendant would stay invisible.

He didn't. He looked up from the open hood of a car, dipstick in his hand, and watched intently as Angel's truck passed, heading on the county highway east toward US 45. In the rearview mirror, she saw him dash into the station office, no doubt to tip off the lawmen.

Angel had been forming a vague idea of disappearing south on US 45 into the thickly forested lake resort country of northern Wisconsin, but she now thought that the police would probably catch her at a roadblock before she got that far. She turned north on a graded Forest Service gravel road she knew would meet a similar track that ran east and west. She'd then turn west, heading for State Highway M64, and drive north to the Wolverines, where she could disappear into the deep woods while the police went haring thirty miles to the east. She knew the Wolverines as well as she knew the woods around her house, and had a good idea where she could hole up in the deep back-country.

As she drove, Angel assessed her situation, her confidence growing.

She relived her experience with Sheriff Martinez, whom she had last seen at the rendezvous two years before. He was a nice enough fellow, Angel thought, but he did not love the Lord. He had been evasive when she asked if he had found Jesus. The color of evil had tinged his slippery words.

She would be caught sometime, Angel knew. If not now, then soon. If she were not a fugitive, she could survive for weeks, maybe months, in the Wolverines. But the police were searching and would not relent until they found her.

Angel made a decision.

She would martyr herself at a last redoubt in the forest.

She would lead the police into a trap and force them to kill her, but not before she had harvested as many of their souls as she could for the Lord.

Especially that of Sheriff Steve Martinez.

CHAPTER THIRTY-TWO

The instant I peered into Sheila Bodey's barn for the second time and saw the now-bare wall and empty desktop, I knew Dan and I had made a serious mistake. We should have parked his Suburban behind the barn and waited for Bodey to come home, however long it took. I kicked myself mentally. It had taken us an ungodly time to decide that we had a serial killer on our hands, and still more time to discover her identity. We could have ended it all in five minutes if we had only had the sense to hang around a while instead of rushing off like Keystone Kops to wheedle a warrant out of a judge.

Now we were going to have to hunt her down, hoping not to lose any of our number—or anyone else—in the effort.

Dan's radio squawked, and he reached in and keyed the mike.

"Garage guy on US 2 saw her half an hour ago. Says she headed east on the highway in a muddy white Ford pickup with a green replacement door on the driver side. Says she's wearing a dark-green parka and a red ball cap. I think she might have turned onto Forest Road 3542. That roughly parallels 2 all the way to Watersmeet. She'd be out of sight of anybody coming from there on 2."

"Half an hour?" I said. "She'll already have reached Watersmeet, whichever way she went. Five gets you ten she's now heading south on US 45."

"What about north on 45?" Dan said. "Lots of places in the woods to hide up there."

"Yeah," I said, "but if you're on the run, Lake Superior would cut you off on the north and you'd have to go east or west. Too easy to get pinched in the middle."

"Let's call Camilo at Watersmeet and have him head south on 45 and ask the deputies at Eagle River to head north. They and the tribals might box her in."

"Good idea," Dan said, and relayed the appeal as well as the descriptions of the truck, of its plates and of Bodey to the Lac Vieux Desert Tribal Police at Watersmeet and the Vilas County Sheriff's Department at Eagle River in Wisconsin. I keyed my own mike and sent Chad south on 45 from Porcupine City so that he'd block Bodey's escape if she'd chosen to head north.

At that moment Sergeant Alex Kolehmainen arrived in his Tahoe from Wakefield with two troopers in tow. I filled him in. His eyebrows rose as we told him who we were after and why. Then he nodded. It all made sense to him.

"Now all we can do is wait," I said. As the troopers cordoned off the place with tape and began their minute forensic examination under Alex's command, Dan and I shifted uneasily from foot to foot.

Now all we could do was wait until Bodey was spotted and caught.

"I don't have a good feeling about this," I said.

"Me neither," Dan said.

All afternoon we waited.

Shortly after four Camilo came on the radio. "Nothing up here but us Indians and mosquitoes," he said. "Nobody's seen a muddy white Ford with a green driver door."

The Wisconsin deputies had no better luck.

"We'll have to put out a general BOLO for her," I said, "while we figure out what to do."

"Got a recent photo?" Dan said, showing me her DMV shot on his cell phone. "This one is pretty old."

"Doesn't look much like her, either," I said. The Sheila Bodey I had met on the Mullet seemed older, softer and friendlier than the woman glaring into the driver's-license camera. "But I know someone who might have a good photo."

I took my cell phone out of a breast pocket and opened it. Two bars, not bad for reception in the middle of nowhere, and good enough.

Horace Wright, as always, was in his office.

"Remember the little quilter at the rendezvous two years ago?" I asked.

Horace the reporter photographs everything that goes on in Porcupine County, and Horace the historian saves the digital files for posterity.

"Sure do. Nice lady."

"Got pictures of her?"

"Sure do." I could hear clacking from his computer keyboard. "Hang on a sec."

"Got three good ones. Give me your cell number and I'll send them."

"Thanks."

Horace had the restraint not to ask if Sheila Bodey was a suspect. I knew he could put things together for himself. And I knew he had taken me at my word that I would give him an exclusive when I was ready. Reporters generally don't cooperate with the police—an unwritten clause in journalistic ethics discourages actions that might change the course of news events the reporter covers—but an exclusive is an exclusive. Situational ethics guide journalists just as they do cops. They may deny it indignantly, but members of both professions sometimes wash each other's hands.

In two minutes my phone chirped and I had three sharp photos of Sheila Bodey in pioneer dress. She was instantly recognizable.

I called Joe Koski at the department and told him to wait for the photos to arrive, then to put them on the BOLO for broadcast all over the Upper Peninsula, Wisconsin and Minnesota.

"Armed and dangerous, right?" Joe said.

"Absolutely. Put in that we know she has a seventy-five-caliber musket called a Brown Bess, a couple of Tennessees, I think a Hawken and I'm sure three or four cap-and-ball revolvers. All of them probably loaded. Possibly a more modern weapon or two—we don't know for sure."

I turned to Dan. "Let's get Emergency Services on alert. I'll call Gil."

The Michigan State Police fields a special weapons and tactics team whose hand-picked members are drawn from all over the state. Emergency Services members are highly trained in forest skirmishing as well as urban warfare. We almost never need to call them into action, but whenever someone, usually drunken and almost always armed, barricades himself in a house, often with hostages, ES is called. More often than not they're able to rout the gunman with tear gas and rescue the hostages unharmed.

"Done already," Gil said on the phone. "They're locked and loaded, and ready to head wherever you need 'em."

I was not surprised. Gil is the kind of undersheriff who is able to anticipate moves on the criminal chessboard. When he learned that Sheila Bodey had flown the coop, he had called the troopers' Upper Michigan regional post and asked them to go on alert.

Now all we could do was wait until something happened.

Chapter Thirty-Three

For a long and frantic hour Angel had driven through the warren of forest roads north of US 2, bearing generally northwest, thanking the Lord that the gravel was still damp from the previous day's steady drizzle, preventing the wheels of her truck from raising a huge and visible rooster tail of dust. But now she had settled down and her breathing had returned to normal. No one, she was confident, had seen or heard her, not even the lone pulpwood cutter she spotted deep in the woods wielding a chainsaw and wearing ear protection.

When her truck finally emerged from the trees and she turned right onto the northbound lane of M64 a mile from Bergland, Angel had formed a plan.

Daddy had taught her never to panic but to think things through, carefully considering the consequence of every action.

Was it better to try to escape?

The truck wouldn't take her far. The needle of its fuel gauge had fallen below the one-quarter mark. The truck, anyway, was too identifiable. The police would be looking for a white pickup with a green driver door. There wasn't time to repaint the whole truck, and even if there were, it would take too many aerosol cans of paint, and hardware stores hereabouts never carried enough cases of the same color. Even if they did, a clerk would remember the customer who staggered out under three cases of olive drab. Or cherry red. Or whatever.

She'd have to dump the truck somewhere.

But could she get far on foot carrying the bulky Hammer of God and a heavy pistol or two? Not out in the open, not if she didn't want to be spotted. She'd have to make her way through the forest carrying a canteen and a couple of boxes of granola bars as well as the weapons. She could stay out of sight and survive for a week, but not much more than that. The distances were just too great. Eventually she'd be spotted and caught.

She soon realized that her first idea—to make a last stand and take as many of the Devil's minions with her—was one of only two choices she had left. The other was to surrender and subject herself to the will of the enemy.

She prayed for guidance.

The Lord answered.

"Defy the Devil," He ordered.

At nightfall Angel headed north for the Wolverines, singing hymns as she drove.

CHAPTER THIRTY-FOUR

The break came almost thirty hours after Sheila Bodey had disappeared in the direction of Watersmeet. A hunter found her truck while getting ready to bivouac overnight and set out at first light on December 1, the opening day of muzzle-loading deer season. It was parked almost but not quite out of sight in a copse of trees off the road at Page Falls in the Ottawa National Forest. Page Falls lies in northwestern Porcupine County, just a mile outside the Wolverines Wilderness State Park to the north. The hunter, thinking the truck might be stolen and abandoned, called the sheriff's department to report his discovery.

A mystery writer I know once described the falls as "a breathtakingly beautiful glade on the Agate River flowing northward through the Wolverine Mountains State Park and eventually Lake Superior . . ." There teenagers smoked pot and drank beer, and adults spooned in the moonlight. Anglers caught trout in the deep pools below the falls. Hunters and hikers used the end of the road to the falls as a parking lot and jumping-off point for forays into the wilderness. Few tourists ever found the falls. Only locals knew about it, and guarded the secret carefully.

"I think she's going to hole up in there," I said, "and try to take out as many of us as she can before we get her." Ten members of the Emergency Services team had crowded into our squad room, having trickled in from around the state during the day while fellow troopers, deputies and tribal cops charged all over four counties and three states fruitlessly looking for Sheila Bodey. The team had stacked its hardware in a conference room. Their boss was Lieutenant Ted Olson, a veteran Marquette trooper who had learned his chops in Army Special Forces. He is a small man—only five feet six—but lean, muscular and fit, able to run a quarter of a mile at full throttle in heavy SWAT armor.

"How do you know she's going to hole up in there?" Alex said. As always, he knew how I knew, and I knew that. And so on ad infinitum. But for a change Alex was not being a smartass. He was just giving me the chance to lay everything out so that the entire team—deputies as well as troopers—understood the reasoning behind the plan I had put together with the help of Ted, Alex and Sue, who upon hearing the news that Bodey had fled for parts unknown had jumped into her car—this time an official state police Chevy—and driven all night up from Lansing.

"Trying to think like a crazed serial killer," I said. "Look, Sue says Bodey probably knows she'll never get away, so she'll try to go out in a blaze of glory."

"It's often what happens when sociopaths discover they're not as smart as they thought," Sue said.

"Sounds like suicide by cop," Ted said.

"Exactly," Sue and I said simultaneously.

I unfolded a topographic map of the area containing the northern reaches of the Ottawa National Forest and the southern boundary of the Wolverines and pointed to Page Falls with a pencil.

"Her truck's right here," I said, "at the edge of the clearing next to the falls."

"Hidden behind a couple of thick hemlocks," said Chad, who had answered the hunter's cell-phone call. "Tommy Bogan, the guy who found it, wondered why it had been stashed there. He said he wondered why it hadn't been pulled in farther so it was completely out of sight. There was plenty of room for that."

"Bodey meant for it to be found," Sue said.

"Bait," I said.

"Precisely," Sue said.

"Which we'll take," I said. "But not in the way she probably thinks. Sue?"

"If I were Bodey," she said, "I'd expect a frontal assault through the woods in a broad skirmish line containing every tactical cop in Upper Michigan, with a pack of bloodhounds along for the ride. The dogs would be howling as they picked up the scent. She'd hear them coming long before she could see them, and she'd very likely dig in at a good defensive point, such as downed logs or rocks on the high ground. She'd want to pick us off one by one as we crawled uphill."

"And so that's not what we're going to do," I said. "Six of us local guys know these woods pretty well, even me, and we are going to go up the trails in pairs, dressed in civilian clothes like hunters, with blaze-orange caps and carrying muzzle loaders. We're going to move slowly and quietly, as if we're looking for deer. If she spots us—and she will, because of the orange— she'll likely not want to waste ammunition on a bunch of hunters but save it for the cops. If she's on high ground and we can find her, we can move around and block her escape to the north while the ES guys move in for the kill."

"Don't much like the idea of the muzzle loaders," said Chad, a member of the hunter team. "I know they're for camouflage, but can't we take real rifles, too?"

"We'll have our Glocks and SIG Sauers. The ES troopers will have their artillery. I'll have Old Betsy here," I said, patting my Combat Magnum in its holster. "And we'll all be wearing Kev-lar."

"Besides," I added, "we're just the scouts. We'll find the

enemy, and when we spot her, we'll hit the ground and dig in, then call in the cavalry for the attack. You ES guys will be just a few minutes behind us, and on my signal you'll move in and assault the breastworks."

They'd climb uphill en masse as best they could in their heavy SWAT armor, firing as they went, and either blow their target apart with a fusillade of high-powered bullets or force her into surrendering. Probably the former.

"Let's take her alive if we can," I said. "I—we—want answers. But let's not lose anybody, either. Use your own judgment."

We spent a few more minutes going over the map and discussing our tactics. Chad left to borrow a cousin's cap-and-ball Tennessee. Dan had his own flintlock Kentucky. A couple of the deputies brought their own muzzle loaders. And Joe Koski, who would stay behind at Page Falls and direct communications, contributed an antique Sharps buffalo gun that had hung over his mantel for decades.

On the way back from Gogebic County I had stopped at Ginny's empty house, let myself in, and borrowed Tommy's Hawken. Now, at the office, I pulled out his powder horn, a patch and a ball, and started loading the weapon.

"You actually think you might want to use that thing?" Ted said. He had absolutely no confidence in antique arms. He preferred modern stuff, and he would have armed his squad with rocket-propelled grenades had any been in his inventory.

"Why not?" I said, placing a percussion cap on the Hawken's nipple and carefully lowering the hammer to half cock. "Might as well have one down the spout. You never can tell, can you?"

Ted grunted skeptically.

"Let's get some sleep," I said. "We'll move out to Page Falls at five."

First light on the first day of December wouldn't come until well after seven-thirty this far west in the Central Time zone, and we'd already have started up the trails by the time the sun rose above the trees.

Most of the ES team—their number swelled by two troopers who had arrived late in the evening by state police helicopter from downstate, landing at the Porcupine County airport—moved into the empty lockup cells, alarming one trusty and a drunken driver who couldn't make bail, and settled down for the night. The rest took couches and chairs and the tops of desks and tried to sleep.

"Sorry, Hogan, you can't go," I told the dog as I replenished his water bowl. "You'll have to hold the fort with Joe."

I turned to Joe, still awake at the dispatcher's desk, and said, "I'll be back by three."

I was not going to be able to sleep. When one is about to go into combat, sleep is impossible. At least for me. But in the Upper Peninsula there is a surefire way to refresh one's body and mind, and I decided to take advantage of it.

I drove through the dark the three miles west on M64 to Ginny's place on the lake, and let myself into a low log building on the shore behind her house.

Swiftly I filled its cast-iron stove with firewood and wadded newspapers, and set them alight. I drew two large wooden buckets of water, undressed to the skin while the heat in the cedar-lined room built up rapidly, then took a seat on a well-worn bench.

I began to perspire as the heat rose, and when I ladled a pint of water on the rocks heated by the stove, a flash of steam burst into the air. Now sweat was dripping from my face.

With the sweat lodge, my Lakota ancestors dealt with stress and adversity and prepared for battle. The steamy, mind-altering heat raised dreams and visions, helping them discover the paths they were destined to follow. Today some Lakota and Ojibwa still follow that tradition. But I am modern and Western-educated, and the spirits do not call out to me in the way they did my forebears. Often I wish they did, but what's done is done. One cannot turn back the clock on personal history.

For an Indian who is about to ride against his enemies, the Finnish sauna is the next best thing, I thought as I poured another ladleful of water on the sizzling rocks, raising a fresh hiss of steam.

I closed my eyes and, as rivulets of sweat coursed down my face and neck and pooled on my chest, allowed Ginny to fill my mind.

What will be will be. Ginny will choose. It is her choice. Whether that will be Lauri Nissinen or me is in the hands of God, fate, whatever spirits there may be, or simple chance. I cannot change who I am, and neither can she change who she is. Nothing is permanent. If I am not meant to be with her, I will accept her decision. Life with her has been good, but if it must end, life will still go on.

Just as the thermometer on the wall reached one hundred forty degrees—my limit—I threw open the door, stepped outside into the frosty air and upended one bucket over my head and shoulders, bellowing as the shock of freezing water rattled my senses to their roots. The second bucket did the same.

I stood tall in the night, naked and exhilarated, every fiber of my being heightened and sharpened. I was ready for battle.

CHAPTER THIRTY-FIVE

The first rays of the sun piercing the screen of trees awoke Angel in her redoubt on a knoll deep in the Wolverines three miles northwest of Page Falls. She huddled under a thick horse quilt she had packed in from her truck along with the rifles, handguns, binoculars, water and two boxes of granola bars the previous afternoon. It had taken three trips over five hours to carry everything in over the stony, root-choked and undulating trail, tiring her so much that she almost instantly fell asleep after a quick supper of two bars and a pint of water.

Despite the quilt, Angel shivered, her breath visible in the cold sunlight. She had not wanted to build a fire whose beacon and smoke might attract unwanted attention—hunters, she knew from previous experience, sometimes camped in the woods the night before deer season opened. She had heard nothing during the night except howls of coyotes, hoots of owls and the snuffle and scratch of small animals.

Angel had chosen her fortress well, as Daddy had taught her. It lay at the top of an almost-circular hill a good hundred feet above the trail that passed around three sides below, with a clear view through leafless birch, sugar maple and ash trees to the path. The steep cliff of a rocky ravine formed the fourth side. Downed logs and rock outcroppings at the top of the hill provided a natural breastworks.

She had remembered Daddy's lecture about the battle of Little Round Top, the granite hill at Gettysburg where Union soldiers had successfully held off a Confederate assault in 1863. "High ground is always a good defensive position, provided one has the firepower to hold it," Daddy had observed. "It also helps when you're hunting. You're shooting downhill with the light behind or above you, and you can see better."

Angel doubted that she could prevail in the end—there would just be too many policemen—but she felt confident that their victory would come at a high cost. Her heart lifted as she dreamed of being celebrated for the skill and bravery with which she fought for the Lord. Her memory on earth would be as immortal as her soul was in Heaven.

She had already drawn blood. At dusk, just before she disappeared into the woods at Page Falls with the last load for her fortress, a lightweight short-barreled Hawken slung over her shoulder, a stranger had emerged a few feet away in the fading sunlight at the trailhead, gazing directly at her. He was dressed in hunter's camouflage garb and a blaze-orange vest. He carried a bedroll, a canteen and a Kentucky rifle.

"That your truck behind the trees?" he called.

Quickly Angel whipped the Hawken off her shoulder, took careful aim, and fired. The stranger staggered, then dropped where he stood. The ball had caught him square in the heart. He died instantly.

Angel hoped the stranger had called the law to report the truck—it would attract her quarry and speed up the inevitable—but there was no telling what else he had seen, and where. She did not want to lose her tactical advantage, meager as she knew it would turn out to be in the long run. She felt no remorse. He was what soldiers called "collateral damage." It couldn't be helped.

She left the stranger's body on the trail. It would warn the policemen what they could expect. And she took his canteen and Kentucky rifle because either or both might come in handy. Daddy would have approved.

Angel was ready.

She fell on her knees and prayed for strength and courage.

CHAPTER THIRTY-SIX

At five in the morning our small convoy of cruisers, SUVs, trucks and vans arrived at Page Falls, having driven the half mile in from State Highway M64 with headlights extinguished under the glow of starlight and a waxing crescent moon. As quietly as we could, we emerged from our vehicles in the darkness and spoke in whispers while we slowly reconnoitered the area with hooded flashlights and nightscopes. Within ten minutes we found a fresh body at the trailhead, and gathered about it, still keeping voices low and lights dimmed.

"He's been dead for only about eight or ten hours," Alex said, opening the man's coat and shirt. "Shot squarely in the heart. Hole looks about fifty caliber. I will wager my next year's salary that it's a muzzle-loading ball."

"Son of a bitch," Chad said. "It's Tommy Bogan."

Tom Bogan was a familiar figure around Porcupine County, a hard-working, once hard-drinking logger who had long terrorized local bars as a young man but had joined AA and stayed sober for a number of years. Everyone liked him.

"Why would Bodey want to kill him?" Alex asked for all of us.

"Probably he saw her go up the trail, and Bodey wanted to silence him," Sue said. She would remain behind with one trooper at Page Falls as reserves as well as to block the road from M64 and turn back any incoming hunters.

"Steve, you really want to try to take her alive?" Gil said.

"Yes, if it doesn't risk anyone's life," I said, my anger and dismay mounting as I fully realized for the first time what we had on our hands: a killer without a shred of conscience or mercy about who she murdered. "If it does—even in the slightest—shoot to kill."

Alex and his crew wrapped Bogan in a body bag and carried him to their evidence van. He could wait until later.

"Let's get a bit more rest," I said. We all sat in the grass, backs against our cars and trucks, and waited for the eastern sky to brighten.

When the first glimmer of dawn finally lightened the horizon at a quarter to eight, we fortified ourselves with sandwiches and coffee and checked our equipment once more. Chad and I, Alex and Gil, and Camilo and another tribal cop all dressed as hunters, donning blaze-orange caps or jerseys over our parkas as hunting regulations required. Underneath we all wore Kevlar vests. We were confident they could stop any slow-moving muzzle-loading projectile. That is, the others were confident. I wasn't so sure. Ballistics theory may be persuasive, but the guy who has to test that theory is nothing but a guinea pig. I knew our quarry was a crack shot, and warned the others there were parts of their anatomy not protected by the Kevlar.

The ES team donned black trousers, jerseys, heavy SWAT body armor and helmets equipped with night-vision scopes. It would still be dark in the forest when we set off. Alex halfheartedly said he wished we "hunters" could wear nightscopes, too, but I pointed out that they were illegal for hunting and would instantly tip off Bodey that we weren't who we appeared to be.

"Time to go," Ted whispered just before official sunrise at 8:24 A.M.

"Lead on, Sheriff," Chad said.

"Just a minute," I said. "Chad, have you ever laid eyes on Sheila Bodey? I don't recall your talking with her at the rendezvous when Gloria Lake was killed."

"No," he said. "Never met her. Never knew what she looked like until Horace sent those photos."

"Then she most likely doesn't know what you look like either," I said.

I made a decision.

"Chad, you're on the point," I said. "I'll be right behind."

The big deputy instantly grasped my meaning and nodded silently.

The sextet of phony hunters set off down the trails that led from Page Falls through the national forest and into the state park. All three trails headed roughly northwestward through parallel ravines carved out of the earth and rock by glaciers many thousands of years ago. High rocky ridges separated the ravines. Chad and I took the center trail, Alex and Gil the southern path, and Camilo and his tribal cops the northern track.

Our plan remained the same: We would act not only as scouts but also decoys, hoping that Bodey would think us genuine hunters and allow us to approach her hideout, maybe even waving us on when we spotted her. We did not think we would run into any bona fide hunters, because we had found only two vehicles at Page Falls—her truck and Tom Bogan's. Anybody we encountered was almost sure to be our quarry.

The twelve-man ES crew would follow on the trails out of sight and not more than ten minutes behind. As hunters we would be walking slowly and deliberately, searching for game, careful where we stepped, quiet as mice, and the ES guys would follow at the same pace. If any of the hunter team spotted Bodey and radioed her location, or gunfire erupted, the ES officers would rush forward up the trails, ready for close combat with M16 automatic rifles and heavy tactical shotguns.

★　★　★　★　★

For ninety minutes we trudged, Chad drawing fifty and then a hundred yards ahead on the trail as I deliberately dawdled, pretending to search for game. The idea was to be widely separated if we saw Bodey—or if she saw us. Twice Chad stopped, whispered into his radio mike, waved at me and pointed through the trees at deer, both young does. We ignored them, shaking our heads for anyone watching. We were veteran hunters after bigger game, a six-point buck or two. That was part of the masquerade.

The morning was biting cold, but I was sweating under the heavy layers of down, Kevlar and wool. I sweated because I was on edge, not because I was overheated. My blaze-orange hunter's cap made a perfect target. Deer might not be able to distinguish the color from forest camouflage, but a human being would. Especially a marksman—*markswoman*. As Chad and I strode deeper into the woods, I began to imagine a rifle barrel emerging from behind every tree. Luckily I had been born with acute hearing, and I listened intensely at every tread for a snapped twig or shallow breathing. The forest had frozen overnight, and so, seemingly, had every sound in it.

I nearly leaped out of my skin when an owl that hadn't yet called it a night whooshed across the trail a few yards ahead, the silken beat of its pinfeathers magnified against the silence.

Every nerve in my body was taut as a bowstring when my ears caught the soft click of a heavy hammer being cocked, then a *skritch-whoof* of flint falling upon frizzen and igniting primer. Just as I dove to the ground behind a downed log, I spotted a small puff of black-powder smoke forty yards uphill. There was no following heavy *whump!* of the main charge sending a ball out of a muzzle barrel.

Hang fire.

Swiftly I rose to my feet, aimed Tommy Standing Bear's

Hawken at the gap in the trees where I had seen the smoke, and pulled the trigger.

The ball lopped a two-inch-thick branch from a sugar maple and sang off into space. I dropped back on my belly and drew my Combat Magnum, at the same time radioing Chad.

"Shooter's up the hill, right in the center, behind a bunch of logs," I said. "First shot was a hang fire."

"Copy," Chad said from up ahead where I could not see him. "Going around to the other side."

"Be careful," I said. "Be damn careful."

Chad did not answer.

"On our way," said Ted, who had heard our exchange on his receiver. "Be there in five."

I should have stayed where I was until the shooter rose and loosed the next shot, then returned fire and waited for backup. But a .357 handgun, powerful as it is, is not terribly accurate over more than ten or fifteen yards, and I am not that good a shot. *Get closer,* my military training told me. *Get closer and you won't miss.*

Without thinking I rose to my feet, hurdled the downed logs and scrabbled uphill on hands and knees, flinging myself right and left from log to outcrop, trying simultaneously to hide and advance. Just as I huddled behind a screen of upturned white pine roots, the shooter suddenly appeared in a gap between two small oaks fifteen yards away, and drew a bead on me. I immediately recognized Sheila Bodey.

"It's her!" I shouted into the radio, and ducked just before she fired and the ball whistled through the void in the air where my head had been. The *whump!* was softer than I had expected, and arrived a split second later. *Also a flintlock,* I thought. *But she'll be using her percussion rifles now. There'll be no delay between ignition and firing.*

I took a deep breath, rose and fired the Magnum again.

Mistake. Bodey had leaped over her protective barricade and was striding down the hill with another rifle. The range had dwindled to ten yards, almost point blank for a long gun, almost clearing the bullet-deflecting branches out of the way. I could see the pupil of one fierce blue eye squarely centered behind the front sight. She fired.

A Peterbilt eighteen-wheeler struck me square in the center of the chest and I collapsed onto my back, stunned, momentarily paralyzed. I could still hear feet scrabbling on loose rock as Bodey scrambled downhill to finish me off.

Somehow I found the strength to shake off the shock, stagger to my feet and face her. She had dropped the empty rifle and was running and sliding toward me in the loose stones and leaves, frantically trying to yank from her belt a cap-and-ball revolver, its hammer caught by a rip in her parka. Carefully and deliberately I raised the Magnum with both hands and aimed at the center of her chest. Five yards. At this range she seemed bigger than a barn door. Couldn't possibly miss.

Slowly I squeezed the trigger.

A millisecond before the Magnum's hammer cleared the trigger sear and dropped on the cartridge's primer, a huge shadow hurtled out of the trees from stage left and slammed into Bodey. My gun barked a split second later, the bullet whining uphill and decapitating a sapling.

"Chad!" I yelled.

Five yards downhill in a pile of leaves the big deputy's broad back rose and fell like a bronc rider's as he pressed his three hundred pounds on Bodey, bucking and twisting under him, spitting and screaming like a trapped wildcat. She was strong, astonishingly strong. Despite his bulk Chad was flung about like a bull rider.

"*Goddam!*" Chad shouted, raising a massive fist and punching Bodey in the ribs, knocking the wind out of her. "*Steve! Your cuffs!*"

Swiftly I leaped over downed branches and clipped the handcuffs onto Bodey's wrists, imprisoned in Chad's iron grasp. Chad remained atop her, one huge knee in her back and one hand pressing her face into the soft earth.

"Son of a bitch," I said quietly. "Chad, I nearly blew a hole in you. You should have blown one in her."

"Is that the thanks I get, Sheriff?" he replied just as calmly.

"That and a medal," I said.

For two minutes we squatted in a motionless tableau, catching our breath, I rubbing the bruise under the Kevlar where Bodey's ball had struck. From time to time Bodey raised her head and hissed.

Then I looked up. A dozen black-clad ES officers ringed us in a circle, weapons trained on Bodey.

"Situation secured," I said. "Stand down."

Under Chad's bulk, Bodey kicked and swore.

"You sure she's secured?" Ted said.

"Stand *up*, Bodey," I said.

Chad and Ted yanked her to her feet. She aimed a kick at me and missed.

In five minutes we had her lashed to a litter Sue had brought up from Page Falls and were on our way downtrail, two burly and black-clad troopers carrying the squirming and bucking burden, a steady train of threats and obscenities spewing from her mouth.

"God will have His justice, motherfuckers!" was the gist of it.

CHAPTER THIRTY-SEVEN

Booking Bodey on arrival at jail had been a struggle, especially getting her fingerprints, and all morning the next day she was hardly a model prisoner. She spent hours in our lone cell for females casting noisy and vicious aspersions on the ancestries of her jailers, including and in great detail mine, and threatening us all with various permutations of the Lord's wrath. She threw her breakfast on the floor, ripped up her bedding and hurled feces at Joe Koski through the food hatch. She missed, but Joe was deeply offended and asked if he could turn the hose on her. I said no, choosing instead to inform Bodey that she could either behave or be put in twenty-four-hour full-body restraints in our rubber room, as we called the padded detox tank.

At that she finally ran out of steam. She did not struggle when we took her to district court shortly after one to be arraigned. During the proceedings she stood calmly while the State of Michigan charges were read. Four of them were charges of premeditated murder in the first degree. The fifth, in the case of Tom Bogan, was murder in the second degree. A sixth was attempted murder for trying to shoot me. There were also lesser charges of fleeing apprehension and resisting arrest. Later we'd add a charge of assault for throwing feces at Joe Koski. When Judge Rantala asked how she pleaded, Bodey stood mute, and an automatic plea of "not guilty" was entered for her.

The judge then assigned a public defender, plucking a name from a rotating list of qualified local lawyers. This time it was

Archie Martin, a stooped, elderly, remarkably colorless but highly competent Porcupine City attorney who never let down his clients. He'd do right by Bodey, I thought, without making unnecessary trouble for the law.

Garner asked the judge to direct the Porcupine County Mental Health Services to send a staff psychologist to the jail to help us decide if Bodey was a danger to herself and if so, whether she should be sent to a facility for mental-health evaluation or remain in our custody.

"So ordered," Judge Rantala said.

After we returned Bodey to her cell, Janis Gilbert, a classmate of Sue's at the University of Michigan and a veteran of jailhouse consultations, arrived from the mental-health office within minutes. I sat her on a folding chair just outside the cell, opening the waist-level food hatch so psychologist and inmate could talk through it. Normally Janis would consult with her subject in our visiting room, three double cubicles separated by reinforced glass, but we didn't want to move Bodey out of her cell. We didn't trust her just yet.

I hoped Janis, a kindly and likable sort whose striking silver hair disguises a steel-trap mind, could get Bodey talking about the demons that had driven her to murder, but that was not Janis's primary task. It was to perform a preliminary exam to determine if Sheila Bodey was mentally fit to remain in the cell.

In an hour Janis came into my office. "Bodey's an interesting one," she said. "Our session was civil and polite, and she seems to have a good grasp of all her faculties. She was enthusiastic when we talked about quilting. But when I tried to explore the charges and what reasons might lie behind them, she simply refused to talk about that. Still, at no time did she seem hostile. In fact, she was actually pleasant."

"A complete about-face from yesterday and this morning," I said. "Think she's yanking our chain?"

"Entirely possible. But I think she'll be OK from now on. I'd like to keep an eye on her, though. Let me know if her behavior changes."

A short while later Archie Martin arrived and, after reviewing the evidence with him, we let the defense attorney have his consultation with Bodey in the visitors' room. Again she offered us no trouble on the way there.

Half an hour later Archie came out. "She's a nice lady," he said, "and she's intelligent. But she's gonna be tough to defend. Just won't talk about the case in any way, shape or form. I may have to ask for a full mental evaluation at Marquette Hospital to see if she's fit for trial."

I knew that Archie was thinking about a plea of guilty but mentally ill, but he is too good a lawyer to telegraph his strategy to the prosecution. He's no pushover.

"Frankly, Steve," Archie said, "I don't think you have a slam-dunk case in Michigan."

"Don't know about that," said Garner Armstrong, the county prosecuting attorney, who had dropped by my office while Archie was seeing Bodey. "I will say it's true that the only forensic evidence we have so far to link Sheila Bodey to the killings is in the murder of Chu Lo Vue, the Wisconsin Hmong."

The imprint of the ferrule on the short starter we found at her hideout in the Wolverines was a perfect match to the indentation in the lead ball taken from Chu's body, and only Bodey's fingerprints had been found on the starter. Alex had had the starter flown to the Wisconsin state crime lab in Wausau and had prevailed upon a friend there to expedite the analysis.

Otherwise there was no scientific evidence to connect Bodey to any of the other shootings, not even Tom Bogan. Ballistics were useless. There had been no witnesses to his death. There had been none to the other killings, either, except to the murder of Marilyn Schneider at the Soo, but the witnesses there would not be able to identify the shooter.

There was, however, plenty of circumstantial evidence. When we captured her, Bodey had in her possession all the rifles of the calibers that had been used in the murders for which she was charged. She had attempted to flee while we were looking for her, and she had tried to kill me.

"No jury would overlook all that," Garner told Archie, who remained impassive.

"And if I should screw up somehow, it doesn't matter," Garner added. "My colleague in La Crosse can most likely get a life sentence with that short starter. And if by some remote chance he doesn't, the judge can still commit Bodey to a mental hospital for the criminally insane, given the circumstantial evidence."

"Too bad Wisconsin doesn't use the needle," Gil growled. Wisconsin has no death penalty, having abolished it in 1853, as Michigan had seven years earlier.

We all knew that if we could link Bodey firmly to the death of Bogan in the Ottawa National Forest, she could be tried in federal court, because national forests are federal property—and the United States of America still can impose the death penalty for capital crimes committed on its public lands. But no federal prosecutor would want to try her first on the wholly circumstantial evidence we had. Generally the feds leave it to the states to try murderers, and if they are acquitted and a federal prosecutor thinks he'll get lucky, then trial in federal district court becomes a possible Plan B.

"We could deliver Bodey to La Crosse tonight so she can be arraigned in Wisconsin tomorrow," Garner said. "Let them have a go first. After she's convicted there, we could try her here if we think we should. Letting Wisconsin go first would maybe save us a little money."

"But that's no guarantee we'll ever hear the whole story," I said. "Our only chance for that is a full confession. Doesn't look like we're going to get one."

Late in the afternoon the defense lawyer, the sheriff and the prosecutor sat around a table in the kitchen. Our small department has no real conference or interrogation room, and we use the roomy kitchen for that purpose rather than preparing inmates' meals there—they are catered by Merle's, two blocks from the department and its jail. Garner leaned his long, skinny frame against the refrigerator, I sat on the freezer and Archie at the small table.

"Them's the facts," Garner said in his folksy way. "Bodey goes to Wisconsin tonight and she's out of our hands, possibly for good. Yours, too."

Archie is a member of the bar in that state as well as Michigan, but he is not employed as a public defender in Wisconsin.

Archie nodded thoughtfully.

"But if she can be persuaded to confess," I said, "we can try her and get her the help she needs in Michigan."

"Yes," Garner said. "If I were Bodey, I'd go for a plea of guilty by reason of mental illness. That would get her psychiatric help as well as protect society from her. Archie, I think that would be the best outcome for all of us as well as for your client."

"Maybe," said Archie. "But she won't talk."

"So there it lies," Garner said.

In the end it was Sheila Bodey who changed everything.

"She's asking for a pastor," Joe said late in the afternoon. "Wants to talk to one."

I thought for a moment. "I'll call George."

The Reverend George Hartfelder arrived shortly after dinner, two Bibles in hand and wearing freshly pressed denims and a clean woolen shirt, as befit a well-turned-out country preacher.

"I am here to minister to the prisoner Sheila Bodey," he said formally, as he always does on such occasions.

"If she assents," I said formally, as I always do.

"Might I ask her myself?"

"Sure."

"Thank you."

"May I see the Bibles first?"

George handed them to me and I riffled through the pages, making sure a shotgun wasn't hidden inside. I handed them back.

"This way, Pastor." I took him to Bodey's cell rather than a visitor's cubicle so that he could pass one of the Bibles to her through the food hatch. There was no way to do that in the secure visitors' room.

Sheila Bodey looked at us through the glass of her cell door with a gentle and welcoming smile. I pulled up the folding chair for George, making sure to keep it six feet away from the cell door so that the prisoner could not suddenly reach through the food hatch and throttle her visitor.

"Let's don't get any closer than that," I said. "For your own safety."

George nodded and sat down.

"All yours," I said, opening the food hatch. "I'll watch on the video monitors, but the audio will be off." The law grants clergymen as well as defense counsel privacy when they visit their clients.

"Thanks."

At the door to the squad room I heard George say, "Miss Bodey, I am the Reverend George Hartfelder. I am a Baptist. As you requested, I have brought you the Lord."

"Thank you," she said calmly. "Is yours the same as mine?"

"He is *One*, you know, Miss Bodey," George said softly.

"Okay," she replied.

After that I gazed at the monitors, able to see but unable to hear them. For a long time they talked. Occasionally Gil or Joe spelled me.

Two hours after his arrival, George sat forward and extended one arm, Bible in hand, toward the food hatch. Bodey reached through the hatch and grasped the book.

George opened his own Bible and read a passage from it, and Bodey did the same with her copy. From time to time she grew animated, jabbing her finger at the book, and each time George slowly shook his head. Twice she leaped up and paced her cell, waving her hands in passionate argument. George just spread his arms as if to say, "Sorry, but . . ."

Then she burst into tears and fell upon her knees. George also knelt and the two of them prayed together for five long minutes.

Afterward George got up and walked to the squad room. His face was haggard and his shirt soaked with perspiration. He looked as if he had gone eleven rounds with the Devil and fought him to a draw.

"She will not repent," George said, his voice heavy with sadness, "for Satan owns her heart. But she says she wants to talk."

I thanked the pastor for his good offices, and he left, mopping his brow with a bandanna.

"Took gumption to do that," I told Gil. "Coming face-to-face with a serial murderer. But he said it was his job."

I immediately phoned Garner at the county building.

At nine in the evening we led Sheila Bodey into the kitchen and sat her down at the cracked linoleum table. Archie sat on one side of her. Instead of sitting across from them, Garner leaned against the refrigerator and I sat on top of a counter. Chad stood casually next to the stove behind Bodey, keeping a watchful eye on her. Gil, Alex and Sue remained out of sight in the squad room, watching and listening on a monitor.

We sometimes arranged ourselves this way during an interrogation to keep things relaxed and casual rather than official and threatening. The technique sometimes encouraged frightened and wary suspects to talk.

I turned on the video camera and told it the date and time, and the names of the people present.

"Will you state your name for the record, please?" I said to Bodey.

"Sheila Eileen Bodey," she said, her head held high.

"You are charged with murder," I said. "Anything you say in this room may be used against you in a court of law," I said. "Do you understand that?"

"I do."

"Mr. Martin?"

Archie identified himself for the record and said, "I have advised my client that she need not incriminate herself. But she wishes to do so. That is her right."

"Do you understand that?" I asked Bodey.

"Yes."

"Very well. Let's start at the beginning," I said, giving the date and place of the killing on the Mullet.

"First," Bodey began, "the name the Lord gave me is Angel . . ."

I glanced at Archie. He nodded almost imperceptibly. He was going to go for an insanity plea.

For three hours Sheila Bodey sat straight in her chair, hands in her lap, and spoke calmly and in minute detail, showing no remorse, even when detailing her innermost thoughts as she planned and executed the shootings of her victims. The sole emotions she showed were delight and pride in having fooled the authorities for so long. The only justifications she offered for her acts were that she was an instrument of God and that her victims had it coming.

Toward midnight she told how on the hill in the Wolverines she had taken Chad for a genuine hunter and allowed him to pass on the trail below. But when I hove into view, she had recognized me immediately through her binoculars.

"If it hadn't been for the hang fire," she said, still quietly and calmly but looking me directly in the eye, "you wouldn't be here today, Sheriff."

After we returned Bodey to her cell, we all sat in the squad room silently contemplating the day's events. Sue was the first to speak.

"It's fairly obvious we're looking at a true psychopath," she said. "Delusion, narcissism, lack of remorse, lack of empathy, and a tendency to violence—all the classic signs are there."

"What caused that?" I asked.

"Hard to say," Sue said, "without a thorough clinical investigation of her history. Sometimes it can be an hereditary illness. Sometimes there are triggers in childhood. One clue is that she talked a lot about 'Daddy.' It was 'Daddy this, Daddy that.' Daddy taught her how to shoot, how to hunt, even how to justify the taking of life to please the Lord—maybe not human, but certainly animal. He was her lord, too. It's possible that he may have been her abuser as well."

"In what way?" I asked.

"Sexually, perhaps just emotionally. Something traumatic may have happened between them to give her those abnormal ideas about sex and sin. I wouldn't be surprised if it was something like Daddy catching her masturbating, then beating her for it, and afterward making her fall on her knees in prayer with him. Things like that tend to unhinge people."

"She didn't mention that at all in the confession," Garner said.

"If it did happen—and I'm not saying it did—it's very likely that she repressed the memory," Sue said. "It might take months or even years of therapy to bring it to the surface. If it exists."

"What about the religious fanaticism?" Chad asked. "Could that have caused Bodey to go round the bend?"

"I don't think so," Sue said. "Generally, religious fervor so extreme that it leads to serial murder is a symptom, not a cause, of mental illness. The Devil did not make her do it, as they say. Something else did. The Devil is just a handy excuse."

"Will we ever know the whole truth?" I said.

"Not unless she submits to a psychiatrist at Marquette," Sue said, "and I have a feeling she never will."

"Well," I said, "remember what she said she felt just before she shot Armstrong and discovered who he was? She was going to apologize to him, saying the shooting wasn't personal. That suggests to me a little bit of empathy has stayed in her head."

"Maybe there's hope for her," Sue said. "A psychiatrist might be able to work on that. Whatever happens, she almost certainly will spend the rest of her life in a maximum-security hospital ward for the criminally insane."

"Meanwhile," Garner said, "Wisconsin will just have to wait its turn."

CHAPTER THIRTY-EIGHT

The next morning our work was done. Shortly after breakfast Chad had set off with Bodey in the backseat of his cruiser for the hospital in Marquette, where she would be held for pretrial psychiatric evaluation at George's request, perhaps for months. That was a load off my mind. We have only the one cell for women, and we usually need it on Saturday nights.

I had called the governor, who offered quiet thanks for my service, and had also informed Sheriff Wayne Champion in Chippewa County that we had solved the case of the murder of Marilyn Schneider for him. Actually, I had informed his under-sheriff. Champion said he was too busy working out his yearly budget to talk to me, and I almost believed him.

Meanwhile, Horace had broken his exclusive—he called it the scoop of a lifetime—in the *Mining Journal,* leaving out no gory detail, and during the day the rest of his colleagues milled about the sheriff's department in the expectable media circus. I felt sunburned from the floodlights. Gil threatened to stuff one arrogant cameraman's equipment up his nether regions, but I think he was kidding. With him it's sometimes hard to tell.

That evening there was one final and mostly celebratory meeting of the team that had tracked down the Hammer of God Killer, as the press was breathlessly calling Bodey, and the last of them had just left the squad room when Tommy Standing Bear dashed into my office.

"Steve!" he shouted as he collided with me and wrapped his

arms around my back. "We came back early!"

"Wasn't expecting you till Saturday," I said, tousling Tommy's hair. I was glad to see the boy. Very glad.

Hogan bounded from his bed in my office corner and showered Tommy with leaps and licks, his massive tail endangering everything breakable in the place.

"What were you doing with my Hawken?" Tommy demanded. "I found it on the kitchen table in Ginny's house!"

"I had to borrow it," I said, "but you weren't around for me to ask and it would have taken too long to reach you in Finland."

"What'd you borrow it for?"

"A good reason. But it's a long story and I'll tell you later, okay?"

The boy didn't answer. He and his dog were tangled, laughing and mock growling, in a squirming heap on the floor.

I looked up and my heart missed a couple of beats.

Ginny stood in the door, a stern expression on her face.

"I have just been to your cabin looking for you," she said. "And what do I find but Alex Kolehmainen and Susan Hemb, um, plumping the pillows in your spare room?"

Tommy looked up with instant interest.

"They what?" I said.

"You heard me."

"There is an explanation," I said, "but as I told Tommy, it's a long story."

"No need for that," Ginny said severely. "I've seen all I need to see."

Then she burst into laughter. "Alex and Sue came into the kitchen and told me what happened the last few days. All I can say right now is 'Wow!' "

Her expression changed to one of deep concern. "You're all right, aren't you, Steve?"

"Never better," I said, unconsciously rubbing my sore chest.

"Thank God," she said.

Both of us stood rooted to the spot, fighting an immense magnetic force between us. We both knew what we wanted, but in the Upper Peninsula of Michigan people are modest and diffident and don't like to put on a show for the neighbors, or have I mentioned that already?

Chad pretended to be busy at his desk. Joe gazed at us with gleeful anticipation. Gil shot a sidewise glance from his office. Garner beamed at us from the center of the squad room. It seemed as if the whole town was peeking in my office door.

"How come Alex and Sue got back together?" I said, just to change the subject.

"Alex said something about having passed the lieutenant's exam," Ginny said.

That brought a smile to my face. A broad, broad smile. I started laughing.

"What's so funny about that?" Ginny said.

"I'll explain someday," I said.

For a long moment we stood gazing at each other.

"Uhm . . . ," I said. "About . . . Finland?"

"That can wait," Ginny said merrily. "Right now, Steve, you're coming home with me. Your cabin's too crowded."

ABOUT THE AUTHOR

Henry Kisor is the author of three previous Steve Martinez mysteries, *Season's Revenge, A Venture into Murder,* and *Cache of Corpses.* He and his wife Debby spend half the year in Evanston, Illinois, and the other half in a log cabin on the shore of Lake Superior in Ontonagon County, Michigan, the real-life prototype for Porcupine County. He is also the author of three nonfiction books, *What's That Pig Outdoors: A Memoir of Deafness; Zephyr: Tracking a Dream Across America,* and *Flight of the Gin Fizz: Midlife at 4,500 Feet.* He retired in 2006 after thirty-three years as a book-review editor, first for the old *Chicago Daily News* and then the *Chicago Sun-Times.* In 1981 he was a nominated finalist for the Pulitzer Prize in criticism.